ICE

Krishna Shastri Devulapalli is an illustrator, cartoonist, graphic designer and writer. He has been in advertising, designed greeting cards, written and illustrated children's books, and is working on several film scripts. *Ice Boys in Bell-bottoms* is his first novel. He lives in Chennai but hails from East Godavari District, Andhra Pradesh, which may be why he's never been able to get a cab.

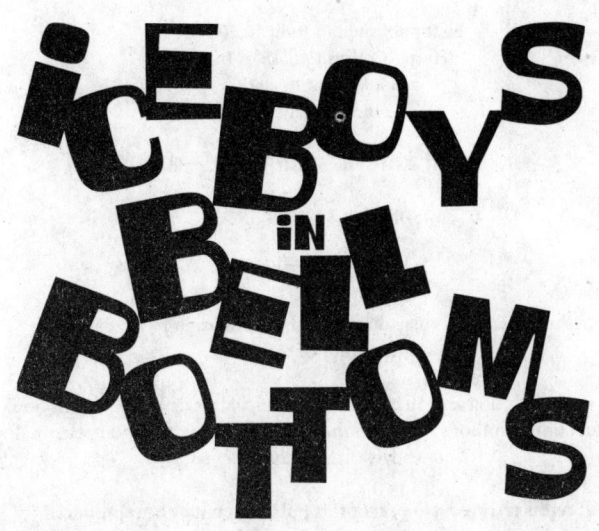

Krishna Shastri Devulapalli

HarperCollins *Publishers* India
a joint venture with

New Delhi

First published in India in 2011 by
HarperCollins *Publishers* India
a joint venture with
The India Today Group

Copyright © Krishna Shastri Devulapalli 2011

ISBN: 978-93-5029-183-2

2 4 6 8 10 9 7 5 3 1

Krishna Shastri Devulapalli asserts the moral right to be identified
as the author of this book.

This is a work of fiction and all characters and incidents described in this book are
the product of the author's imagination. Any resemblance to actual persons, living
or dead, is entirely coincidental.

All rights reserved. No part of this publication may be reproduced,
stored in a retrieval system, or transmitted, in any form or by any
means, electronic, mechanical, photocopying, recording or otherwise,
without the prior permission of the publishers.

HarperCollins *Publishers*
A-53, Sector 57, NOIDA, Uttar Pradesh – 201301, India
77-85 Fulham Palace Road, London W6 8JB, United Kingdom
Hazelton Lanes, 55 Avenue Road, Suite 2900, Toronto, Ontario M5R 3L2
and 1995 Markham Road, Scarborough, Ontario M1B 5M8, Canada
25 Ryde Road, Pymble, Sydney, NSW 2073, Australia
31 View Road, Glenfield, Auckland 10, New Zealand
10 East 53rd Street, New York NY 10022, USA

Typeset in 11/15 Minion
Jojy Philip New Delhi 110 015

Printed and bound at
Thomson Press (India) Ltd.

For
Naanna, my hero

ONE

The first time I saw our new house, it looked like it was lying down.

But that's the way most things looked from my favourite place in the world, the upper berth. The 'upper berth' was the space between the back seat and the rear windscreen of our Ambassador, where I lay sandwiched as our family of seven journeyed back and forth between Madras and Hyderabad, trying to figure out which was home.

On these expeditions, it came to be understood that that space belonged to me and no one else. But it wasn't as if there hadn't been a tussle. Soon after I discovered it, christened it and became its de facto proprietor, my younger sister, Kavi, pitched for my ouster with that failure-proof younger sibling ploy, the 'why does Gopi always get everything' whine. Her success was short-lived. Being younger than me by half-a-foot, she was rattled about like a pebble in a tin can by the moving road and slid right back onto my mother's lap in under five kilometres. My elder sister, who had first dibs on everything in our family, did not enter the fray. I wouldn't have stood a chance if she had. What Lalli wanted, Lalli got. The two reasons for my good fortune: she was one size too big for the upper berth and wore glasses.

So our places in the car were fixed. It was Father and Grandfather in the front seat along with Ramayya the driver, Mother, Grandmother and Lalli at the back, with Kavi doing musical laps among the adults. As for me, I ruled the upper berth with the sovereignty of the class bully. No one else wanted it and no one else could have it.

It was a perfect fit. It was as if Hindustan Motors had sent over an engineer, taken a plaster cast of me and decided to leave that exact shape between the back seat and the rear windscreen of their Mark II Ambassador. It was my home with the ever-changing view.

While my family watched the road, the trees and the cows go by from one side to the other, my world moved vertically. The only reason I didn't die of deep vein thrombosis was because Grandfather made us stop every few kilometres to show us a field, a brook or a man balancing water pots on his head. I was six or seven and didn't get what all the fuss was about. I wondered if it had anything to do with his being a poet.

Truth was, all of us just wanted to get home as quickly as possible and were waiting for Grandfather to decide where that would be.

If stopping to stare at ducks and bullock carts was bad, detours to see Grandfather's never-ending supply of admirers in strange-sounding places like Bitragunta and Garladinne were worse. Our grey Ambassador, stuffed fuller than a purohit at a death ceremony, teetered off the highway and took us, bobbing and weaving through winding dirt roads, to depressing little towns that barely made it into maps. We ate and slept in strange houses, empty classrooms and, once, even in a vacant marriage hall. Wherever we went, there was always a mob jostling around Grandfather, the all-night conversations providing a mournful background score to my dreams. I woke up those mornings craving for the stability of the moving car and the constancy of my blurry background. When we finally left, with bladders emptied and the radiator refilled, it seemed the entire village had come to see us off. It was obvious that Grandfather was not just a poet. He was a *famous* one.

On those rare stretches where the journey continued uninterrupted, my residence at the upper berth was sometimes cut short by my mother yanking me out without warning, stiffer than a constable's shorts, not so much to hug me as imprison me in her lap.

'If you lie there all the time, you'll look like this!' she'd say, her hand making a "Z".

But I would clamber back as soon as her attention was elsewhere. So it was no surprise when we approached our new house in Madras one summer day in 1973 that it looked like it was lying down.

But before I tell you about the new house, I have to tell you about Grandfather. Otherwise, my story wouldn't make sense.

TWO

Grandfather was *the* Meghamala Radhakrishna. Meghamala for short. Anyone who paid attention knew he was the most famous living Telugu poet *ever*. From the fuss made over him, you'd think he was seven feet tall.

To us, in his all-white ensemble and matching cap of wild hair, he was certainly a magnificent specimen of grandfatherhood. He looked like a dhoti-clad Einstein or a clean-shaven Tagore – take your pick. Also, he couldn't speak and breathed through a hole in his throat.

But this hadn't always been the case. Till a few years ago he could talk and, by all accounts, had done more than his share of it. At about the time I was born, Grandfather was diagnosed with throat cancer. People had shaken their heads sombrely when my horoscope was written up because of my birth star, the dreaded moola. In astrological circles it was believed that the moola nakshatram could do more damage to the family elders than a twelve-bore fired at close range. But Grandfather's cancer probably had more to do with the fifty or so Lanka cheroots he had been smoking every day for over thirty years than my poor birth star. When the doctors in Hyderabad and Madras gave a collective shrug and looked skywards, Grandfather was taken to Bombay. There, a great doctor operated on him and saved his life but had to remove Grandfather's larynx in the process. When he returned to Hyderabad, voiceless but alive, the same astrologers who'd predicted his speedy death did some quick thinking and reinterpreted my horoscope. Apparently, the Saturn in my birth chart had furtively moved into the servant's quarters while the surgery was in progress thereby changing everything.

'Your grandson is the reason you are alive, sir! He possesses a mahadjatakam,' went the chorus as Grandmother tearfully doled out hundred-rupee notes. My mother, on the other hand, suggested they take the planets and insert them into their black holes. It was unlikely she meant this in a purely astronomical sense.

Except for Lalli, who was a few years old when he had had his operation and claimed to remember speaking to him, Kavi and I had never heard Grandfather's voice. So it seemed perfectly natural to have a grandfather who wrote on a scribbling pad when he needed to talk and wore a white bib to cover a hole in his throat. Our name for him was CG, short for 'Cloud Garland', a loose translation of 'Meghamala'.

Grandfather wrote songs for films. The problem was he lived in Hyderabad while the films were made in Madras. Tired of going up and down for his songs, it was the film people who asked him to come and live in Madras. But Grandfather wasn't about to make up his mind that easily. In fact, as Father used to say, very early on, the one thing Grandfather had made up his mind on was on *not* making it up. This accounted for all of us moving from Hyderabad to Madras when CG had an assignment and returning to Hyderabad when he was done.

You may ask why the bunch of us moved, armed with kerosene stove and baby food, when only my grandfather was required.

From the day my father was born, so the story went, Grandfather had never spent a day apart from him. So bizarre was his obsession with his son that Grandfather had snatched him from my bewildered grandmother's lap and taken him along on his never-ending travels even before Father had uttered his first words. The joke among his writer friends was that the crazy poet sprouted a pair of breasts in the night and secretly breastfed his son. Whether this was true or not, one thing was. Teluguland's most literate man had a son who didn't go to school.

When anyone dared venture into the realm of his son's future, Grandfather would say 'Bah! Who needs school! Travelling with me is education enough. He'll turn out just fine.'

Grandfather's prediction had mostly come true, but not for his reason. Far from ending up illiterate, Father miraculously learnt the alphabet in both Telugu and English all by himself. I say miraculous because the darkened theatre was his classroom, Humphrey Bogart and Rita Hayworth his tutors and comics books his curriculum. On what must have been deadly boring days in unknown towns (much like the ones our car would halt in, radiator spouting steam, thirty years later) my father also discovered that, like most kids, he enjoyed drawing. With all the time in the world and a never-ending supply of art material provided by an apprentice poet, unlike most kids, he didn't give up. Before long he was a freelance illustrator. When the cheques began to arrive, he had no choice but to pick up arithmetic as well.

The problem was, even though he had made a name for himself as an artist, married my mother and had the three of us, the one thing Father hadn't taught himself was saying 'no' to Grandfather. So, every time CG went to Madras, in a tradition that had been established from his infancy, Father had no choice but to go along. And, like the tail on a whimsical kite, we followed.

In the summer of 1973, after half a dozen bone-rattling trips to Madras and back, the final decision was made. Well, *almost* final anyway. And a *decision*, if you could call it that. We would move to Madras – for a couple of years. The house in Hyderabad wouldn't be given up – at least not immediately. We would continue paying rent – till we figured out something. And the kids would be educated in Madras – for the time being.

If you imagine a family seated in the living room after the kids had gone to bed all concerned about their future, thrashing out the pros and cons of life in the two cities and finally arriving at a decision – that's not the way it happened. I have no memory of the day but chances are Grandfather yawned, a bunch of Telugu movie producers took that as a 'yes', packed our belongings, put them on a lorry and pointed us towards Madras before he could change his mind.

In the ensuing confusion, if at all there was a decision made, it was by Mother: No home schooling for her children. They would go to a proper school in Madras and be educated like normal kids.

THREE

Once I got off the upper berth, I realized that our first real home in Madras – and the rest of the city – was far from horizontal. The owner of the house was a retired railway stores-in-charge who had somehow been convinced by a fast-talking production manager that it was okay to let his property out to a seventy-six-year-old Telugu poet who couldn't speak. Our landlord, Raghavan, had built the rambling grey two-storey house with scrupulous savings and judicious pilferage from the Indian Railways. He stayed on the ground floor, and the first floor and the maidan-sized terrace were ours. Our rent was fixed at three hundred rupees which, when converted to Grandfather's exchange rate, was significantly less than a song. (He was being paid a thousand for those.)

On inspection it was revealed that the house was designed by someone who had the heart of a maharaja and the bowels of a titmouse. The bedrooms with their high ceilings, the living room with its cathedral-sized windows, the dining room and the kitchen were each big enough to house a small family. However, the sole toilet of the three-thousand-square-foot house was a 5′ × 5′ concrete cubicle with an eastern-style closet which proved beyond doubt that you could take a man out of the railways but not vice versa. Only a token system would ensure accident-free ablutions for seven quirky bowels. About a furlong away from the toilet, keeping apart those conjoined twins of early morning endeavour, was another tiny room meant only for bathing.

The lorries arrived shortly thereafter, bringing hastily chosen articles from Hyderabad while leaving half our life behind. Dishes arrived without their lids and chairs came in odd numbers. Apprentice film directors and aspiring playback singers doubled as movers and worked tirelessly, placing things exactly where Grandfather wanted them, expecting no payment from him other than a leg up. The Persian wine jugs went on the stand in the living room, the brass Nandi, a writer's wedding gift to my father, found its place on the windowsill. For a man who couldn't make up his mind about where he wanted his house to be, CG was definitely house-proud.

The master bedroom with a sit-out that overlooked the street would be his. Lalli, his first-born grandchild, would sleep in his room as always. The room accommodated the three large beds of varying heights and yet didn't seem crowded at all. Bedroom Two went to my parents, Kavi and me. The room held its breath a bit with the four beds. No one paid attention to my space-saving suggestion of placing Kavi's bed in the kitchen. The undefined room adjacent to the living room was a perfect studio for my father, its big open windows a perennial source of bounce light from one direction or the other.

Maybe it was a defence mechanism or maybe it had to do with the ever-present horde of admirers who were willing to walk on a bed of nails for CG, but Father had a princely detachment of all things mundane. He had allowed the relocation to happen, like most other things in his life, as though it was an occurrence at the neighbours'.

But when his material arrived, he magically came to life. He stood downstairs and supervised its unloading like it was the Kohinoor. If you wanted to elicit a violent response from my normally placid father you could ruffle his patent-leather hairstyle or mess with his stuff. After accidentally dropping a bottle of Camel 99 Indian ink, a forty-year-old production 'boy' saw this side of Father and slunk off sobbing like a little girl.

I watched fascinated as his dismantled studio from Hyderabad was reassembled in Ramalingam Street by the trembling hands of unpaid help. One by one, the easel, the carefully packed poster paints, the squirrel and sable-haired brushes wrapped in a plastic sheet, the blue-bordered ceramic plates for mixing colours, the Fuji Photo Colourbooks, Berol Venus pencils, Pelikan erasers, the 11″ × 14″ pre-cut sheets of drawing board, the rolls of Gateway tracing sheets – enough ammo to draw twenty picture stories – were put in their clearly designated places. This was not the material of an artist who had anticipated a move to the next room in the near future, leave alone another town.

Equally precious to Father were the boxes upon boxes of reference material consisting of comic books, Hollywood film magazines, pulp fiction and pocket cartoon books I had been trying to get my hands on for as long as I could remember. Fleeting glimpses of the forbidden Technicolor world was all I had managed so far, when Father brought them out for an airing. He knew that if his treasure was in any danger, it was from me. Finally, my father's Foldelux chair was positioned behind the easel and his ratty cushion placed on top. If the upper berth was my most favourite moving place, the moda right beside my father's easel was its stationary counterpart. When the lorry carrying our things had left Hyderabad, it was the one thing I'd made sure had gotten on. Once it was placed to the left of Father's chair, the studio finally looked complete. Now we were both ready. Soon he would begin drawing his valiant folk heroes atop wavy-maned horses and I would prepare to be the greatest artist in the world.

FOUR

The wait was over and it looked like we finally had a home. APW 5252 stood quietly in the garage adorned by stray frangipani. Its grey body gave no indication of the torture CG had put it through. Ramayya had gone back to Hyderabad or, to be more precise, escaped in the dead of the night, informing only my mother.

'Amma, please tell ayyagaru,' he had pleaded. 'I have a wife and kids back home in Hyderabad.'

The house was buzzing with film folk relieved to have finally pinned down Grandfather. Now, all we needed were some friends. Sekhar, the pencil-thin son of our landlord, we realized, wouldn't quite do. At eleven, he was nearly six feet tall and didn't look like he played I-Spy. It wasn't difficult to visualize him peering at a chessboard through his thick black frames though.

The house, on the other hand, was built for playing I-Spy. A garden that looked like a Tarzan movie set surrounded the house on three sides, wild and green, the foliage about to burst with chattering apes any minute. Evidently, Raghavan's sticky fingers included a pair of green thumbs. The frangipani by the gate was as good as a ladder to the top of the garage. Even

Kavi the fusspot climbed up the tree in a second. The asbestos roof with its bed of rotting flowers was a great hiding place. It was also a crow's nest that gave us an unfettered view of Ramalingam Street and, more disturbingly, our eighty-year-old neighbour's bathroom. There were areca nut trees that looked uncannily like Sekhar. A gaudy collage of hibiscus, December flowers and parijatam covered the soil all along one side. The curry leaf tree grew next to the tulasi in its concrete box with niches for lamps. The backyard was a fruit salad. Chikkoo, mango and jackfruit hung low enough to be plucked by a kid, and there were more coconut palms than you could count.

The hiding place of all hiding places was the abandoned outhouse at the back. Time and the branches of the enthusiastic chikkoo had knocked the tiles right off a part of the roof. It was easy to climb up the tree and lower yourself into the outhouse. It was filled with what looked like the final pre-retirement haul of S. Raghavan, Esq.: girders, rotting wooden doors, fishplates, boxes upon boxes of god-knows-what, metal commodes, taps, burglar-proof aluminium tumblers with chains and everything you could think of that went into a train except perhaps the coach itself. Maybe poor old Raghavan had just been fulfilling a childhood dream of having his own train set.

The fourth tree-free side of our house had an impeccably marked cemented badminton court. Yes, we could use it if we wanted to. On the other side of the court, with no compound wall in the middle, were two houses, one behind the other. Newer and smaller than Raghavan's heaving, sweaty monster, they belonged to his sisters. Tenants: one Gujarati family, one Telugu family. Kids: zero.

It was summer and there was talk, mostly from my mother, about finding schools for us. But that was a good forty-five days away. It didn't make sense to have all this and no friends. The three of us took up the job on a war footing and hung around outside our gates advertising our wares.

Within a couple of days our campaign showed signs of success. We interested a gang of two boys and a girl enough for them to walk up and down our street five times in an hour. All three of them were barefoot, had tight curly hair and sported bruises in various shades on their reedy bodies. They seemed perfect for I-Spy, though. I made a note never to get into a fight with them.

I approached them with a subtle opening gambit.

'Want to play I-Spy?'

The three kids exchanged looks and broke into uncontrollable laughter.

'You mean Ice Boys?' said the biggest of them, the boy.

I was taken aback. I retreated and consulted Lalli. She was already reading Agatha Christie and had a wider vocabulary than mine.

'What's Ice boys?'

Lalli thought for a while and said, 'I think that's what they call I-Spy in Madras.'

I went back to them and asked again.

'OK. So, you want to play Ice Boys?'

And so Pandu, Chanti and Padma became our friends. They were nine, eight and six and would have stayed on our street had it not been cut in the middle by a main road. The three of them lived in a one-room house along with an older brother, two older sisters, and their mother. Their twenty-one-year-old brother was the only earning member in their family. They were the first kids I knew who didn't have a father.

We'd offered them a massive compound, courtesy Raghavan, to play Ice Boys in. The three kids probably felt a need to return the favour. And they did it in a spectacular manner. One by one, completely unaided by any apparatus, Pandu, Chanti and Padma climbed a coconut tree in our house. Having reached the top they dangled fearlessly from the branches. Pandu, the oldest, became my hero by waving to me with one hand. Recruitment of new playmates was instantly taken off our hands. Three deliriously happy kids hanging from the branches of a coconut tree was advertisement enough. Soon, half a dozen more kids landed up as much to play hide-and-seek as learn the finer points of palm tree climbing. And Raghavan had the first of several nervous breakdowns.

A couple of days later, when the raggedy trio hadn't turned up, I walked up to their place to see what was keeping them. The three kids were sitting on the floor, all concentration, and eating rice mixed with a delicious-looking brown curry. The aroma of their meal was like nothing I'd ever smelt before.

'Want to eat some?' said Pandu giving the back of his hand an even coat with his tongue.

I really did and was wondering how to say 'no' unconvincingly.

'Don't be silly,' his mother said. 'They're Brahmins. They don't eat meat.'

'That's not true. My mother and father won't mind,' I said, without having the faintest idea about either. (It turned out we were and they didn't.)

Pandu pulled a plate from the little stack behind him and indicated to his mother to serve me some of the stuff. I mixed the pungent brown gravy with the rice and chewed the deliciously rubbery meat. That day is permanently etched in my memory. After all, how can you forget the day your tongue loses its virginity?

FIVE

A few months earlier, in a brief moment of rebellion, when Lalli had refused outright to leave Hyderabad and her tiny circle of friends, Father listed the wonders that Madras had on offer in the following order.

'Madras has a beach. English movies get released first in Madras. Most importantly, Auntie Renu lives in Madras.'

Under these circumstances apparently only a fool would refuse to move.

The truth was Auntie Renu was not really an aunt. She was the daughter of a writer, a distant relative of Granddad's. Back in the days when CG lived in Rajahmundry, the man had died suddenly leaving behind his wife, daughter and a dozen unpublishable manuscripts under his care. Unlike Father, CG's surrogate child was given stepmotherly treatment and put through school and college. Eventually, she moved on to the more commercial pastures of Madras. But the influence she exercised over Grandfather, Grandmother and Father was considerable.

From the time we were born, CG and Father put up such an attractive advertising campaign to sell this connection the three of us ended up believing that Auntie Renu was our only 'aunt' and her kids were our only 'cousins'. The small matter of the real aunts, uncles and cousins from Mother's side, all of whom lived in Hyderabad, was completely ignored. They were conventional folk who worked in banks and offices and that wasn't a selling point at home. My mother, who hated Auntie Renu, didn't bother launching a counter campaign. She figured we would like who we wanted.

There's a subtle difference between a circus and a train wreck. A circus has clowns, elephants and acrobats, but it also has a ringmaster who knows what to do when the elephant has diarrhoea. A train wreck, on the other hand, is far more laissez-faire, where everybody is doing their own thing. Our house followed the Barnum & Bailey touring model with Grandfather playing ringmaster while Auntie Renu's family favoured the railway disaster approach.

No one could accuse our family of being traditional. It wasn't as if Father rushed off to office six days a week and insisted on quiet family dinners with everyone present at seven o'clock. Nor was my mother, heaven forbid, the typical housewife. Above all, Grandfather was the furthest thing from the benevolent family patriarch who went off on annual pilgrimages to Kasi, wife in tow. But when it came to unconventional, we were no match for Auntie Renu's family, the Bankas. They countered each innocuous quirk of ours with a demented fetish of their own.

For starters, no one in the Banka household really worked. But they, too, somehow lived in a sprawling house, set in the middle of ten grounds. It was conveniently situated a street away from our place.

Auntie Renu's husband, Uncle Anand, had last been employed in the '40s as the unlikely sales rep in a company that sold Ayurvedic medicines. Since then, snuff-box in hand, he had kept himself busy with the following: supplying Auntie Renu the wireless technology necessary to produce four children without once exchanging a civil word, walking a distance equal to several times the earth's circumference without once leaving his living room, disagreeing with everyone at all times on all subjects without once losing an argument.

Auntie Renu, Banka Renuka Bai to the music world, was an accomplished Carnatic singer. Family lore, usually the victim of gross exaggeration, had it that as a child she could play the veena with one hand and a sitar with the other while operating a sruti box with her toes – blindfolded. None of us kids witnessed this. But what we did see frequently was Auntie Renu playing anyone who crossed her path like a ghatam.

The Bankas' first child, Niranjan, was a pint-sized chap with gigantic ears. He was a Bharata Natyam dancer by profession, and life in their household revolved around fixing recitals for mother and son. When Niranjan wasn't rehearsing, we were used to seeing him lounging about in a nightie, a string of dried-up jasmine hanging from his head, absently practising his mudras.

Next came the twins, Damodar and Sachu. Damodar, Dodo for short, also with elephantine ears, was the founder-lead singer of Madras's first-ever rock band, Atomic Lingam. When Dodo realized his true interest lay in agriculture or, to be more specific, grass and its beneficial effects, he dropped out of medical college. As a result, the Banka home became a definite stopover for every unbathed, draft-dodging American flower child, and Dodo, the karta of a global 'joint' family. To complete the picture, he had a dusky and voluptuous Anglo-Indian girlfriend called Bliss who pretty much lived in his room. Sex, drugs and rock & roll – Dodo was on a first-name basis with all three. Without doubt, he was the first Telugu Brahmin boy living the American Dream in Tamil Nadu.

When Dodo's rock band jammed, they played Led Zep, Deep Purple and their own unintelligible compositions. Their audience – a bunch of American teenagers in beads, goggles and kurtas chanting '*Hare Rama, Hare Krishna*' out of tune and carrying enough grass for a small herd of cows.

Sachu, Dodo's twin sister was a curly-haired walking hormone who had changed from a skinny buck-toothed kid into a buxom teenager with a permanent pout in six months flat. The neighbourhood boys who'd been chucking stones at her when she walked to school were now throwing themselves at her feet. Continuing in the musical tradition of her family, Sachu played them all like a giant fiddle.

The youngest Banka kid was Rishi. Needless to say his ears prevented him from wearing anything with a turtleneck. I had once overheard a writer friend of CG's say that if Uncle Anand's tadpoles were examined under a microscope, each little bugger would have flapping ears.

Rishi was a couple of years older than me but about my size. With his family constantly visiting us in Hyderabad, he was somebody I had known all my life – sort of like the older brother I never had or wanted. If memory served me right, I received my first beating from him. These were followed by booster doses at regular intervals. When Rishi got tired of beating me, he kept in shape pushing, teasing and taunting me. As soon as we went home, I used all that I'd learnt and endured on Kavi with great success.

As Rishi constantly reminded me – he was stronger than me, could run faster than me, climb higher than me, sing better than me and knew words that I didn't. I agreed wholeheartedly because my pain threshold was low.

I don't know why but the one claim Rishi didn't make was being able to draw better than me.

Our first summer in Madras, when Pandu's gravity-defying feats got repetitive, I strolled across to Rishi's house with not just permission from the folks at home but their unconditional approval.

Father: Where are you off to?
Me: To Rishi's.
Father: Oh, all right, then.

I didn't get it. Here was my father, the same guy who scowled when I tried to get my hands on his French cartoon books, giving me a pat on my head and sending me off to see the Sex Pistols.

The only hitch was that Kavi followed me like a whiney pig-tailed shadow.

On the average day, if I wanted to play with Rishi, my course went thus: start by elbowing my way through the living room where Niranjan was practising for his next recital; dodge Uncle Anand as he jay-walked between the several members of his son's dance troupe snorting snuff and telling everyone that they were all doing everything wrong and would amount to nothing; slink past Auntie Renu playing the veena with one hand while she aimed a brass utensil at the bobbing head of her husband with the other; tiptoe past Dodo's room through a curtain of sweet smoke hoping to catch a glimpse of Bliss's exposed bubby; make sure I didn't trip over Sachu's latest boyfriend, prostrate and professing undying love, and find Rishi in the only sane place in the house – on top of the guava tree in the backyard.

SIX

Summer flew by in a flash with Ice Boys, new friends and our first passive inhalation of grass. It was now time for school. In a covert operation not entirely supported by Grandfather our parents managed to find the three of us admission. I don't know if it was sexism or just plain old protectiveness towards the girl child that my sisters found themselves in a little school less than a hundred metres away from home while I was admitted to the poshest new school in Madras – the rather unposh sounding Vidya Vihar Boys' School. The fee Father had to fork out for one term at my school was more than the combined annual fees of my sisters. I loved it. I wasted no time in telling my sisters that I was better than them, my school was better than theirs and that they were both not my real sisters, having been picked up by my parents from an orphanage in an ill-judged move. My sisters thought I was an idiot because they clearly had the better deal. They could wake up and amble along to school in less than three minutes while I had to trudge nearly a kilometre. I was quickly brought back to sea level.

Vidya Vihar Boys' School was affiliated to the ISC board. At my admission interview there was mention of Cambridge Senior, imported textbooks and a school blazer, all of which would, naturally, cost extra. Father's face fell as he briefly considered the wisdom in his father's home-schooling method. My mother gave him that special look that usually preceded a well-aimed throw of a blunt instrument at home. My face lit up like a neon sign at the thought of parading in front of my sisters, striking a variety of poses that would showcase my monogrammed blazer.

The first few days in Vidya Vihar Boys' School were pure magic. Our uniform was navy blue shorts, a cream half-sleeved shirt worn with the blue school tie, black leather lace-up shoes and navy blue socks. We were to wear the blazers on special occasions. Every morning I couldn't wait to leave home in my swish new uniform. By the time I finished tying my shoelaces, my sisters were as good as invisible. I walked out of my house in as Cambridgean a manner as I could muster and made it a point to ignore everyone I saw on the road. Who *were* these guys? Did they know I was doing Modern Maths?

In school the male teachers wore jackets and ties and many of the female teachers wore skirts.

T.V. Suresh, the first kid who spoke to me, pointed out: 'The lower the class taught, the higher the skirt. That's how it is in Cambridge.'

I heard names like Miss Phillips, Miss DeCosta, Mr Manuel and Mr Daley. Even the school peon was called Stanley. It was all very refined.

Earlier, I had nearly botched my chances at the interview. After I had read out a passage satisfactorily from an English Reader, the headmaster, Mr Amalraj, asked me, 'Are you interested in sports?'

'Yes, sir!' I mumbled.

'What's your favourite sport?'

'Ice Boys,' I said.

Sports was obviously very important at Vidya Vihar. Cricket nets, where a former Tamil Nadu player corrected the grips and fine-tuned the stances of his wards, greeted people at the gates. There was also a basketball court, a volleyball court and a play area each for the primary and senior classes. There was a sports room with a ping-pong table. And there were two teachers in charge of Physical Training.

The funny thing was, two PT masters, a respected cricket coach, acres of space, and a large sports budget notwithstanding, the favourite sport of Vidya Vihar Boys' School was one that required nothing more sophisticated than a rubber ball and a yogic detachment to one's privates. It was a game called Holly Golly, and must have been invented by a simple-minded sadist (probably a close relation of the chap who'd designed the toilet at home). This is how it was played. There were two teams. The aim of each player was to hit any member of the rival team as hard as possible with a rubber ball. Any player who got hit was out of the game not to mention out of order for several days. Whoever survived was the winner. Every day, to my parents' alarm, I trotted off to a posh school all tie-clad and shiny-shoed and returned looking like an escapee from some medieval torture chamber.

At about the same time the multicoloured bruises began to fade I realized that things weren't all that chic at Vidya Vihar. Several of the suited teachers that I was so impressed with when I'd joined came to school on bicycles, ties askew, sweating like hogs. One of them, I realized when I happened to look under the table, wore Hawaii slippers. It seemed, with their pay scales closer to Basin Bridge than Cambridge, the poor fellows could barely afford one jacket each. With the cycling, and the Madras heat, each teacher's jacket sported salt-rimmed patches of dried-up perspiration in patterns so distinct that we could almost identify the teacher by his sweat map.

I also realized, to my disappointment, that Miss Phillips, Miss DeCosta, Mr Manuel, Mr Daley and even Stanley the peon were not American or, for that matter, even English. They were all as Indian as our landlord Raghavan.

SEVEN

Children go through everything that adults do: jealousy, pain, love and even lust. You could have asked any eight-year-old in Vidya Vihar what he thought of Miss DeCosta and watch him squirm with his phantom libido to confirm my theory. The one thing though that's the exclusive bastion of adults is nostalgia. And thank God for that. That is why children lamenting the passing of the old days, when they were microscopic swimmers in their dad's testicles, is a rarity. But, thanks to Father, I experienced what no child before me had or was capable of experiencing – the best times I never had.

The '50s, when the family was living in Madras, had been a terrific time for Father by his own admission. It looked like Grandfather's self-centredness hadn't had any obvious side-effects. Father had survived a childhood without formal education and emerged seemingly unscathed. He had a lucrative career going as a sought-after children's illustrator. He was in his twenties, had his own money and could spend every last paisa of it on himself because Grandfather was happy taking care of things at home. Young men Father's age, whom he'd envied while they went to school and college, were earning a fraction of what he was after spending the entire day in a stuffy office.

If the blurb on his book covers was right, Father was a pioneer in many ways. He was, it claimed, the first comic book illustrator in India, the country's youngest children's book publisher, the first one to win awards in three languages and so on. What the blurb didn't mention was that, in the conservative '50s, it's quite possible he was also the country's first serial consumer. Unfettered by responsibility, coddled by his father and powered by earnings that far exceeded anyone of his age or background, Father indulged himself silly. He watched every Hollywood movie that came to town, flitting giddily between Casino and Minerva, and bought any English film magazine he could lay his hands on. He developed a taste for fancy clothes and treated himself, as he boasted to us so often, to a new rayon bush-shirt every week. He had owned fifty pairs of shoes and god-knows-how-many hair-care products. That he didn't get into 'booze and broads' like the gumshoes of his staple entertainment must have been more an indication of our familial propensity for inaction rather than any inherent saintliness.

Then came responsibility in the annoying form of Mother and the three of us. Whether he liked it or not, baby food cut into his shirt budget. Father realized that he couldn't magically turn into a bachelor every evening and disappear to a matinée with a friend. (Not that he'd stopped doing that entirely but had cut down to about once a week). So he did the next best thing. He continued to live in the '50s.

Any conversation with him invariably led to the Golden Age of Hollywood. All we heard was about Lauren Bacall's voice, John Wayne's gait or Tyrone Power's profile. Every little fancy of ours, which naturally had to do with *now*, was pooh-poohed with the help of a bigger, better, more beautiful '50s' example.

> *Father*: What are those ridiculous trousers you're wearing?
> *Lalli*: Bell-bottoms.
> *Father*: Only sailors wear bell-bottoms. Don't you remember Gene Kelly in *On the Town*?
> *Lalli*: They're in fashion now, Naanna. Everyone in school's wearing them.
> *Father*: Why don't you wear those dresses like Debra Paget in *Ten Commandments*? They look so nice.

Apparently, Father was under the impression that the Old Testament had unfolded in the '50s.

Father was a terrific storyteller and, on the odd rainy evening, forced to stay indoors, he could be coaxed into telling us stories. While other kids heard of Krishna's love for his childhood friend Sudama or the brave exploits of Bhima from their grandmothers, we were narrated the plot lines of such movies as *A Place in the Sun* or *Bad Day at Black Rock*, sound effects and all.

Father's jealously guarded library was a shrine to '50s pop culture. There were issues and issues of *Picturegoer*, *Screen Stories* and *Photoplay* arranged chronologically and maintained in mint condition. There were equally well-stocked sections of pulp fiction, pocket cartoon books and comic books. If Martians had blown Earth to smithereens and the only thing that survived was Father's library, they would have had a pretty good idea of what Americans were up to in the '50s – provided they could read English.

It was only natural, what with the running commentary on the fabled '50s, that I found myself drawn to Father's collection of books. On weekends, after having learnt to jimmy the lock to the cupboards from the ever-resourceful Pandu, I quietly disappeared with a stack of well-chosen mags and comics to the little room at the top of the staircase. In that little oven of a room, where the hot air of the entire house was trapped, I spent hours looking at Gina Lollobrigida's magnificent cleavage, Alan Ladd's fading good looks and publicity shots of a nineteen-year-old starlet on the verge of discovery called Joan Collins. I read the columns of Walter Winchell and Hedda Hopper. I was mesmerized by the black-and-white illustrations of Sun Comics featuring the adventures of a sanitized Billy the Kid. Somehow, American comic book manufacturers had turned the notorious real-life outlaw into a masked crusader of the poor and downtrodden. All by myself, I laughed out loud at the exploits of Tubby, Little Lulu, Iodine and Donald Duck. And though I didn't fully get the humour of the French cartoons, the topless women made it amply clear that they were all about the same subject. The variety of illustration styles on display was incredible, and I made it a point to note the names of the artists. Campaign's style was meticulous, almost sculpture-like; Hogarth's figures had lithe bodies and adopted near-impossible poses; Marge and Cavalli, the funny guys, used very few lines but their pictures were just as terrific, while Jimmy Hatlo seemed to enjoy drawing excruciatingly ugly kids.

It's common for older siblings to pass on an old geometry box or a pair of trousers they've outgrown to a younger member of the family. Those can be put away in a dusty corner of your cupboard. But the hand-me-down fixation of an obsessive parent is impossible to discard. Maybe it was because I listened harder or maybe it was because Father was aloof and I wanted his attention. But it was I, far more than my sisters, who became his willing and enthusiastic slave.

Father was my hero. He could draw, he was a walking Hollywood dictionary, and owned the best comics in the world. He was the King of Hep.

Like most kids, I didn't realize this was all stuff *he* considered important. I never did consider whether I'd have been similarly infected had his thing been nuclear physics.

I constantly quizzed him on 'our' favourite subject, and he was more than happy to give me his unshakeable opinion.

'Naanna, who's handsomer? Gregory Peck or Cary Grant?'

'Neither. It's Tyrone Power. Gregory Peck's cheeks are too hollow and Cary Grant's lower lip sticks out. Tyrone Power is flawless.'

Like a big-eared parrot, I repeated everything he said to my friends at Vidya Vihar who didn't know Hollywood from balsa wood.

When I wasn't listening to Father talk films, I loved to watch him draw. My small moda was a permanent fixture in his studio. It was set to his left, so as not to hinder his drawing hand, in the tiny space between his easel and the comic-filled cupboard. It took the place of the 'upper berth' in my life.

I knew from the comics I read that putting one together was a team effort. If you looked at the credits at the bottom of the first page, there was a storywriter, a penciller, an inker, a colourist, a letterist and an editor. Sometimes the comics carried little bios of them. They were all professionally trained, had gone to art school and got all kinds of degrees.

How come Father, who'd never seen the inside of a classroom, did all these jobs himself?

Watching Father draw was like witnessing a daily magic show from a dress-circle seat. A typical page of comic art that he put together took shape in this manner. Taking the crisp machine-trimmed page, he first divided it into three equal rectangles drawn one below the other. Then he pencilled in the script into the boxes. Oval bubbles with a pointy tail directed towards the speaker encompassed speech and cloud-shaped bubbles with steadily shrinking tiny circles at their bottom indicated thoughts. Even-toothed starbursts surrounded Indianized sound effects, *Dham* for 'Crash' and *Bhal* for 'Splash'.

Having got the words out of the way, the artist took over. This was the part I liked. Using a Venus HB pencil, Father made people and places appear magically on the page in their rough form. Construction lines that wouldn't appear in the final drawing fixed features in their proper place on faces, and limbs in their right proportion on the bodies. Expertly, Father alternated close-ups with long shots and mid-range shots to best convey the drama in the story. For instance, the opening panel of a comic book was invariably a long shot.

'How will the reader know where the story is taking place unless you establish the location and atmosphere right in the beginning?' he would say.

People reacting in surprise or fear was almost always a close-up.

'The reader needs to see the expression of the character.'

And a close-up very rarely followed another close-up.

'Monotony! You've got to mix it up. Change the angles.'

Then came the inking of the picture.

This was the time for hard decisions. A line once inked would remain there for eternity. Father detested using Poster White to opaque out errors. Using a variety of nibs and brushes dipped and redipped in Camel 99 Indelible Ink, he miraculously chose the correct line among the mess of pencil strokes and construction lines of the sketch. With every stroke, the wet ink from the nib caught the light and glittered for a magical fraction of a second before being sucked in by the thirsty paper. Shadow and highlight appeared seamlessly as the drawing progressed.

When the inking was done, and the page was suitably dry, I was called in for a job that has never been credited on the pages of any comic book – the Eraser.

As Father had his mid-morning coffee, I carefully erased all the pencil lines and shook out the rubber crumbs while staring in wonder at the page. Magicians betrayed princes, horses came back riderless to castles and beautiful bustier-clad damsels wept, imprisoned in dungeons. The slim lithe hero, with a scimitar hanging from his waistband, always sported an impeccable hairstyle, like his Brilliantine-saturated counterparts from Father's Hollywood.

In the last box of every page was Father's groovy signature: 'Baloo', with little dots in the corner of the two 'O's that made them look like a pair of mischievous eyes.

The colouring style Father adopted for his comic strips was almost childlike, flat, even coats of prime colour filled in carefully so as not to breach their ink line boundaries. For this, he used something called 'photo colours', originally created to colourize black-and-white publicity stills of films to make multicoloured posters. It seemed there was no keeping apart Father and films. He had figured out somehow that photo colours, with their vibrant, transparent nature, suited his comic book art.

Instead of the usual bottles or tubes, these colours came in books. These fascinating little books, roughly the size of a cheque book, contained sheets of metallic paper with names like Peacock Blue, Vermillion, Chrome Yellow and Leaf Green. When a small piece of the required shade was put on a plate and a few drops of water added, the colour would bleed onto the plate in dreamy tendrils. It was just about the neatest trick I'd ever seen in my life. However many times I saw this, it continued to amaze me. I wondered who the genius who invented photo colour papers was.

The colouring itself was an organized affair. Instead of finishing up all the colours in one panel and moving to the next, it was done clinically, colour by colour, several pages at a time. The yellows were filled in first in all the pages, then the blues, the greens and so on.

One day, having been served up with an imposition in school, I got into trouble for incorporating this method in the hope of finishing it quick time. My writing task – 'I will submit my homework on time' – to be written a hundred times. Instead of writing the entire sentence once and moving on to the next line, I tried writing a hundred 'I's first, followed by a hundred 'will's, and so on. I was caught by my teacher who seemed mad for some reason. My punishment: another imposition that went 'I will write impositions line by line and not word by word'.

Sometimes, Father dabbed the colours on an overlay sheet of tracing paper instead of applying them directly on the page. Then the Gateway sheet would shrivel up like CG's skin and the resultant blurred multicoloured quilt of an indefinite pattern wouldn't make much sense to me.

One day I asked him: 'How's anyone going to make out which colour goes where, Naanna?'

Father gave me a knock on the head, turned the page around, and held it up to the window. As light passed through the tightly stretched overlay sheet and the drawing, I could see the hero's tunic in red, the foliage in green and all the colours exactly in their place – clear as a printed page! Now, how in hell had he figured *that* out?

When I told him I wanted to be a children's illustrator when I grew up, Father told me three things: that the key element in a children's drawing was expression, that I should never hesitate while drawing a line even if it was going wrong and, most importantly, that he'd kick me in the bum if I ever entertained the idea of becoming an artist.

EIGHT

Father drew every day between ten and one and on some days again between three and five. That is, every day other than Saturday and Sunday. But before I tell you what he did with his weekends, I'll have to tell you about Raymond Simmons.

Raymond Simmons wasn't tall or blond. Nor did he look like the illegitimate offspring of Raymond Burr and Jean Simmons. He was five-foot-three, wore his trousers a couple of inches below his nipples and was what matrimonial ads described as 'homely'. About that there was no controversy. As to all the other details about him, there were two versions available at home – Mother's and Father's.

In Father's version, Raymond 'Call me Ray' Simmons was a hero, a cross between Tyrone Power and Edward R. Murrow. He had picked up Father from obscurity and put him on the national map by giving him an opportunity to draw for *The India Journal of Arts*, of which he was editor. His generosity hadn't stopped there. Seeing that the gauche artist from Andhra needed a mentor, Simmons had volunteered for that role. Then, selflessly setting aside giant gobs of his valuable time, Simmons (who had now become 'Ray' to Father) took it upon himself to teach his protégé everything a young man of high society needed to know. In other words, he was Professor Higgins to Father's Eliza Doolittle – without the sexual tension.

In Mother's version, Raymond Simmons was Rayamandalam Narasimhan, a schoolteacher from small-town Tamil Nadu. He had conned a rich widow, eloped with her to Bombay, had his moniker anglicized, used his wife's contacts to get a job as a reporter, brown-nosed his way up the journalistic ladder and bumped the poor woman off.

Next, to amuse himself, Narasimhan had tried to introduce her fool husband to the joys of wine and women. When his young protégé exhibited neither the liver nor the libido required for these pursuits, he hadn't given up. He presented his last option – horse racing.

When Father won a thousand rupees on his very first visit to the race course, he was hooked – and that took care of his weekends forevermore.

I liked Mother's version better.

I remember the first time I heard Uncle Ray and Father discuss racing. It was in Hyderabad.

'Pity my horse came in second,' said Father to Uncle Ray who was nodding sympathetically, 'it was by a whisker.'

Father could ride a horse? All I had seen him ride thus far was on the pillion of his friend's Vespa, that, too, side-saddle, like a girl.

This was fantastic. I had to tell my friends. Then Uncle Ray spoke about *his* horse. *He* could ride, too? This was too much. Maybe Father and Uncle Ray had their own band of Merrie

Men who raced up and down the hills of Hyderabad righting wrongs.

I wanted in.

'Naanna, can I join?'

'Join what?' Father looked surprised.

'You know, the Race Club, to ride along with Uncle Ray and you.'

Father thought for a bit.

'Sure, you can,' he said, 'but not now. You'll have to be eighteen.'

'Why?'

Father did some more thinking.

'Because they don't have horses your size,' he said.

With my membership in the club more than ten years away, I lost interest.

I wasn't to know that what Father had taken up was something far more dangerous than galloping across the jagged Deccan terrain on a highly unpredictable beast. And, unlike Robin Hood and his Merrie Men, he belonged to a band that helped rob the foolish to pay the rich.

When I think about it, it wasn't really all that bizarre that Father picked up gambling. It ran in the family. CG was a gambler, too, except he didn't go to the racecourse. And, as it turned out, Father's entire life was a bookie's delight. If an adventurous punter had been secretly betting on him, he'd have made a fortune. After what CG had done, what were his chances of learning the alphabet, finding a wife, having children, having a successful career or, for that matter, having a career at all? Bookies would have offered a minimum of a hundred to one on anything normal happening in his life.

Though it was Simmons who introduced him to the delights of the turf, Father took it to the next level all by himself. When a person takes up drinking as a hobby, it's not enough to just buy a bottle of booze and knock it back. The fun is in getting proper glasses, a nifty ice bucket, chilled sodas and salty snacks. To jazz up the principal hobby of losing money, Father picked up a delightful range of sub-indulgences like numerology, astrology, and the study of the effects of Rahu Kalam.

On Fridays, with the last panel coloured, whatever the weather, Father rushed off to the news-stand in Pondy Bazaar to pick up a little pink book which contained the details of the races scheduled for the weekend: the names of the horses, the parentage of the animal, the names of the owners, trainers, the jockeys riding them with mention of their weight and the colours they would be wearing, the publisher's choice for winner. This became Father's favourite reading material, taking the place of his *Picturegoer*s and James Hadley Chases.

NINE

I don't know if the celestial town-planners went 'Let's put all the freaks in a neat little cluster' or whether we would have ended up being instantly surrounded by nut jobs even if we had built ourselves a log cabin in Death Valley. But, somehow, that's the way it looked from home. At Ramalingam Street, if you threw a tranquillizer dart, chances were it would find a psycho.

The neighbour to our right, the same one whose bathroom our garage roof played viewing gallery to, gave us no reason to look into his bathroom at all. Not that we didn't try. But the freak show he had in mind was far too spectacular to be conducted within its four walls.

On the second Sunday of every month, the octogenarian stripped down to a loincloth and seated himself on a stool in his garden. This was a pretty scary sight in itself but I was bored, nine years old, and would have watched a nose-digging competition if there had been one.

The first time I saw our neighbour this way, I was puzzled by his two-toned complexion. His face looked normal but his body was white as a polar bear. Closer inspection – though why I wanted to examine the body of a shrivelled, semi-naked eighty-year-old in a more thorough manner beats me

– revealed that the whiteness wasn't his skin so much as a bullet-proof rug of hair covering every visible square inch of his body. What followed was something that would have shocked even Auntie Renu's family.

An efficient-looking gentleman, who had been standing around quietly, poured a bucket of hot water on the old man. As tendrils of steam rose off the old fellow, the man proceeded to lather his entire body using a creamy soap and what looked like a giant shaving brush. Soon, the old man, who'd resembled the mythical Yeti a few minutes ago, looked like a miniature cumulus cloud with a human head coming out of it. The man then pulled out a knife from his toolbox and proceeded to sharpen its 8" blade on a rotating wheel powered by a foot pedal. All the while, our neighbour stared impassively at passers-by who'd been paralysed into spectators.

After several minutes of flying sparks the knife gleamed like the principal weapon in a horror film. With the skill of a sheep shearer, not to mention the stoicism of a Sister of Mercy, the barber then shaved the old man with smooth, even strokes that Father would have envied. Each deft stroke removed a little pincushion of foam and hair to reveal a bald strip of eighty-year-old skin till there was a giant ball of furry lather on one side and a naked, hairless geriatric on the other. Finally, all that remained untended was the real estate within the loincloth.

The audience waited, even as the last vestiges of their sanity fought a losing battle with their frozen eyeballs. There was a murmur in the crowd as the barber put his big knife back in his tool box and pulled out a smaller one. In a sudden show of coyness, the old man got up, turned his back to the spectators and opened his garment to the kneeling barber. Then, though we couldn't see much, there was the unmistakable sound of knife on soapless hair.

Krrrk. Krrrk.

It was obvious the barber knew his craft. Soap meant obscuring his view, a chance he couldn't take in this region. Delicate operation complete, the old man faced his audience but not before covering his shiny new loins while leaving his rear exposed. With this, the kneeling barber finally shaved my neighbour's ass to conclude operations. An hour or so later, after the stragglers had left, the maid swept the tonsured off-white fur, baked dry by the Madras sun into one big mound before disposing of it. I don't know about the other people who witnessed this event but I never, ever again ate son papdi.

Which really was a pity, because the best-ever son papdi I tasted was made down our street in the corner house where the Dikshits lived. Not just son papdi, the samosas, gulab jamuns, and anything you could get from Bombay Halwa House in Luz, the Dikshit kitchen did better.

Old Man Dikshit owned a pharmaceutical company and they were easily the richest people in the neighbourhood. They had a big games room with a ping-pong table. The Dikshit kids, Bunty and Chunky, became my friends and we played TT once in a while. But, for some reason, Pandu & Co., their palm tree climbing skills notwithstanding, were not welcome in their house and I didn't like that. But, loyalty apart, it was very difficult to turn my back entirely on the goodies. So I began two-timing Pandu very early on in our relationship.

When they had a birthday party for the younger son, Chunky, the gifts they gave us cost more than what Father spent on any of our birthdays. The Dikshits were a close-knit family and did everything together: movies, vacations... Well, almost everything, anyway, because they never could get into a lift together. Otis elevators came with the standard warning: 'Not to exceed eight people or 600 kg'. Together, the four Dikshits weighed a little more than that.

If the Dikshits were not elevator-friendly, it was mainly because of Maharaj, their cook, who insisted on adding pure butter to everything (including, I suspect, the coffee). Which is why the stuff he made was leagues ahead of Bombay Halwa House fare.

Mother spoke fluent Hindi. If you were south Indian, it meant that you could communicate with any north Indian because that's what they all spoke. Mother was easygoing and befriended, among others, Mrs Dikshit, and soon managed to get Maharaj's wife and second-in-command to come over on Sundays so that our wheat-challenged family could learn how to make chapatis that didn't taste like footwear. One such day, a most amazing lifestyle detail of the Dikshits came to our attention.

'How come you're free today, Lila, do Saab and Memsaab go out of town on Sundays?' my mother said, showing off her Hindi.

'Nahin, didi! Sunday, na, nobody eats.'

'Some religious fast?'

'No. They go to the bathroom on Sundays.'

My mother was horrified.

'They go to the bathroom *only* on Sundays?'

'No, didi, they go on other days. But today, they *only* go.'

'What do you mean *only* go?'

I remember Lalli telling me the average human being sets aside about seven to eight minutes a day for his bowels. In our one-bathroomed house, we were lucky if we got three. But what if you are fed by Maharaj? Was it fair to have just about three-quarter of an hour per week to get rid of nearly 16 kg of stubborn butter and maida that has set like a 23-foot concrete snake in your intestines? It was natural that the Dikshits dedicated all of Sunday to the evacuation of the week's backlog. Their marathon effort – patience and peristalsis apart – was apparently aided by the best the R&D Department of Dikshit Pharma could provide.

That day, as I ate Lila Devi's terrific chapatis a tad more circumspect than usual, I told myself that I wouldn't judge anyone too quickly. Here I was thinking that the most unfortunate man in the world was my eighty-year-old neighbour's barber when there was a chap who cleaned the Dikshit septic tank every Monday.

My patchy friendship with the Dikshit children ended completely that summer when they caught Pandu acting suspicious outside their gate one day. When Pandu ran away, they looked around and found that he'd altered the posh brass nameplate, which read 'THE DIKSHITS' in an elegant font ever so slightly. Pandu had scratched out the 'DIK' and written the word 'BIG' above it.

The pharmaceutical experiments of the Dikshits were tame compared to the ones conducted by Dr C. Sarathi, our seventy-five-year-old family doctor who conveniently lived a street away. Like all social contacts in our family, the good doctor, too, was sourced from that cup that kept on giving, the Telugu film industry. Dr Sarathi's claim to fame was that he had been the great N.T. Rama Rao's physician in the '60s. The thespian had moved on but our doctor hadn't. No visit of ours was complete without Dr Sarathi telling us about the glorious days of his youth when he'd treated and cured a young, and apparently very sickly, NTR of a variety of ailments. The doctor told us stories of his heroism and selflessness as he saved the unfortunate actor from a fate worse than anything the mythological demons he'd encountered in so many films could put him through. Though we were appreciative of fantastic stories, thanks to the occasional bedtime efforts of Father's, the three of us somehow didn't enjoy the experience as much as we should have. Maybe it had to do with Dr Sarathi's repeated attempts to puncture our exposed behinds with his one and only hypodermic, circa *Raja Harischandra*.

We survived Dr Sarathi's attempts to make our rear ends look like pointillist art but I don't know how we survived the Magic Medicine he administered to treat anything from common colds to weakness. For a man who lived in the '50s, if his stories and syringe were any indication, Dr Sarathi was all for keeping up with current trends where medicines were concerned. Whatever our ailment, other than the usual antibiotics, he always prescribed a booster dose of little pink pills. He called them 'Vitamins of the Gods'.

Grandfather could write moving poetry about dying moons and living stones and Father could make talking animals spout wisdom but, as far as common sense went, they were in the same league as the village idiot. That their children who'd been wheeled in on a stretcher were fit enough to take part in a half-marathon after taking the Magic Pills didn't strike them as suspicious.

The high point of Dr Sarathi's medical experiments took place when Grandfather decided one day that his favourite granddaughter looked a little too weak. Dr Sarathi said it was no problem as he had a 'new, improved, super-power magic medicine with extra vitamins' that would have my emaciated older sister pulling our Ambassador up St Thomas Mount with her teeth after just twelve doses.

Dose One went fine. Lalli said that she felt good.

After Dose Two, she said, 'I feel better!' but in a voice that sounded a bit like she'd taken up smoking on the sly.

Slow as they were, when my sister began to sound like Amitabh Bachchan, Father and Grandfather figured out something was wrong and decided to get a second opinion from a doctor who'd not passed out of the film institute.

The new doctor looked carefully at the prescriptions of Dr C. Sarathi and thought for an entire minute as Father waited. Then he calmly took off his stethoscope and gestured to Father to come closer. As Father leaned towards him, wondering what the secrecy was about, the doctor coiled the steth around his neck and tried to garrotte him. When he was subdued by his staff, the doctor made Father promise him that he'd never, ever take his kids near Dr Sarathi ever again.

The 'Vitamins of the Gods' that Dr Sarathi had been pumping us with were apparently industrial-strength steroids.

Just as we thought things couldn't get any more exciting in our neighbourhood, we were informed that the bungalow in front of our house lying vacant was going to have new tenants, the Maharani and the Crown Prince of Devagiri. Apparently, they owned the place and were moving in. This was fantastic. A real live Queen and Prince in our midst. Maybe they were moving because the evil Prime Minister had poisoned the benevolent king. Maybe they'd park their horses in the vacant space where we played cricket once in a while. Why, they could park an elephant, too, if it was an Asiatic elephant. Anyway, it would have to be an Indian elephant because I'd heard that African ones couldn't be tamed. I was so excited that I told all my friends. I wondered if they'd be dressed like Father's drawings – Walt Disney meets Ravi Varma. That would be terrific. Or, would they be dressed like the drab kings in our history books? Shirtless chaps with lopsided turbans who looked more like medieval milkmen.

'Naanna, you don't have to go to the races any more,' I told Father one day. He stared in alarm at me. What in hell did I mean, not go to the races?

'All the references you need – for horses – will be available right across our road, once the Maharani moves into her bungalow. Isn't that great?'

'That...er...may be so, but...you know, when you draw as many horses as I do, you'll need variety. So I guess I'll still have to go to the racecourse.'

'Maybe not so often.'

'Um.'

I was too excited to be disappointed by Father's reply. I had so much to do. I wanted to ask them (after I got to know them better, of course) whether the king had planted shady trees all along the roads in his kingdom. That would be a subtle way to find out if he was a good king or not. From Rajaraja Chola to Akbar – all good kings planted shady trees. Everyone knew that.

The lorries arrived first, full of cardboard boxes all carefully lowered by workmen. Probably contained rapiers, armour, antique medallions and royal seals. None of the workers looked like soldiers, though. Maybe the soldiers would come in the cavalcade preceding the car, definitely a Rolls-Royce, carrying the Queen and Prince.

The first people to arrive in a rickety two-toned Fiat were a man and a woman. The man was unshaven. The woman looked slovenly in her nylon saree, and walked with a stoop. Must be the servants. They opened the boot, pulled out a couple of suitcases, and went in. The Maharani and the Yuvaraj couldn't be far behind. I waited. As day turned into evening, I'd brought down my expectations considerably. I was willing to let go of the horses, the elephants, the Rolls and the convoy. Just one turbanned prince in a zari sherwani with a sword, or even a knife, in his waistband. That's all I asked for.

No one came. I gave up my wait and went to sleep.

The next day, I went to school and forgot all about the Prince and Queen. There was no activity in the house to rekindle my interest. A few days later, I wondered about our royal neighbours and asked my mother, 'Ma, what happened to the Queen? Wasn't she supposed to come?'

'What do you mean, supposed to come? They came two days ago. Don't you remember, you were on the terrace watching as they drove up.'

'When!? *Where!?*'

'The old lady and her bearded son. Don't you remember?'

TEN

Inspired by the adventures of the Famous Five, the three of us decided we needed a dog. But we had a problem. CG hated dogs almost as much as he hated making up his mind, and was quite free expressing this feeling. Street dogs of T. Nagar retracted their tails into their rectums and took off wailing like a convoy of ambulances at the sight of Grandfather taking an evening stroll, walking stick in hand. The compassionate poet (sometimes referred to as the 'Andhra Shelley') who wrote of flowing streams and gentle deer turned into a red-eyed maniac at the sight of strays. Screaming in a voice that only the dogs could hear, he charged at them like a medieval warrior and cleared the road in ten seconds flat. When Grandfather visited friends who owned dogs, the instructions were clear: chain the sons-of-bitches. The same horror of dogs percolated down to Grandmother and Father who reacted with either a 'Chi, po!' or a 'Help!!' depending on whether their encounter involved a feeble mongrel or an Alsatian that had come loose.

Mother's was a different story. She had loved dogs all her life and loved them even more when she realized that the enemy hated them. So when we told her that we'd like to have a dog, she rubbed her hands in glee and let out a cackle of delight.

Our lucky break came in the form of Bonkers' litter. Bonkers was a jet-black stray that had walked into Auntie Renu's household and stayed on against better judgement. Maybe that's why she was called Bonkers. When Bonkers' unprotected liaisons with multiple partners resulted in a steady stream of hideous-looking pups, the Bankas had to do something and assigned the job of litter clearance to Dodo. This he did by putting them in a box, transporting them on a borrowed motorcycle and abandoning them on the streets of St Thomas Mount. This scheme worked out okay in the beginning. But, on one occasion, having left with two pups, Dodo returned with six pups, two kittens and a goat. Investigations revealed that, in his hunt for a suitable spot to abandon the pups, Dodo had stumbled upon a peddler of Grade A pot. Naturally, he had smoked a joint, and another till he was seized with a serious case of the guilts and decided to atone for his previous crimes by providing sanctuary to homeless animals.

'When all else fails, sucker a Meghamala.' The Bankas knew this as well as the rest of Andhra Pradesh. One day, as we were playing with the latest batch of plug-ugly pups that Bonkers had spewed out, Auntie Renu put her arms around Kavi and me and said, 'Hey, kids, choose one and take it home. It is my gift to you!'

Kavi and I whooped with joy at the rare show of generosity from the old skinflint. We quickly came back to earth when an image of Grandfather rhythmically stomping the pup to a furry pulp popped simultaneously into our heads. Auntie Renu somehow saw the gory animated film clip running in our minds.

'Don't worry about your grandfather. I'll take care of him!' she said.

Without wasting a second, Kavi and I picked out a coal-black male pup with a stub of a tail from the mess of tongues and paws on display and ran home with our brand-new pet before Auntie Renu could change her mind.

At home, CG, who'd already received a call from her, was in the expected state. He was twirling the walking stick like a scimitar and threatening to kill everybody starting with Grandmother. It was family tradition for Grandmother to get right of first refusal whenever CG thought of inflicting pain on anyone. But his dance of death was mere posturing because the wily Renuka Bai was one of the few people who could twist my grandfather like a coir rope. The three of us secreted the whiney little pup in our room and decided to name it while Grandmother ducked flying objects of metal and stone.

I was keen on 'Buster' – after the clever little black Scottie that belonged to Fatty in the Enid Blyton mysteries. So 'Buster' it was.

Within its first month in our house, Buster survived several assassination attempts at the hands of CG. The first was with a Godrej Seven Lever Navtal that missed the pup by a whisker. A javelin throw of his walking stick was next. The pup escaped but the assistant director on duty didn't. He swore off films and took the next bus to his native village. But Buster seemed to have borrowed a few lives from the neighbour's cat and survived every single stealth attack with not a scratch on its tar-black body. But the same couldn't be said of the poor mutt's mind. Grandfather's surprise strikes, the strict vegetarian diet of dal and rice with a spoon of ghee, the steady flow of perverts in the Meghamala home who called it anything from 'Bhaskar' to 'Bastard' and three children who de-ticked it on a twenty-four hour basis made it take the *Gaslight* route of Ingrid Bergman.

For the uninitiated, the conventional doggie greeting accepted around the world more or less follows these four steps.

Step One: The waggy-tailed run-up.
Step Two: The two-legged stand, front paws resting on human.
Step Three: Head lift to accept chin scratch pat.
Step Four: Depart with waggy tail.

Buster got Step One and Step Two right but altered the dynamic of the greeting by inserting a Hitchcockian Step Three of its own. That was: urinate on leg of human.

ELEVEN

I'm pretty sure that someone had pasted wall posters all over Andhra Pradesh that went 'Attention, aspiring singers, actors, musicians and sundry no-goods looking for a break in Telugu films! Absolutely no talent required! Contact Meghamala Radhakrishna. Free boarding and lodging available!' because the response was terrific. Every week our doorbell would announce the arrival of a fresh candidate from Teluguland's underbelly. He or she would be fed, clothed, housed and taken off in our Amby to do a round of studios and film companies. Some took a month, others took a year but every talentless petitioner was found employment in the film industry. Such was CG's goodwill. It was a matter of detail that aspiring singers found themselves in the camera department and hopeful actors found succour as assistant directors.

Once, there was this flautist who stayed with us for what were the most excruciating five days of our life. At his 'audition' he proved that while he was a man of many talents, none of them had to do with music. Armed with nothing more than an innocuous wooden pipe, he produced what sounded like a dead-on imitation of a bird sanctuary reeling under an attack of nerve gas. Grandfather promptly welcomed him into the fold. Taking this as a sign of encouragement, at four o' clock the following morning, the piper pulled out his flute and practised his interpretation of avian anguish for a full hour. On Day Three, Buster thought it fit to join in. Day Four – Raghavan was diagnosed with tinnitus and hospitalized. The flautist, however, left in a huff on the fifth day. The reason – when he woke up, took a deep breath and blew into his flute no sound came out. Inspection revealed that the other end had been stuffed with a ball of maida that had hardened into stone overnight. The culprit was never found.

Within a year, the flautist was so successful that he bought a house in Madras, which his mentor, my grandfather, couldn't manage in his lifetime. He achieved this not so much through his exhaling skills as his inhaling ones. Grandfather had found him a job as production assistant in a film company. The sudden death of his boss saw him promoted to production manager. The erstwhile piper, putting his breath control to maximum use, sucked away in under a year what he wouldn't have been able to make in ten years playing background bits. In his second year, he produced a film, was ripped off by *his* production manager, sold the house and went back to Andhra.

If our home was the confluence of several streams from Andhra's mythical Glacier of Freaks, Father fed it with a few local rivulets of his own. Sourced from the elite precincts of the Madras Race Club and Udipi Sri Shanta Bhavan, he regularly brought home people who were as talent-free as CG's candidates. The only difference was they weren't all Telugu. That my sisters and I escaped molestation, not to mention having our throats slit and our organs harvested by this conveyor belt of delinquents, can only be attributed to divine intervention.

There was Saikumar, a schoolteacher from Chirala, who quit his job and came to Madras to become a playback singer. He couldn't have reached our home faster if someone had picked him up at Central Station and driven him over to our place. Those wall posters now probably had a map to our house as well. Within fifteen minutes of his arrival he had belted out two off-key renditions of Grandfather's most popular songs, was calling him Thaathagaru, my grandmother Baammagaru, while Mother had become Akkayyagaru. This caused a fair amount of confusion in my young mind. Was this stranger with a bad voice my brother or my uncle? Worse still, did this mean that my father had married his sister?

It was a time of transition for film music in Andhra. The ageing Ghantasala who had been the voice of N.T. Rama Rao and Akkineni Nageswara Rao was running out of breath. The Telugu film industry, known for sticking to the tested over the original, was scouring light music troupes and hotel bands for failure-proof clones. Aspiring singers, rather than develop an individual style, modelled their voices along the lines of the bell-toned Ghantasala, hoping to be instantly accepted. Saikumar was no different.

In reality, the erstwhile schoolteacher was pretty thin-voiced but hoped to achieve the Ghantasalesque timbre through a series of ingenious steps. In this scheme, Saikumar's first co-conspirator was his tailor in Chirala. Apparently, he had been instructed to fit Saikumar's shirts with a collar two sizes too small. The first thing the singer did before a formal rendition was to suck in his neck and button up his collar. As a result, his face instantly turned a hot pink. The next step – a giant swig of boiling water prepared and kept ready by my mother aka Akkayyagaru. This deepened his face to a tandoori maroon. Step Three involved cutting off the remainder of the oxygen to his lungs by clutching his throat with his right hand. Finally, Saikumar closed his left ear tightly shut with the free hand and waited in this pose for a second or two. When he turned the appropriate shade of purple the singer began his performance. For the next five horrific minutes, Saikumar's head fought maniacally to break free from the death grip of Saikumar's hand. The song itself tortured forth, sounding like the venerable Ghantasala begging for mercy from a particularly sadistic assailant. A lone tendril of smoke escaped from Saikumar's free ear. By the time the song was done, so was Saikumar – in the manner of gutthi vankaya kura, a stuffed brinjal preparation cooked directly over the fire. After the polite round of applause, which had more to do with relief at Saikumar's survival from his own masochistic assault than his rendition, he was ready for his next song.

When Saikumar was not singing he was kept busy in the guru-sishya parampara of yore. He accompanied Mother vegetable shopping, was assigned small carpenterial and plumbing projects, re-copied CG's manuscripts in his schoolmasterly hand and baby-sat us on occasion.

One day, I was having a bit of target practice with a homemade bow and arrow. The bow was a combination of coconut sticks and industrial twine (from Raghavan's booty) put together following instructions from Arthur Mee's *Children's Encyclopaedia* and my own latent sadism. For the arrows, I switched to the feathery broom. The dried fronds were ripped off and the naked stick was sharpened to a needlepoint. An empty cylindrical calendar box served as a quiver. On the whole, this was no child's toy but the product of a disturbed mind brought up on Sitting Bull comics. Soon, I was busily shooting off arrows at a target made with pilfered cardboard and paints from Father's stock.

Saikumar seemed free that day. No music director to torture, no drain to unplug. So he picked on me.

'What's so great about shooting at paper?' he said scornfully.

The picture of obsequiousness with CG, Saikumar showed a lot more of his true self to us. He told us off whenever he could, sang bawdy versions of Grandfather's songs and mocked us when the adults weren't around. He was somehow sure we wouldn't rat on him and he'd been right so far.

'So what do you suggest I do?' I said.

'I'll stand in front of you with a target on my head. Let's see you shoot then!'

Before I could protest, Saikumar returned with a tomato from the kitchen and placed it on his head. He had obviously read a less-than-faithful translation of William Tell. Arms akimbo he sniggered at me.

'Go on...or are you scared?' he taunted.

I didn't get it. Why would I be scared? He was the one being shot at.

So I took careful aim and let fly.

Just because I made a mean bow didn't mean I was a good shot. The arrow missed the tomato by about 5″ and embedded itself into Saikumar's septum with a thwack, quivered for a few seconds and stopped.

A lone drop of blood trickled down the singer's nose.

I guess the pain induced by self-inflicted torture is quite different from pain inflicted by someone else. Saikumar, survivor of a thousand stranglings by his own hand and super-cool drinker of super-hot fluids, screamed in a voice reminiscent not so much of Ghantasala as his partner in love duets, P. Susheela.

That marked the simultaneous end of my archery practice and Saikumar's taunts.

The next direct-from-Andhra import was another singer. But the similarity between poor Saikumar and this one ended there. The new entrant had a husky voice with no help whatsoever from tight collars – though if anyone needed a collar *and* leash, it was this one. But we'll come to that later.

Her name was Lanka Jhansi and, boy, could she sing. Out of the blue, she landed up at our place, sat at Grandfather's feet and belted out song after song with the ease of the seasoned stage performer she was. In fifteen minutes everything was fixed. She'd stay with us and more or less use Saikumar's template as far as relationships went. Grandfather was Thaathagaru. Grandmother became Baammagaru. Mother was Akkayyagaru and as a final confirmation of the rampant incest in our family, Father was Annayya.

Lanka Jhansi was the first person to bring breasts to our house. And by that I don't mean that Mother and Grandmother were mammary-free. Nor was the concept of breasts alien to me. The *Picturegoers* and the *Photoplays* from my father's '50s' collection had a fair amount of cleavage on display. But Lanka Jhansi's breasts were the first three-dimensional ones I noticed. As the rest of my family closed their eyes and appreciated her rendition of Grandfather's songs, I was riveted by her breath control.

I don't know if it was joy at my family's response to her singing or the prospect of a free stay in Madras but Jhansi went on a hugging spree. Even Father wasn't spared. She caught me just as I was about to run away.

With a 'Where do you think you're going, you cutie pie!' she shoved my embarrassed face into her breasts and held me there for a full minute. It felt like being asphyxiated by jasmine-scented cushions covered by sequinned nylex cushion covers. I came out gasping for breath and ran away, not unlike Buster on seeing the postman. I realized that day with a great sense of relief that the chances of my ever being gay were slim.

Lanka Jhansi had a profound effect on the women in my house as well. To begin with, my older sister's knowledge of the birds and the bees was advanced by a good three years. It wasn't via a soft-voiced Moral Science approach which began 'When a man loves a woman…' Jhansi's birds and bees wore the Andhra equivalent of leather boots, and cracked whips. One day, when I was spying on the two just out of earshot, Jhansi showed my saucer-eyed sister a dramatic re-enactment, complete with vigorous hand movements and thrashing head, of a bird–bee situation she'd been in. Lalli's spectacles shattered.

Mother, on the other hand, went for a wardrobe change. ('Akkayagaru! These drab cottons are for old people. You should wear nylex. It's in.') Mother took to wearing sequinned nylex saris in copper sulphate blue and monkey bum red. Lunch hours at school turned nerve-racking. While other children ate their meals out of dabbas brought by drab dowagers, I was lovingly fed by the Nylex Nightmare.

With Mother's wardrobe change, what had once been mind-numbingly boring trips to the homes of CG's buddies now became harrowing episodes of the *Twilight Zone*.

Long shot of Venerable Poet getting out of his car.

Cut to people greeting him.

Pan across faces of three hunted-looking children.

They get out of the car, one by one.

Cut to low-angle shot of a woman's foot swinging out of the car and landing on the ground to kick up dust.

Quick cuts in extreme close-up of horrified people.

Tilt up slowly to nylex-clad figure of Mother coming into full view to Bernard Herrmann's shower theme in *Psycho*.

Even before Lalli could have her glasses repaired, Lanka Jhansi moved her moral instruction classes to the next level.

Rajakumari was a neighbourhood theatre that showed an eclectic mix of movies. Tamil movies were the staple. Sunday mornings were reserved for Laurel and Hardy, Tarzan and other kiddy films. When business was dull, Rajakumari showed, to a packed house, that genre of Malayalam film Adoor Gopalakrishnan never quite got the hang of. The posters, which looked like lingerie ads for plus-sized drag queens, regularly caused accidents on the busy Pondy Bazaar road. For the convenience of the non-Malayalam speaking pervert, they also had crisp English titles. *Rape the Typist*, *Lissy's Coconuts* and *Blouse Fever* were among the more popular of these shoestring epics. For some reason Jhansi thought that eleven-year-old Lalli's education would not be complete unless she saw one of these movies. And off they went to *Blouse Fever*, if memory serves me right, with assorted lungi-clad, beedi-smoking sexual deviants from Aminjikarai to Adambakkam for company.

Father somehow got wind of this and stormed into Rajakumari Theatre with a face redder than Mother's saris. The 'House Full' board and a watchman who told him not to panic as tickets for the evening show were still available made him shift to Saikumar purple. The five-foot-two-inch illustrator of children's books kneed the watchman in the nuts, kicked open the door, caught my sister by her ear and dragged her home.

Lanka Jhansi was asked to find alternative accommodation with immediate effect and Lalli's glasses were washed in phenyl.

Unfortunately, Lanka Jhansi's exit to a woman's hostel didn't magically restore Mother's wardrobe to normalcy. The nylex saris continued to haunt us long after. Lalli survived her tour of Jhansi's Den of Depravity and ended up having an average adolescence aided, no doubt, by the guardian angel for squares. Grandfather, quite used to an array of felons zipping in and out of his life for over seventy years, continued with the crossword in *The Madras Mail*. Poor Father ended up having the roughest time. Every night he woke up in a cold sweat from a nightmare starring his oldest child dressed like Sheela in *Chemmeen*.

Just when he thought things were settling down, Lanka Jhansi returned. The woman was not her old self at all. Her sequins seemed to have lost their shimmer. Everyone felt sorry for her and all was forgiven. She sang, was fed and before we knew it, was fast asleep. Everything was back to normal or so we thought.

That night, Father was woken by something much worse than a miscast Malayalam nightmare with Telugu subtitles. It was to the sound of Raghavan's wrought-iron gate being clanged violently. Furtive inspection from behind the curtains of CGs bedroom window revealed the perpetrators to be a medium-sized band of thugs. The Meghamala bowels, already at the mercy of our minuscule toilet, froze – threatening never to thaw in the near future.

But, thankfully, the railway-issue metal monster proved to be a worthy adversary to the gang who were high on arrack and low on coordination. When we crawled out from under our beds the next morning, long after the drunken lorry-load of hooligans with Molotov cocktails and sickles had left, Lanka Jhansi sang like a canary. In the last six months the young lady had been quite busy. Apart from visiting recording studios, surgically removing whatever aesthetic sense my mother possessed and introducing my sister to the finer points of debauchery, she had also been juggling the libidos of half a dozen men. Unfortunately, one of them happened to be a politician's son, and didn't take kindly to being six-timed. He had come a-calling after visiting hours at the hostel in a fully loaded tempo, leading to her expulsion. With nowhere to go she'd come to our place and the chap had followed, albeit with scaled-up operations.

Without wasting a minute, Father did what any sensible father would. He rang up Pistol Rangarao, writer of detective fiction.

With his vast experience in solving fictitious crime, Pistol Rangarao interrogated all of us, smoking cigarette after cigarette. I broke under pressure and confessed to copying the answers from a classmate in the maths test. Rangarao let me off the hook and offered a couple of solutions. One – we leave Madras en famille, settle down in Chandrampalem under assumed names and take up agriculture. Two – we double padlock our gates.

Lanka Jhansi was dropped off at the Madras Central with a one-way ticket to Waltair and we implemented Solution Two.

TWELVE

'Amma, I don't want to go to school!' I said, coming to this decision one evening when we were assigned homework in three subjects.

'Why?' she said.

'It's a waste.'

'How's school a waste?'

'Well,' I said, pointing to my Modern Maths textbook, 'what use is a venn diagram to me? Artists don't draw diagrams, they draw pictures.'

Mother wasn't convinced.

'Whether you become an artist, bank manager or doctor – school's a must. You can't stop going to school!'

Whenever Mother was like this, I pulled out my deal sealer.

'But Naanna didn't go. He's doing fine, isn't he?'

I knew the look on Mother's face. It usually preceded a whack. But instead she changed her approach.

'Maybe. But if you don't have an education, no one will marry you.'

'But *you* married him!' I said, thinking I'd closed the case.

'That's because I was forced to,' said Mother.

'What do you mean "forced to"?'

What was she saying? This was Father we were talking about – my horse-drawing hero who knew everything about Hollywood.

'What's wrong with Naanna?'

Mother was halfway to the kitchen by now. All she said was, 'Finish your homework quickly and go to sleep, you have school tomorrow.'

Mother had lost both parents when she was three or four and was raised by her grandfather. When she was sixteen, the old man had zeroed in on Balakrishna, better known as Cartoonist Baloo (with the two 'O's), who also happened to be son of the poet Meghamala. Mother didn't get it. Why would her industrialist grandfather pick a crazy artist who'd never been to school for her?

In spite of a spirited revolt, Mother lost the battle and married Baloo, eight years her senior, in 1960. Rather than any fear of the patriarch, this had more to do with the gentle coaxing of her sister, Malathi, the only person who ever had any influence on her. But that didn't mean she was about to give up the war. She'd stood up to her grandfather, she sure as hell wasn't about to be cowed down by some poet.

CG was used to twisting people till they looked like corkscrews. Anything was okay so long as he got what he wanted. In Grandmother, he'd found the perfect mate. She never once questioned him. If he said, 'Ratnamma, jump off the building,' her reply would have been 'Please have your coffee. I'll jump as soon as I wash the cup'.

Muttering under his breath, Father had mostly gone along with CG, for two reasons. One – he knew no other way, and two – the horde of sishyas that came with the territory offered him a smokescreen to get away from it all undetected every once in a while.

As for everyone else, they were either charmed off their feet by CG or intimidated into submission. What Grandfather hadn't bargained for was Mother. Though it was impossible to convert CG to her ways, Mother did the next best thing. She didn't allow him to intimidate her for a second.

Mother hoisted the flag of her small independent republic at the very beginning. When my sister was born, there was a big to-do about naming her. CG had a sister who had died young and, on seeing the newborn baby, he decided she was a dead ringer for his dead sister. Mother's feelings were thrown aside by the chorus of thick-skinned hangers-on: 'Exactly like Kasturi! Kasturi's born again!'

Eighteen-year-old Mother fought CG and his hardened bunch of yes-men and named my sister Lalita, after her mother, registering her first victory.

Team Sharada – 1, Team Meghamala – 0.

What interested me in this story was, if the faded picture of CG's sister was anything to go by, infant Lalli looked like Ernest Borgnine.

When I was born, I was automatically named Gopal, for CG's father, Meghamala Gopalakrishna. Mother let that one go to Team Meghamala but got her way by calling me Ramu all her life. Her father, my other, equally legitimate, grandfather, was called Ramarao.

CG may have been the poet and Father the artist but Mother was no less an original thinker. One of her first creative exercises was a non-invasive sex change operation on her first-born. She gave Lalli a crew-cut and dressed her up in boys' clothes. The result, though initially enjoyable, wasn't entirely satisfactory because Lalli insisted on going back to being a girl. Her next target was me. Mother had my hair grow shoulder length and began dressing me in sweet little frocks. I was told, so complete was my conversion that, in under a month, I was bringing a bottle of coconut oil and a comb and sitting on the floor, waiting patiently to have my locks oiled, combed and plaited. Mother would plait my hair, make a pretty little bow out of ribbons which matched my frock, add a small garland of jasmine and send me off to play. How other infants in gender-appropriate gear didn't clobber me to death with their rattles beats me. Instead of opaquing over this phase of my life with Camel Super White, Father recorded it minutely with his camera.

Mother later developed the unpleasant habit of producing these photographs of me in a variety of hairstyles favoured by the mod '60s' woman, wearing frilly frocks *and nothing else*, at the most ill-timed moments. Somehow she was under the impression that they'd enhance my cuteness factor. Prospective girlfriends suddenly remembered a forgotten chore and disappeared, never to return. Miraculously, I buried this traumatic chapter of my life, and didn't turn into a transsexual beautician called Daphne later in life.

Mother was a complete movie freak. If a Lithuanian movie with Swedish subtitles was playing at a theatre near her, she'd be there. If someone told her a movie was lousy, she'd watch it to see how lousy it was. She had had all three of us in the first five years of her marriage. In those years, the only movies the Meghamala women had seen were the ones that featured CG's songs. That just wasn't doing it for Mother any more. With Kavi and me dangling from each arm, my older sister tagging along, she saw an average of two movies a week. This was a covert operation in which an intrepid band of housewives with synchronized watches disappeared along with her on the same days at the same time, reappearing in their kitchens by the time their husbands returned from work. Had we remained in Hyderabad, I'm sure there would have been an unusually large number of divorces in Adarsh Nagar.

Grandfather, not that he'd ever admit it, liked Mother. When she insisted on sending us to school, that was the first display of gonads he had come across in a long time. As time passed, strangely, Mother's outgoing nature matched Grandfather's wanderlust and they became unlikely allies. It was she who'd accompany him on all his mad tours, leaving us to enjoy the rare quiet at home. But this didn't mean Mother had been co-opted by Team Meghamala. CG and she continued fighting like mean children, and she continued playing for her own team of which, I later realized, I was vice-captain.

Father might have been the artist in the family but it was Mother who went through 'phases'. There was the sequinned nylex phase. Then there was the 'fruit only' phase. Every now and then, just as we had begun developing immunity to her latest 'hobby' – bam! – Mother would deliver a haymaker with a new one. Like the doll-making phase.

One Saturday afternoon, with the three of us fed, Mother disappeared in a blaze of parrot-green nylex. The shock waves that the nylex used to send down our collective spines had become a dull, bearable ache of late. We waved an absent goodbye and went back to our lazy afternoon activities. That evening, when she returned with a large jute bag and a new glint in her eye, we knew that something terrible was about to happen. Mother upturned the contents of her bag and looked at us.

'What do you think?' she said.

Strewn all over the floor were the dismembered limbs, torsos and faces of several small men and women who seemed to have met a gruesome end at the hands of a megalomaniac dictator. Kavi screamed and ran away. Lalli and I didn't reply.

'Doll-making! I've joined a doll-making class and I'm going to make and sell dolls!' said Mother triumphantly.

'What about the embroidery?' I asked weakly. 'You're…er… pretty good at it. What about all those sequins you bought in Town?'

'Bore, ra! That was just a hobby. This could turn into a lucrative business, you know.'

To me, the only business opportunity apparent was the trade of human spare parts.

Whether Mother would have a thriving business or not, we came to know that deep in the bowels of George Town someone did. It was a bunch of traders who sold heaps of pink plastic body parts, mounds of artificial hair in every possible shade, expressionless faces of stiff calico, and a variety of fabrics, miniature buttons and bows to thousands of women who were suddenly seized by the urge to make dolls.

My mother's doll-making guru was a neighbourhood housewife called Mrs Neelakantan who ran her show in a quiet street in T. Nagar. For reasons I'm unable to recall, I found myself accompanying Mother to a class one day. Ten women sat on the floor with an array of small body parts, eager to put them together into attractive mini humans while Mrs Neelakantan's own creations, dressed in a variety of costumes, stared blinklessly out of their glass prison in the living room. Using pins, needles and foul-smelling glue, Mother and her classmates painfully produced small nude women, thankfully devoid of genitalia. It was like watching a bizarre ritual of an obscure central African tribe under the guidance of a Brahmin witchdoctor. After hours of toil, the end products resembled a Nazi experiment gone terribly wrong. One woman's doll achieved effortlessly what B.K.S. Iyengar had been trying to do in vain for years – look at its own buttocks. Another woman unintentionally created a hermaphrodite. As for Mother, her first work of art had two left feet.

Not in the least bit discouraged by the grisly results, in a couple of months Mother had produced a total of twenty dolls. They were proudly lined up in seemingly impossible positions along a windowsill for all to see, and hopefully buy. Her favourites were the 'Shakuntala with Deer' and 'My Fair Lady'.

It wasn't as if Mother was particularly bad with her hands. Her embroidery on the nylex saris, though a tad lurid, was actually quite painstaking and original. It was that even Michelangelo would have fared only slightly better under Mrs Neelakantan's guidance with the raw material sourced from George Town. Had the real Shakuntala looked anything like Mother's version, you couldn't blame Dushyanta for his amnesia or, for that matter, electing for a quick lobotomy in case his memory returned. As for poor Eliza Doolittle all dressed-up for Ascot, one look at her would've had Professor Higgins going 'Cor, blimey!'

Mother's twenty dolls gathered dust, scared the crap out of us when the lights went out and finally died a tattered death on that windowsill in Ramalingam Street.

With clockwork regularity, Mother picked up new 'hobbies' to establish her individuality, make a bit of money and, most importantly, annoy the hell out of Team Meghamala.

Mother was a terrific cook of authentic Telugu Brahmin fare. One day, she decided that her repertoire needed to be poshed-up and enrolled herself in a cookery & bakery class. Soon, exercise book upon exercise book was filled with recipes entitled 'Pineapple Pandemonium' and 'Caramel Coma'. She also came back with tasty, if minuscule, morsels of cakes and biscuits from her class. When Mother got herself one of those metal boxes with a glass window – the kind you put on a gas stove and pretend it's an oven, we knew the day she would be delivering her pièce de résistance was near. We weren't disappointed.

One Sunday, Mother announced that she'd be making chocolate burfi. Not quite what we expected after the drum roll, but it was a start. The trauma of the nylex and the dolls had faded and, after all, Mother had always been a good cook – so, finally a hobby of hers that wasn't going to damage us physically or mentally. On D-Day, when she began work on the burfi, she realized that there had been a small oversight. She had covered all the ingredients needed in the 'burfi' part of the dish meticulously, but she'd omitted to buy one ingredient for the 'chocolate' portion of the dish, i.e., the chocolate. Now this would have sent the average person scurrying to the market for Cadbury's Cocoa Powder. But Mother was not the average person. Rummaging around in the kitchen shelves, she found something she thought would do just as well – a tin of Protivita, the powdered chocolate health drink. It was the must-have beverage for any patient within kicking distance of a bucket. Doctors prescribed Protivita, 'The Tonic for the Catatonic', when all else failed because it produced results. It was believed that after a glass of steaming hot Protivita, a patient would either bounce right off the hospital bed singing '*Top of the World*' by The Carpenters or die instantly.

Mother emptied the tin of Protivita into the mixture and produced a tray full of delicious-looking brown-and-white diamonds. Innocent to the last-minute switch in the principal ingredients, we gobbled up the burfis while they were still hot. Though the burfis tasted a bit odd, we energetically congratulated Mother and told her that her days of being a restaurateur were just around the corner. The three of us felt so energetic, we cleaned up our room without being asked to and followed it up with a two-hour game of shuttle – all without so much as breaking into a sweat. Father, who walked a couple of kilometres every evening, broke into a jog before he reached the end of our street. We found out later that he'd sprinted all the way to the Parthasarathi Temple in Triplicane, outrunning buses along the way. As for CG, he was seized by the urge to rearrange the furniture in the house, moving the sofas and dining table into the verandah and his own gigantic bed into the living room single-handed.

We became aware that things were really wrong only when we found Grandmother missing.

It was odd because Grandmother never left home on her own. A frantic search found her in the backyard climbing down the jackfruit tree under the guidance of Chanti, who informed us that this was her fourth successful attempt in the last hour. Later, when we finally awoke from our forty-eight-hour slumber following three absolutely sleep-free days, Mother told us that she'd quit the cooking class.

THIRTEEN

It was a good time for cloth merchants. Not so for Father. In the earlier drainpipe era, 1.1 m of cloth could be comfortably tailored into a pair of pants for the average man. Two metres was all you needed for a full-sleeved shirt. But with the birth of the bell-bottom and the 'Bobby' collar, not to mention shoulder flaps and button bands, overnight, tailors became expansive with their estimates for cloth.

Father dreaded our trips to the cloth shop in T. Nagar to buy me pant- and shirt-lengths for a birthday or Deepavali. To begin with, I had begun demanding pants, not shorts, for special occasions and, if that wasn't bad enough, they had to have flared bottoms. That instantly trebled my wardrobe outlay. I had a sneaky suspicion that my father had always hoped that we would be a one-time-only expenditure – like his easel, for instance. After all, he'd spent good money for our births, vaccinations and education. But, unlike the easel, we kept coming back for more.

After I chose the cloth (the loudest checks I could find from the faux double-knit range displayed in the 'janata' section of the store), my father thought he'd try getting past the salesman.

'Okay. We'll take one metre.'

'For shorts, sir?'

'No, full pants,' my father said, pointing to me, 'for the boy.'

'You want bell-bottoms?' said the salesman, addressing me directly. Father clenched his teeth.

'Of course.' What did the sales guy think – that I was some tight-pant-wearing square?

'Shirt, ordinary or latest fashion?'

'Latest,' I said, 'with Bobby Collar, button band, two flapped pockets and shoulder flaps.' Imagine me wearing a frill-free shirt like Father!

Having confirmed my impeccable fashion credentials, the salesman went back to my father who was now gripping his wallet like a drowning man clings to floating wreckage.

'Sar, you'll need 1.4 m, actually, 1.5 to be on the safe side, for the pants and two metres for the shirt.'

My father turned the shade on Page Five of his Fuji Colour Book.

'But he's ten years old! The tailor uses less cloth for me!'

The chap had made the sale. Father wasn't going to break my heart before Deepavali. He should've let it go. But he was a salesman and decided to pitch for the sale of another three metres of cloth via pant- and shirt-lengths for my father.

'You should also wear bell-bottoms, saar. Will give you personality.'

The carefree '50s with no pesky kids – when tailors made do with reasonable amounts of cloth and, more importantly,

Cary Grant and *not* some presumptuous salesman decided what looked good on him – flashed through Father's head like the montage from *It's a Wonderful Life*.

Proving that he hardly needed bell-bottoms to give him 'personality', Father jumped onto the counter, caught the salesman by his non-Bobby collar and heaved him up. Then, in a curious mix of English, Telugu and very ungrammatical Tamil, he asked the salesman a series of questions all of which were anatomically quite specific, involved his immediate family and the creative use of certain carpenter's tools.

It was a good Deepavali that year. The manager of the shop gave us the material at 50% discount in lieu of the anguish he'd caused my father. I learnt very interesting words in three languages which I immediately taught Kavi.

But the joy of my 22" flares lasted only a day.

It never failed. We could count on a Banka to upstage us at any given opportunity.

When Sachu, the curviest Banka offspring, sashayed into our house, the flicker-free spotlight that had been trained on my gargantuan pants died abruptly.

Sachu was wearing 30" bell-bottoms.

They were astounding, like a tent cut in half.

'Nice trousers, Gopes,' she said, ruffling my hair, 'just a little wider at the bottom and they'd look like the ones I got last year. Rishi's wearing them now.'

Father looked stricken. How many salesmen did he have to assault before this fashion insanity ended?

Sachu was the final authority on all things. Everything she did was hep and, however hard we tried, the three of us younger kids just didn't make the cut. She had boyfriends and was doing it (whatever 'it' was), if gossip was to be believed. She was a model at a time when 'model' referred to the year of manufacture in one-horse Madras. ('Our Amby is a 1960 model.') She had cleavage rivalling the *Picturegoer* covers and, when all else failed, she had the ultimate trump card – French.

Sachu constantly peppered her non-stop chatter with words that ended in open-mouthed vowels accompanying them with lavish hand movements. For all we knew, she could have been speaking Oriya but according to her it was French. It was very impressive and very annoying.

My own knowledge of French was limited to the French cartoon books without captions and Anne French (a cream that magically made silk scarves glide down Anna Bredmeyer's legs if the ads at Safire were to be believed). On account of her reading, Lalli's was a little better. Unable to take Sachu's Gallic onslaught, poor Lalli murmured something about Alexandre Dumas one day. When Sachu didn't pay any attention, Lalli loudly proclaimed that she loved Dee-art-tug-nun in *The Three Musketeers*.

Sachu burst out laughing.

'It's not Dee-art-tug-nun, silly goose. It's pronounced Darr-ta-nyan!'

There was no winning with Sachu.

She also knew a few neat tricks. Like how to make calls when a telephone was locked. It was brilliant, really. If the number you needed to dial was 446785, all you had to do was tap the knob four times first, leave a gap of a second, tap it four times again and so on till you completed the number. And – *bam*. You could call anyone you wanted to. What was tough was dialling a zero. You had to tap the knob ten times without missing a beat. But in less than a day, under the able guidance of Sachu, the three of us were tapping away like experienced Morse operators.

Besides this, Sachu was an adept shoplifter, too. She used her rat-a-tat speaking style and her partially unbuttoned blouse with clinical efficiency to cut a swathe through the unsuspecting retail trading community of Pondy Bazaar. On one occasion, when a salesman caught her trying to swipe a pair of ear-rings, without missing a beat, Sachu opened one more button on her blouse and began screaming in French.

'Brochettes de Poulet à la Jambalaya! Comment allez-vous!! Je vais très bien, merci et vous!!!' She wagged an accusing finger at the sales guy, with a final 'You…you…*D'artagnan!*'

The shopkeepers were a timorous lot, as Father had proved. They were no match for Sachu's blitzkrieg, and French-kissed their ear-rings goodbye. Ironically, the shop in question, owned by a Marwari who had never travelled further than Parry's Corner, was called Petit Paris. Pronounced Pe-ti Puh-ree, *s'il vous plâit*.

Any fears the three of us might have had of our education not being well-rounded enough were put to rest. That part of the curriculum that had been left unattended by Lanka Jhansi's sudden departure was completed by Sachu.

I realized my 22" flares were just not going to do it any more. I had to either learn Swahili or get wider bell-bottoms to silence Sachu. The latter seemed easier but the question of asking Father didn't arise at all. If his molestation of the salesman was anything to go by, I would be lucky if I got a loincloth for my next birthday. It was really unfair. Mother and Grandmother could get yards of cloth in the name of sarees, but I couldn't get myself a measly two metres for proper bell-bottoms.

Dejected, I went off to my research centre, the oven room. Maybe looking at Robert Taylor's tights in *Knights of the Round Table,* a time when men didn't need garments with leg-room to look good, would ease my aching heart. I sat there browsing through my stash of *Picturegoer*s when my attention was diverted by a Telugu magazine. It had Grandfather on the cover being fêted at some event. A large sweaty man was wrapping CG in a giant shawl. The old guy had the look of a silver fox cornered by a fur trapper. I just didn't get it. Why would you present someone in Madras with a shawl? It was like giving my friend Rusty Mistry a book of crossword puzzles. There must have been at least a trunk full of shawls at home collected by CG at various celebrations.

Suddenly, a klieg light came on in my head, floodlighting the fashion possibilities at my disposal. Metres and metres of unwanted cloth wrapped in mothballs available absolutely free. Not long after, with the help of Grandmother who had the keys to anything worthless at home, I made my choice – three Lal Imli shawls of pure wool, in navy blue, maroon and khaki that leaned towards yellow. Each shawl was a glorious three metres, giving me the freedom to use the equivalent of an entire pant length for each leg – no questions asked. Let

Sachu try and beat *that*. Before I rushed off to the tailor, I extracted a promise from my grandmother.

'Under no circumstances will you mention this to Kavi or Lalli.'

I didn't see the point in their depleting what could take care of my bell-bottom needs till I was forty.

As I rushed off towards Gentleman's Society Tailors with nine metres of shawl, I realized something that took the air out of my inflated sartorial dream. How was I going to pay the tailoring charges for my gigantic pants? I didn't have a rupee.

I was ten years old, I had enough cloth to put up a shamiana. I wasn't going to let something like mere economics come in the way of my vision. I decided to cross that bridge on the delivery date.

At Gentleman's Society Tailors, Arumugam, my father's costumier for the last twenty years, looked suspiciously at the giant parcel wrapped in newspaper that I had brought along.

'Ennappa,' he said, 'what can I do for you? Where's your father?'

'Oh, just need some pants tailored,' I said. 'He's busy so I came by myself.'

'Show me the cloth,' he said.

I opened my parcel and presented my cache to Arumugam. The tailor picked up the yellow shawl and opened it out. He held it with his arms stretched as far as they could go. You could have projected a 16 mm movie on it. His assistant pedalled away on the Singer, suppressing what sounded like a cough.

'You want pants made with *these*?' Arumugam sounded doubtful.

'Yeah, what's the problem? Not enough cloth?'

'But these are *shawls*,' he said.

'So?'

'But they are made of *wool*,' he said, pointing at the Madras sun. The assistant suppressed another cough.

I had come well-prepared for this line of questioning.

'I'm going to Kashmir...for higher studies.'

'Okay.' He gave up and pulled out his measuring tape.

After he took down my waist, hip and inseam measurements, it was time for the big one. He held the tape against my minuscule bell-bottom.

'Same? Twenty-two?' he said.

'Bigger,' I said.

'Twenty-four?'

I saw Sachu's smug face and shook my head.

'Twenty-eight?'

'No.'

'Thirty? Really, *thirty*?'

This was taking too long.

'Thirty-six,' I said.

Arumugam paused. He wanted to see if he was getting this right. A ten-year-old boy barely over four feet was asking him to make trousers that had 36" bottoms out of a woollen shawl.

'Don't you think it's too big?' he said. 'How will you walk?' I looked at Arumugam kneeling at my feet, a measuring tape in his hands, his tone almost pleading.

'I'll be fine,' I said.

'Okay,' he said, 'but I have one condition.'

'What?'

'You will never tell anyone, not a soul, that you got the trousers tailored here, okay?'

I obviously wouldn't. Why would I tell my friends that my clothes were made at Gentleman's Society Tailors in downmarket Pondy Bazaar when they were under the impression that my clothier was Syed Bawkher of Mount Road?

'Also, for safety,' added Arumugam, 'I will make only one pair of pants for you. We'll see how that goes, then we'll make the others, okay?'

I agreed. Now I had the option of widening the flares to forty for the other two pants.

The week went by in slow motion. All I could think of was Sachu's French-accented laughter and her 30" flares. I used the time to plan the grand unveiling of my pants. I would cycle over, my flares fluttering like the multicoloured satin flags on the Marina and come sliding to a halt. Then I would stride out from a cloud of dust, my matchless bell-bottoms flapping wildly and Sachu would be silenced forever.

On the date of delivery, I rushed off to the tailor's not unduly perturbed by two facts: I didn't have the twenty-five rupees to pay him. (I did have a couple of rupees, though. That was for the cycle I was going to hire.) And it was ten o' clock in the morning. (Delivery time was always six in the evening.)

What I did have was a plan.

Arumugam received me with an 'Ennappa?' It was preceded by a long expulsion of breath.

'My bell-bottoms. Are they ready?'

Arumugam's shoulders sagged a bit. He pointed wearily to the little sign on his wall. It said: 'Delivery after 6 p.m.'

'Why don't you check? It might be ready.'

Arumugam gestured to his junior. It was the same chap who had had a bad throat earlier. He stopped pedalling and went behind a screen and there was the unmistakable rustle of brown paper covers. Then he came out carrying a cover all stapled and impressive, placed it on the counter and, for some reason, ran back behind the screen to have a coughing fit. His bad throat seemed worse. I tore open the cover and held my world-beating new pants along my leg. In the mid-morning light, they definitely looked more yellow than khaki. But I didn't care because my flares stretched from heel to eternity. I could have easily hidden Buster under them.

I had done it. Revenge was now only minutes away.

I noticed that the inside of the waistband, which usually had the tailor's label, was bare. Gentleman's Society Tailors for some reason did not want to be associated with these pants. That suited me fine, because the first thing I did anyway was to rip off the label on any new garment to prevent nosy friends from finding out that I didn't go to Syed Bawkher. I thanked Arumugam and was about to leave when he stopped me.

'Bill?' he said.

'Finish the other two trousers and I'll pay for all three.'

'But...'

Before Arumugam could reply I was off. That had been my plan all along.

I rode like the heroes of Father's comics, my brand-new shawl pants tucked away in the carrier of the hired BSA *SLR*. At home I tried them on. They looked even more impressive than they had at the tailor's. When I walked into his studio, my flares preceding me by a few seconds, Father took one look at me and said, 'You have finally gone mad.' I didn't need further proof of their magnificence. I would have presented him with a few poses except that my legs suddenly felt as if they were being colonized by a small swarm of red ants. I put my hands inside my pockets and scratched myself discreetly.

'You are a bigger idiot than I thought,' Father said. 'Not only do you look ridiculous but you'll contract some tropical skin disease. That's wool you're wearing. Thaatha got the shawl fifteen years ago at a function in Vizag.'

The ants had now brought in fresh troops. I danced from one foot to the other but continued to keep the smile plastered on. Just because they were woollen or smelt of mothballs or were made of material much older than I was, didn't mean I was going to give up. I had to show Sachu. Lalli and Kavi, who were in on my pants by now, watched me with open mouths.

Taking a deep breath, I got back on to the cycle and took off in the direction of the Banka residence. Though every nerve-ending in my body begged me to stop, take my trousers off and scratch myself with coconut fibre in the middle of the road, I pedalled with gusto. People on the road stared at me. My bell-bottoms flapping away in the wind, I flew like I was on Mother's burfis.

Quite often, elaborate schemes are undone by minor oversights. I had got the material, I had got the pants made, I had managed to get the biggest flares T. Nagar had ever seen but I had forgotten one thing – the metal trouser clip that you could get for a rupee in Pondy Bazaar, a must-have accessory for anyone who was a bell-bottom-wearing cyclist. It was a ring-like contraption, open at one end, which you could clip around your trouser bottom to prevent it from getting entangled in your cycle chain.

In a tradition established by Wile E. Coyote, my high-speed journey came to an unplanned and instant halt as my unfettered pants got entangled in the cycle chain. There I was, a yellow streak of lightning racing towards victory one moment – a mangled fashion victim with a mouth full of dirt the next. The traffic around me came shrieking to a halt. I looked around and got up gingerly as a couple of drivers echoed Father's sentiments of a few minutes ago. I was wearing only half my trousers. Most of the right side of my pants had been ripped off by the cycle and eaten up by the chain. There were no broken bones, only ears singed by public opinion, a bruise on my knee that looked like the Warner Bros logo, and a hire-cycle that would only go around in circles.

I did not get revenge on Sachu that day. As a matter of fact, I never did. Sachu moved to Bangalore to pursue a career in, of all things, Kannada films. What I did get was two more bell-bottoms of hundred per cent wool, this time with 40" flares.

Father paid the tailoring charges on the condition that I wouldn't ask for any new clothes for the next two years.

I managed to stave off irreversible skin damage by dusting myself generously with Johnson's Prickly Heat Powder every time I wore my woollen pants.

My record for having the biggest pants in T. Nagar remained unbroken.

FOURTEEN

It was in the summer of '59 that Mother reluctantly met Father for the first time. As he skulked behind his old man, accompanied by my invisible grandmother and the very visible Auntie Renu, she was sure of one thing. She wasn't going to be part of this burlesque routine – her grandfather be damned. But politeness prevented her from walking out of the room as the old men held forth and Auntie Renu checked out my mother's hip-length plait.

'Is it real, my dear?' she asked.

Before Mother could respond, she was diverted by a name that popped up in the conversation between the old men. Retracting, at the last moment, what would have been a life-altering right hook had it landed on Banka Renuka Bai's wagging chin, Mother asked, 'Did you say Pistol Rangarao?'

Everyone turned towards the teenager in surprise. She could speak.

'Yes, he's Baloo's close friend,' said CG, who still had his voice back then. 'Why, do you like his books?'

According to Mother, the reason she married Father – as also the reason Auntie Renu's jaw didn't need to be wired up – was Pistol Rangarao. The fact was, had my father walked around the streets those days, yelling, 'Hey, I know Pistol Rangarao,' any number of young women or, for that matter, old widows, middle-aged men or mystery-loving transsexuals would have done the same. Such was the popularity of the creator of Detective Savyasachi, the greatest Telugu-speaking crime fighter of all time.

In the '50s and '60s, the adventures of the enigmatic Savyasachi (accompanied by his young assistant, Hussain) were Rangarao's answer to Sexton Blake. They were self-published under the imprint Pistol Publications and, at eight annas a book, sold faster than they could be produced.

One day, a year or so into the marriage, Dad mentioned that the elusive Rangarao was in Hyderabad and would be landing up at home for lunch. 'Ah, finally!' thought Mother, as she visualized his arrival. A tall, impeccably dressed man, cigarette dangling from his mouth, would walk in through the door to eat her carefully prepared brinjal curry. She wondered whether he'd be bringing along his assistant, Hussain, too, before she realized that she was getting confused. So fine was the line between the creator and his creation. But she didn't lose heart. Hadn't she heard somewhere that writers and artists modelled their heroes on themselves? After all, Father did sometimes look like the diminutive wisecracking foxes he drew. By the same yardstick, Rangarao couldn't be that different from Savyasachi.

My mother wasn't disappointed – initially. A gust of rich tobacco preceded the arrival of the writer, as Mother hid behind the curtains to get the first glimpse of her hero. Through a haze of smoke, Pistol Rangarao made an entrance.

Or was it him? Because the person who walked in was a small, fidgety fellow with a shock of grey hair. Then, in a voice most unlike Savyasachi's much-written-about baritone, the man proceeded to chatter non-stop, sitting padmasana style on the sofa.

'Hey, Baloo, you rascal,' he said, giving Father a thump on his back, 'how's married life treating you?'

This was Pistol Rangarao? Looking at the animated writer of detective fiction, who looked more like her husband's creation than his own, Mother shook her head.

'Case closed!' she muttered as she went in to get him coffee.

Mother told us this story many times but Pistol Rangarao (Pistol Mama to us) was far from disappointing as far as we were concerned.

Considering that he wasn't actually an uncle, Pistol Mama was the best uncle we had. His life revolved around his only son Bharani who was born late into his marriage. Pistol Mama's pet name for him was Bullet. He had, after all, sprung forth from the loins of a firearm. His wife, Auntie Vani, had no choice but to go along as Option Two was Sonofagun. So Bharani was Bullet to everyone. Everyone other than Pistol Mama's eighty-year-old father, that is. He called Bharani and everyone else by any name that popped up in his failing mind. Every now and then, he also walked around the house stark naked.

Bullet was a couple of years younger than Kavi and the four of us could do anything we wanted in Pistol Mama's house. Any bizarre scheme we came up with was immediately approved with minimum paperwork. Bullet, instead of being interested in pulp fiction like any self-respecting son of a crime writer, was an avid fan of Indian mythology. While we read *Tubby* and *Little Lulu,* and Mickey Spillane on the sly, eight-year-old Bullet had bulldozed through the Amar Chitra Katha collection. Having done that, to the exasperation of the publishers, he had begun suggesting names for new titles so obscure they would have had even Vyasa scratching his head.

When they didn't take him seriously, Bullet decided to take his passion for mythology to another setting – the stage. This was in an 'all the world's a stage' kind of way – with the Pistol living room, backyard and godown serving as venues. He had an enthusiastic producer in his father who was in it in the best 'art for brat's sake' tradition. He had a reluctant supporting cast in the form of us, neighbour kids and domestic help. The villain was usually played by his semi-lucid grandfather who didn't always stick to the script.

Now, all Bullet needed was costumes. As budget was no constraint, he didn't need to resort to old curtains, stolen saris and cardboard cartons and went straight to Krishco, the costume supplier for B-Films and mythological plays.

This tiny shop in Panagal Park looked as if a lorry carrying god calendars from Sivakasi had had a head-on collision with one loaded with Amar Chitra Kathas. There was enough papiér-mâché weaponry to restart the battle of Kurukshetra. That it would've been a bloodless coup with the Krishco arsenal is another thing. Saffron robes, yellowing beards and kamandalams were stocked together in case someone needed a hundred sages at short notice. There were also more crowns than a swayamvaram could accommodate. When Bullet entered the shop he had the same expression on his face Father might have had on finding Liz Taylor sitting next to him at the Madras Race Club with Richard Burton nowhere in sight.

Thus geared, with Bullet as hero (after all, he was the producer's son), we put up many mythological plays, all within the Pistol compound. These played to a far smaller audience than the exploits of my hirsute neighbour. This wasn't due to any lack in the histrionics department on Bullet's part. On the contrary. It had more to do with his lacklustre supporting cast. While Bullet knew the script by heart, us junior cast members constantly fluffed our lines. Bullet's grandfather, who moved seamlessly from his dialogue to select sections of the Negotiable Instruments Act (on which he had been an authority) as he stripped off his clothes layer by layer during rehearsals, ruined any chance we might've had of making it to Broadway.

When things went completely out of hand, Pistol Mama intervened.

'Why don't you fellows take a break and play cricket?' he would suggest.

To the neighbours' disbelief, a bunch of kids wearing faux metal crowns and ratty beards, their bows slung over their shoulders, would trudge across the road to the nearby maidan to play cricket – with a sulky Bullet batting first.

Bullet soon recognized he was working way below his league and decided to go solo. Pistol Mama heaved a sigh of relief because the costume budget would reduce drastically and he wouldn't be called in to defuse potentially incendiary situations every five minutes. We were happy, too, because, in our hearts, we knew the Meghamala brand of melodrama was better suited to real life rather than the stage.

Bullet didn't have to wait long. His big break was around the corner.

The Andhra contingent of Vidya Vihar was small and every year, at about the time of the annual day celebrations, the ten or so kids who took Telugu as their second language fell mysteriously ill. In fact, at around this time, I was in demand as a writer of creative leave letters and was charging a small fee to help kids avoid the humiliation of being part of the school's sole Telugu presentation.

```
Dear Sir,
Please excuse my son, Srinivasulu Reddy,
from the Annual Day play because of our
family curse, which stipulates that if
any one of us steps on a stage, the
Telugu teacher in the nearest school
will die instantly.
Yours faithfully,
Bantireddy Ranga Reddy
```

* * *

```
Dear Sir,
My son, G. Ravi Babu, is allergic to
artificial gold and will break out in
pustules if any fake jewellery were to
come in contact with his skin. Financial
```

> constraints restrict me from buying him a real gold crown. So I request you to please cast another boy in the role of Krishnadeva Raya.
> Yours faithfully,
> G. Kantha Rao

* * *

As luck would have it, Bullet, too, studied at Vidya Vihar. In fact, the two of us had joined the school on the same day. The only reason I was there was because of Pistol Mama, who insisted that Father put me in a reputed school, whatever it cost.

'A good education is everything, Baloo. Put Gopi in a good school,' he had advised my reluctant father.

Bullet's enthusiasm to don greasepaint was directly proportional to our willingness to hospitalize ourselves before an annual day. When he volunteered to take care of the Telugu item on our annual day, the other Telugu kids shivering with stage fright, the Telugu master who was at his wit's end, not to mention Bullet himself – everyone was ecstatic. From then on, year after year, Bullet played a variety of mythological heroes in thankfully solo acts to a captive audience of hapless parents at the annual day function. Every year, as curtains rose to Bullet playing a scrawny high-pitched Arjuna, Drona, Bhishma or Abhimanyu, the loudest applause was from the Telugu boys who'd been permanently let off the hook.

Not long after, Madras was abuzz for a different reason. The West Indians were coming! And they were going to play at Chepauk! And it was going to be aired on television!

This was unbelievable.

Doordarshan was to commence operations in Madras by relaying the Test match. But how were we going to watch the match? No one we knew was going to buy a TV, other than the Dikshits – and after the nameplate incident I wasn't welcome there.

The newspapers were full of ads for TVs. EC, Crown, Krish, Televista, Gemco, Dyanora – exotic names with promises of non-stop free home entertainment. Our lives were going to change. We didn't know what to expect. A couple of rich kids in class bought TVs but, sadly, I didn't get an invite.

When we'd all but given up on the double joy of watching a Test match *and* television, we got a call from Pistol Mama.

'What, kids – want to watch the match on TV?'

We didn't bother replying.

Leaving Rangarao with a silent receiver in his hand, wondering whether he ought to inform Savyasachi about 'The Case of the Missing Meghamalas', we ran all the way to their house, which was a kilometre away. And there it was, sitting gloriously in its wooden cabinet – a brand-new Gemco television set!

'What do you chaps think? I did my research – this is supposed to be the best model in the market,' said Pistol Mama, tapping the cabinet. He switched it on and grey static filled the screen with a hiss. It looked uncannily like the fabric in the economy section of Avinash Dress Emporium. We watched it for a full five minutes.

We went home wondering how in hell we were going to wait four days.

We didn't have to. Two days later there was a call. It was an inconsolable Bullet.

'The TV's missing,' he said between sobs, 'it's been stolen.'

FIFTEEN

Who'd think of stealing from Pistol Rangarao, creator of Savyasachi? Other than Rusty Mistry, I couldn't think of a single person who could be that stupid. In his seventy-six books, be it murderer, arsonist, kidnapper or thief, there had never been an instance when Pistol Mama hadn't got his man – even when it was a woman.

A real live mystery was better than anything TV could possibly offer. The three of us were back at Pistol Mama's place on the pretext of consoling Bullet. Their living room had a funereal air with our friend wailing like Arjuna on finding the Gandiva gone. I didn't know why; there was no doubt in my mind Pistol Mama would have the Gemco back in its place by the evening.

The crime writer was sitting at his desk, his hands hovering above his beat-up Remington. An unlit Panama dangled from the corner of his mouth. There was no welcoming wave, no affectionate 'Hi, kids!' from him.

I thought it was a strange time to write.

'Did you inform the police?'

Pistol Mama's head jerked up to see where the suggestion had come from. With the suddenness of the move, the cigarette flew out of his mouth.

The speaker was Lalli, who was now biting her tongue.

What was she thinking? Hadn't she read his books? This was the guy the *police* called.

Pistol Mama put a fresh cigarette in his mouth and lit it this time with the Zippo lighter that travelled everywhere with him. He took a drag so deep his cheeks touched inside his mouth. The lit end glittered like Jhansi's blouse.

Then, without preamble, the writer bounced off his rickety chair and walked out of the door and up the staircase. The three of us and a sniffling Bullet scurried behind him, pushing each other to be the first on the narrow staircase. On the terrace, Pistol Mama just sat on the parapet and continued smoking his cigarette. He seemed to be deep in thought, his eyes panning the cloudy January horizon. We watched silently as he took a final drag from the filterless stick. The flame now almost touched his lips. Pistol Mama threw the minuscule butt down and stubbed it out with his bare foot.

When he turned to look at us, he was smiling.

Three minutes later, Pistol Mama, Dilli (his beefy driver-cum-handyman) and four clueless children strode down Thanikachalam Road. Our journey was short. We stopped at a house at the end of the road. Pistol Mama turned towards the direction of his house and turned back to look at the house outside which we stood. He did it a couple of times like he was making a mental calculation. Then, nodding to himself, he strode in and rang the doorbell. Dilli, who was right behind his boss, looked like he meant business. We waited.

An old woman opened the door. Pistol Mama pushed past her and walked into the living room. We followed. Sitting there shamelessly, in its glorious wooden cabinet, was Pistol Mama's Gemco TV. Bullet ran over and hugged the TV. The old woman stared at us.

I couldn't believe it. I had given the man till evening and he'd wrapped it up before lunch?

'Now, look here,' said Pistol Mama to the old woman, 'we can do this the easy way or the hard way. Which would you prefer?'

The woman looked around. Six strangers stared at her with varying degrees of menace.

'Er...the easy way, I think,' she said.

'Good, there's no point involving the police,' said Pistol Mama gesturing to Dilli who had already unplugged the TV.

In ten minutes the TV was back where it belonged. While Bullet continued holding it tight, his granddad stared at it suspiciously.

'What's it doing back here?' he said.

There was one thing to be said about the Pistols. All of them, including young Bullet, were never impatient when the old man got this way. They were probably grateful he was wearing something.

'It was stolen, Thaatha. Dad got it back for us,' said Bullet, his arms still around the prodigal TV set. The old man looked like he wasn't buying it.

I was dying to know how Pistol Mama had cracked 'The Case of the Missing TV' that fast. I didn't have to ask. The crime writer sat on his chair and lit another cigarette with the air of someone who was willing to let us in on his greatness.

The four of us sat on the floor and waited patiently. Bullet's granddad wandered off, mumbling something that sounded like 'It can't be!' repeatedly.

'Well, it goes like this,' said Pistol Mama. 'The TV was stolen in the morning between six and seven. That was the time your aunt and I had gone for a walk and Bullet was asleep. About that there's no doubt, right?'

'Right!' went the chorus.

Who were we to poke holes in Pistol Mama's theories?

'When we came back, we found the door ajar. This was not surprising because we don't usually lock it. So the thief must've walked in around then and walked off with the TV. He had a full hour to do it.'

'But how did you find out where it was?' I asked.

'Patience, boy, patience,' said Pistol Mama, giving my hair a ruffle, 'I thought I'd get some idea if I sat at the typewriter. When that didn't work I went upstairs. There, quite by accident, I noticed that the skyline looked different. I knew because I look at it every day as I have my mid-morning cigarette. There was a *new* TV antenna a couple of furlongs away which wasn't there yesterday...'

'But how were you so sure they hadn't bought a TV today?' asked Lalli.

'I wasn't,' said Pistol Mama, blowing a plume of smoke, 'so I rang up the sole distributor of Gemco televisions and asked them how many sets they had sold. Can any of you guess the answer?'

'One!' I jumped in before anyone else.

'Good,' said Pistol Mama, giving me a pat on the head, 'so I took a gamble. If the house had a Gemco it would have to be ours. It *did*, and, from the lady's reaction, it *was*. And there you have it.'

I wasn't about to give up.

'But what if it hadn't been a Gemco? What would you've done then, Pistol Mama?'

'Taken it from there, my young friend,' said Pistol Mama, closing the case comprehensively, 'taken it from there.'

On the first day of the Test match we arrived at Bullet's place a good hour in advance. The Pistols were already seated, staring blinklessly at a geometric pattern on their TV. It was accompanied by a steady background hum that would have had Buster pissing buckets. Only Bullet's granddad looked disconsolate. He sat all by himself on the sofa wearing nothing but his vest. We knew from the strategically placed newspapers.

For five days we watched the Indians battle it out with their western counterparts. Vishwanath missed a century by three runs, Prasanna got five wickets and India won by 100 runs.

At the end of it everyone was ecstatic *and* exhausted. India had won and we could blink again. But all I felt was disappointment. Where were the close-ups, the reactions of the spectators, the angles, the drama? Why such flat staging? If only they'd put Father or me in charge of direction.

A few days later we got a call from Pistol Mama. He wanted to know if we wanted a TV absolutely free, because they had two sets now. One was their own while the other was the one we had extorted from the old lady down the road who had moved house without notice.

Apparently, there had been a couple of fatal flaws in Pistol Mama's deduction. For one, he hadn't considered Bullet's senile grandfather. When Pistol Mama and Auntie Vani were out on their walk, the old man had taken it upon himself to lug their new TV downstairs, buck naked, to their storeroom far from the sticky hands of the giant purple lizards that came every night in tempos and whispered among themselves in Punjabi. To make doubly sure that it remained safe, he had packed it neatly in wrapping paper and hidden it behind a large stack of books. This was why Dilli had taken a few days to discover it.

Flaw Two was how the crime writer had deduced the TV was his based on the sales figures made available by the sole distributor. Apparently, this didn't include the people who had purchased sets directly from the factory, of whom the old lady was one.

SIXTEEN

The thing about speech is it's ephemeral. You speak, the words come out of your mouth and disappear leaving no evidence. But that's just as well because mostly people say stupid things, like Rusty Mistry who once asked, 'What colour's an orange?'

This wasn't the case with Grandfather, though. Everything he said was there on the 4" × 5" pages of his scribbling pads for eternity. From the time CG had his tracheostomy, the scribbling pads had substituted for speech. It's a good thing that it was Grandfather who lost his voice, as opposed to Rusty, because he rarely said anything stupid. Mean – maybe. Profound – on occasion. Funny – always. But stupid – no way.

If there had been a poll for who the greatest Telugu poet was, Grandfather would definitely have been a contender. Had there been a poll on the best damned Telugu orator ever, he'd have won outright. We were told that in the '40s and '50s thousands of people packed stadia in Andhra Pradesh *for two to three hours at a stretch* to listen to him speak about *poetry*. He must've been good. Either that or they must have had naked ladies juggling daggers in the background.

Grandfather loved to talk but he also loved to smoke – a lot; that, too, foul-smelling cheroots that had more tar than the Grand Trunk Road. He didn't realize, even as his voice changed from an effeminate trill to a Bogartish rasp, that one didn't necessarily go with the other. After thirty years of conflict, the cheroots won, and CG was diagnosed with throat cancer.

After the removal of his larynx, Granddad didn't mope around and feel terrible for himself like ordinary folk. He just picked up a scribbling pad and a ballpoint pen and went on as though nothing had happened. The speeches continued. They were no less enthralling. They were a bit shorter and read by his writer friends, and sometimes my older sister, to equally packed auditoriums.

Speeches aside, Grandfather was a talkative man. So this meant a lot of scribbling pads. At two to three pads per month over ten years, he'd exhausted about three hundred and fifty little books. While these caused storage problems, what with the bursting library at home, they livened up Mother's afternoons.

When there was no bad movie to watch or disturbing doll to make, Mother relaxed on her bed with one of CG's scribbling pads for company. She scoured the pages not so much for any literary gems as for less than flattering tidbits about herself. To her surprise, she didn't find too much ammo. Hmmmm, the old man appreciated her, after all. Not bad, she thought.

Though that may have been marginally true, the real reason for the relatively low percentage of complaints about Mother had more to do with CG's timely self-editing. A healthy fear of Mother and a deep respect for her sleuthing abilities had Grandfather periodically ripping out any page that had an uncomplimentary reference to her. Had this editorial policy been general, the spines are all that would have remained.

For Lalli and me, the scribbling pads taught discretion and the ability to ad-lib at an early age. CG was sarcastic, impatient and a prankster to boot. These three qualities, not to mention a complete disregard for what was appropriate for children, put my older sis and me in tight spots on occasion. Grandfather was the picture of charm with old writerly friends or bright young people, his 'conversations' animated and direct. They spoke, he showed them his response.

But, like most artists, Grandfather hated anyone who wanted to give him money. In his case these were film producers. When one of them made an obsequious entrance, CG sometimes called for an 'interpreter'. The interpreter's job was to read out what he'd written. Sometimes it would be Mother, sometimes a random 'disciple' and sometimes it would be us kids. The triangular conversation that ensued would go along these lines:

> *Producer:* Sir, we are making a film and it would be incomplete without a song of yours.
> *Grandfather:* Ask him why he looks so uncomfortable. Does he have piles?
> *Translation:* Thank you, but I'm a little indisposed right now.
> *Producer:* I will not take 'no' for an answer, sir. You must write at least one song for us.
> *Grandfather:* Okay. In that case, you must have your haemorrhoids removed immediately.

Translation: I need a little time. The doctor has asked me to rest.

Producer: No problem, sir. Take a month.

Grandfather: Why don't you make *Frankenstein* in Telugu and act in it? I could write a love duet for you and Wolf Woman.

Translation: Please call me tomorrow. I'll be in a better position to tell you.

Everybody in Ramalingam Street was having a jolly old time or so it seemed. They were home all day, eccentric writers and musicians drifted in and out, there was talk of movies, songs, dance and poetry, there were books to be read, drawing board to be stolen, colours to be mixed, comics to be copied.

With all this I couldn't think of one good reason to go to school.

As the masochistic pleasures of Holly Golly and the novelty of the sweat maps in Vidya Vihar wore thin, I got into the habit of playing hookey. If it drizzled, I didn't go to school. If there was a preview of a film, I didn't go to school. Imaginary colds, maths tests, song sittings, undone homework – life seemed to be full of reasons to not put on my uniform. This got Mother livid.

For some reason, I was her favourite child. She camouflaged it well enough, giving impartial smacks to all three whenever one of us misbehaved. But she didn't fool me. *I* was her boy. Seeing me turn all Meghamala on her must have caused her some anguish. Considering my attendance, my academic performance was quite decent; she hoped that I'd go the banker–doctor way in the manner of her people.

'What's wrong with you, Ramu?' she said, using her special name for me when things got serious. 'How can you ever be successful when you grow up if you keep cutting school like this?'

'Naanna's never been to school. He's fine, isn't he?'

Somehow that was a theory Mother never bought.

How I got away skipping school that often had as much to do with Father's non-committal attitude as the naivety of the authorities at Vidya Vihar. After each absence, I handed over a grisly leave letter to my class teacher, hangdog expression and weak cough in place.

> Dear Sir,
> My son, M. Gopal of Class VI, was unable to attend school from Tuesday the 21st to Friday the 24th of August as he had a mild fever accompanied by cough and a runny nose. But that was only on the first two days. When he set out to school on Thursday, he unfortunately swooned on the staircase and fell down. In the process, he twisted his ankle and had to rest for two more days.
> I request you to grant him leave for these days.
> Yours faithfully,
> *M. Balakrishna*

Rather than Father, the chronicler of these misfortunes was me in my best adult handwriting. Though I was a first-time writer, I used all the tools employed by the Sexton Blake Detective Library and the forbidden James Hadley Chase to great effect. There were double-whammies, triple-crosses, red herrings and changing MacGuffins, all leading to a thrilling if improbable climax. I managed to elicit willing suspension of disbelief from my stupefied teachers to the extent that they worried about me and my periodic run-ins with fate. A disapproving Lalli, who never once failed to top her class right through school, was my editor. She helped me get the spelling and punctuation right. And these letters were signed with an expressionless stare, lasting for about a second, by Father. Not once did he tell me that what I was doing was wrong and that I would pay for it later. And not once did he consider the fatherly option of catching me by the ear and dragging me to school.

At school, my teachers got more and more concerned as the excuses got more and more bizarre.

'What is this, Gopal? Last week you had nausea and loose motions. Now, you say you were scratched by a cat. But didn't you say you had a pet dog?'

'Yes, sir. I do have a dog. It bit our neighbour's cat...which got angry...and scratched me.'

'How terrible. You must see a doctor.'

They were right. It wasn't just me, all of us at home needed to see a good doctor. But not the kind they meant.

The occasion that topped the hookey list was the song sitting. Every time there was one, Kavi (my occasional 'dumma' partner) and I would go to Grandfather and say, 'CG, please tell Amma we won't go to school today. We want to see you write the song.'

Grandfather would be overjoyed. Finally, the grandchildren he had always wanted. Admiring *and* striving towards illiteracy. He didn't need much persuasion. He would hide us away under his cot till it was past school time. On a couple of occasions he even hijacked us on our way to school to some production house to hang around while he wrote.

But when Kalyan Babu, Andhra's first cowboy, sent a flunkey over to request CG to write a song for his latest production, I shot off my resignation to Vidya Vihar. Unlike my leave letters, it was a pretty straightforward effort.

```
To
The Headmaster,
Vidya Vihar Boys' School

Dear Sir,
As of today I will not be coming to
school ever again. I find no reason to.
Nothing that you have on offer can match
the experience of spending time with
Kalyan Babu.
Please consider this my official
resignation.

Yours faithfully,
M. Gopal
```

One look at Mother, and I thought it would be wise to hold on to the letter for the present.

'Telugu Terence Hill' Kalyan Babu was the producer-director-hero of *Six-Gun Sampath* and its sequel, *Holster Harnath*, India's first Westerns. The movies, referred to as 'Southerns' by wags, had busted box-office records in Andhra Pradesh. All of a sudden, no boy could run straight any more. We were all doing it at an angle, going clippety-clop, pretending we were on horses at full gallop.

If I remembered right, Kalyan Babu had asked CG to write for both films but he had declined. I wondered why. It couldn't have been that hard for him to come up with a love song for a Telugu-speaking cowboy riding the Pallavaram hills dressed in a red velvet-corduroy suit and contrasting green boots. Whatever the reason, the good news was CG had caved in this time. He'd agreed to write a song for Kalyan Babu's latest film and the sittings were going to be conducted in *his* office which *had* to be full of cowboy memorabilia. I was in like Flynn. Nothing was going to stop me. Not wild horses, not even Mother.

It was probably my luck that the initial sessions coincided with a couple of holidays. Mother reinserted Father's belt into his trouser loops as there was no use for it, at least for now. My lucky streak continued on the day I accompanied CG to Kalyan Babu's office. Kavi was down with fever.

Kalyan Babu's company was called Sri Venkata-Revolver Combines. To the average person, the name might have sounded incongruous. But for a man who made films about cowboys battling it out in Amalapuram, it wasn't much of a stretch. The logic was that he was a great devotee of Lord Venkateswara of Tirupati *and* he specialized in making films with guns. It was a good name. Fear of God or fear of the gun – either way the audience would flock in.

On reaching Kalyan Babu's office, it appeared as though my luck had finally run out. Firstly, there was not a single tobacco-chewing gunslinger or whooping Apache in sight. Next, Kalyan Babu, who received CG with a namaste, looked more Yul Brynner than Clint Eastwood without the bullet-proof wig he wore in his films. He was also dressed in a spotless white dhoti and kurta with matching chappals, making it obvious that he didn't intend mounting a horse anytime soon. The disappointment continued inside the air-conditioned office filled with pictures of Lord Venkateswara. Mrs Kalyan Babu, the actress Jaya Bindu dressed in a Conjeevaram, served us yucky buttermilk with floating curry leaves. Considering she'd played barmaid in *Six-Gun Sampath*, the least she could've done was pretended the floor was the bar counter, the buttermilk whisky, and slid it across.

Two hours later, CG was ready to leave. I had been ready an hour and fifty-five ago, when I realized the movie Kalyan Babu was making was not a sequel to *Holster Harnath* but a 'social'. What was wrong with the guy?

As we got up to leave, CG wrote something on his pad and showed it to Kalyan Babu. The former cowpoke looked at me. I tried hard to picture him on a horse. All I got was a disturbing low-angle shot of his dhoti flying open as he mounted it.

'So I hear you like cowboys,' he said.

I nodded. Who didn't?

'Ramu!' he called out. A flunkey appeared out of nowhere.

'Take the young man to our costume department. Let him take something back home,' he said.

Was he serious?

The next thing, I was in a gigantic room that smelt of naphthalene balls and was filled end to end with costumes and props. Its contents looked like they had been ordered by Sergio Leone after he had had a head injury. There were purple Stetsons, parrot-green boots with gold spurs, long-haired wigs that looked like they'd been made with coir dyed blonde, a Red Indian chief's headdress put together with chicken feathers and a poncho made of Benares silk. There were also patently fake six-guns (the seven chambers gave them away) carved out of cheap wood, bad thermocol replicas of Winchester '73s and enough cardboard bullets to recreate the Alamo in Pallavaram.

I didn't waste a minute. I picked up the green boots, the red velvet corduroy cowboy suit and a plain cream-coloured straw hat for myself. After all, there was no point in overdoing it. For Kavi, the choice made itself. It was the chicken feather headdress.

The costumes arrived at home all dry-cleaned and altered the following day. With me playing The Tabasco Kid and Kavi dressed like Sitting Chicken, Ice Boys took on a different complexion for the next few days. Though Kavi was sent home from school to get rid of the odour of stale poultry that she was letting off, and she took off the headdress every five minutes to scratch her itchy scalp while at home, my joy was short-lived. One day, as I negotiated the chickoo in our yard in my red suit and green high-heeled boots, my rusty spurs got mixed up with its branches. I fought in vain to disentangle myself when I heard hysterical laughter. It was coming from the neighbour's. I turned around as best as I could with my foot stuck above my head and found the octogenarian who lived next door clutching his stomach.

When a man who had his privates tonsured in public on a regular basis thought *I* was funny, I realized it was time to kill the cowboy. Meanwhile, Mother, who had got sick of giving Kavi Dettol baths every day, set fire to the headdress.

A month or so later, when the frenzied glee of the old man had faded from my memory, I wondered if it was time for The Return of Tabasco Kid. But to my alarm I couldn't find my outfit. I threatened Kavi with dire consequences but she maintained she knew nothing of their whereabouts. For a while, I consoled myself with my shawl pants.

One day, when I'd forgotten all about Kalyan Babu, and we were about to embark on yet another session of Ice Boys, Pandu asked me a question that put everything in perspective.

'Hey, guess what, I saw a picture of Sachu in a film mag wearing boots just like yours.'

SEVENTEEN

It was the '70s and a five-rupee note went a long way. If you had a car, it could get you two litres of petrol. For a housewife it was three kg of Ponni rice. For the scholar, it could buy four ruled eighty-page Wisdom notebooks. For an out-of-towner in search of work, it meant four limited-meal tokens at RR Meals Centre in Pondy Bazaar. For Father, it was the price of a jackpot ticket at the Madras Race Club. And for me it was the complete movie experience. Therein lay the rub.

Father was reluctant to part with five-rupee notes at regular intervals because it compromised his punting power at the tote counter. On weekends, even requisitions from Mother for household items were processed unenthusiastically, approved sulkily with cuts or, better still, passed on to Grandfather. What chance did I have? Forking out of any cash on my account was usually preceded by a mention of the obscene amount of money being misspent on my school fees, my irregular attendance, my wildly fluctuating results and the extra cloth for my bell-bottoms.

But, by the time I was twelve or so, I had reached a stage where I needed a fix of at least a couple of movies a month and was going to get the money one way or another.

I sometimes wondered what the source of my addiction was. Was it the surfeit of celluloid influences in my life – Father forever talking films, the stacks of carefully guarded *Picturegoers*, Grandfather's movie connections or, for that matter, Mother's own regular noontime excursions? Or was it that I was a little rotter who refused to get his priorities right in spite of not being a complete cretin? Though it was easier to believe it was entirely the former and blame the adults in my family for tainting my impressionable mind, an indication that it could have been a bit of the latter was that my sisters were perfectly happy, making do with the occasional family outing to a wholesome entertainer like *Chitty, Chitty, Bang, Bang*.

There was a new English film almost every Friday. Father took us to two-three movies a year. How in hell was I to watch the others? If I used the unrealistic techniques favoured by the protagonists of my Moral Science textbooks, I'd have at best got to see a couple more in a year, maybe one as a reward for improving my attendance and another for standing first in class. But that seemed terribly long-winded. Besides, what was the guarantee I'd be rewarded? I needed money and I needed it now. So, I looked to the hard-boiled heroes of James Hadley Chase and Mickey Spillane and, closer home, our landlord, Raghavan, for inspiration: a little blackmail here, a little misappropriation there, with a bit of pilferage and reallocation thrown in.

I was ready to do anything for five bucks.

There are advantages to being part of a large and inefficient family. You tend to collect a lot of junk. And junk, I came to realize, was money. Up in the little room adjoining the terrace where I examined the French cartoon books, sat a treasure trove of junk.

One Saturday afternoon, in spite of several heartfelt petitions, I failed to relieve Father of five rupees.

'I don't have any money!' he said unconvincingly as he got into his friend's car to rush off to Guindy Racecourse.

I muttered an expletive loud enough for him to wonder if he'd heard right but a tad too late for him to come back and kick my ass. With this minor victory I retreated to the junk room at the top of the stairs with Pandu.

'Bloody unfair, *he* can go to the races, but I can't see *Breakout*,' I complained to my friend who happened to be five rupees richer than me that day. 'He bloody knows I love Charles Bronson!'

'We can still see the movie, you know,' said Pandu.

'How, you idiot? You only have five bucks. Who's going to pay for my ticket?'

Pandu didn't reply. Instead, he pointed to the pile of junk lying on one side of the room.

'This'll get you eight to ten bucks,' he said, pointing to a treadless tyre that had seen a lot of highway.

'Three-four kilos of this should get you five bucks,' he said pointing to the piles and piles of newspapers and magazines. We had a larger collection than the average family thanks to Father's contributions to various periodicals. Other than this, there were car horns that had lost their voice at about the same time as Grandfather, Father's fetid footwear from the

'50s, forgotten manuscripts of nameless novelists given to CG for his comments that never came, superseded schoolbooks from classes passed, ferrous-oxidized furniture frames – in short, junk worth at least a hundred movies by Pandu's estimate.

With no moral dilemma whatsoever, I hatched the plan. The two of us walking down three flights of stairs past Mother, Grandfather and two incredibly pesky sisters didn't seem like such a good idea. I asked Pandu to go downstairs and wait near our garage. My plan: take deep breath, throw tyre down, have Pandu catch it, sell tyre, see movie.

As the tyre was halfway through its descent, Raghavan appeared out of nowhere. I watched in horror as my rubber contraband dropped silently towards his bald, gleaming head. Thankfully, it missed him by an inch, landed on the concrete with a *thwack* and bounced about a couple of times before Pandu managed to grab hold of it. The landlord looked up and saw my face peering guiltily from behind the parapet wall. He then looked at Pandu who was pretending to dust the tyre in what he thought was a nonchalant manner. It was all over. The old coot would call my folks out and rat on me...

Close-up of my face, sweat dripping off nose. (music begins)

Cut to close-up of Raghavan's face looking at me, hand cupping chin, thoughtful. (tempo increases)

Cut to Pandu's hands gripping tyre, knuckles white from pressure. (tempo increases further)

Cut to my face, cut to Raghavan's, cut to tyre, my face,

Raghavan, tyre in sequence several times at high speed. (music reaches crescendo, ends with clash of cymbals)

Instead, Raghavan gave me a thumbs-up and walked off. I wondered if he was paying forward the favour of a vigilance inspector who'd ignored his own reallocation from the railway stores.

Nobody found two boys rolling a tyre down a T. Nagar street on a Saturday afternoon remotely suspicious. The sale itself was closed by Pandu who knew the vulcanizing shop that would be interested in our wares. We got six rupees for the tyre.

And there you had it. One day, a prolific writer of crime fiction (via my leave letters). Next day, with the blessings of my landlord, a full-fledged criminal. That day we saw Charles Bronson in *Breakout* with our own hard-earned money. It was fantastic.

I soon realized I had a flair for crime. To Pandu's frustration, I didn't dip into the treasure trove every time we needed money for a movie. It would have been the easy way, but Mother would have noticed the difference.

I realized that school-related expenses were a good source, too. Anytime a book, a geometry box, chart paper or sketch pens needed to be bought, I added my margin. Father was going to curse under his breath anyway. What was a couple of rupees more? Ignoring Pandu's advice, I kept it at a believable ten to fifteen per cent. The only unfortunate thing was that my school fee was paid by cheque. I'd have made a killing otherwise. At any rate, commissions thus collected added up to about one movie a month.

I saw business opportunities in everything. Gullible classmates like Rusty Mistry added to the kitty once in a while. Once, I heard Rusty lamenting the tattered state of his textbooks and offered to have them bound for him at a throwaway price.

'Five bucks for ten textbooks,' I said, 'but in advance.'

Mistry was sold. I did the binding myself with rice paste, pieces of Grandfather's old dhotis coloured in Cobalt Blue poster colour (standing in for calico), and old packing paper re-stolen from Raghavan's stockpile.

The result was hideous.

Rusty got a thrashing from his father.

I settled out of court by giving him a kickback of two bucks.

Net profit – three bucks.

It was a time when jeans were a rare and precious commodity. And it wasn't enough to have any pair, they *had* to be Levi's or Wrangler. The rest were pretenders. When my well-to-do classmates went off on an excursion to Sri Lanka, I saw business opportunity written all over it. I asked my buddy Gulab Chand to pick up a pair of jeans for me.

'Hey, Gulu, remember, da, it has to be Wrangler or Levi's, okay?' I said.

'Okay, da. I get it, I get it.'

Gulab sounded tired. Maybe because this was the fifth time I was telling him.

I had already lined up Kanika Krishnan, an unattainable nineteen-year-old friend of Sachu's as prospective customer, and given her waist measurements to Gulab. It was a sealed deal. Gulab would get me the jeans, I would add a margin of fifty per cent and hand over the merchandise to Kanika. She would ruffle my hair and pay me my price. I'd pocket my profit and pay up Gulab. I saw myself coming out with funding for at least ten movies in this deal.

Gulab didn't disappoint. He got me a pair of Wranglers, all wrapped in plastic. The waist size was 26". Perfect. That was what Kanika had wanted. Gulab wanted a hundred-and-ten rupees for it. I told him I'd pay him the following day. I ran to Kanika's house and gave her the jeans.

'What a sweet boy you are,' she said, ruffling my hair in advance.

She went in to try on the jeans. I sat in her living room thinking of the fifty-rupee profit I was going to make. Had this transaction taken place three or four years later, I would have foregone not just my profit but poor Gulab's investment as well to see Kanika Krishnan getting into those jeans.

But the thing next best to seeing Kanika Krishnan without her jeans was seeing her in jeans one size too tight. Even at twelve, I fully understood that this was a moment I was not going to forget that easily.

'Well, what do you think?' she said, turning round and round like an otter, her head craned to catch a glimpse of her own behind.

What I saw made my blood run cold. No, it was not the sight of Kanika's near-perfect rear threatening to bust the seams. It was the label on her jeans. It read 'Rangler'. It wasn't a wonder that that philistine Gulab had been gypped. His spelling had always been lousy.

What if she realized I was trying to palm off a cheap Sri Lankan fake? Where the hell was I going to find another buyer at such short notice? How the heck was I going to pay that cold-blooded bastard Gulab his hundred-and-ten bucks? Not to mention the interest he'd charge if I was late, coming from a family of 'financiers'?

Kanika went in and changed back into clothes she could breathe in. I waited. The Ranglers were folded neatly and she had my hundred and sixty rupees. She handed over the money to me as she looked at the label.

'Isn't Wrangler spelt with a "W"?'

I thought hard.

'Depends...' I said.

'On what?'

'On...er...where it's made,' I said, desperately calling on the repository of bullshit at my disposal, 'for instance, in Sri Lanka, it's spelt without the "W". In the US, it's with the "W". In the UK, it's with two "R"s. W-R-A-N-G-L-E-R-R.'

'Oh, really? That's interesting.'

It was my good fortune that Kanika's mind hadn't developed the way her rear had. It looked like I would get away with it.

'The thing is, Kanika,' I said, closing the deal with a line Chase would've been proud of, 'no one's going to be looking at the label when you're wearing those jeans.'

'Smooth talker,' she said, giving my hair a final ruffle.

I thought it was not prudent to tell her that her Ranglers would shrink a good two inches after their first wash.

When business opportunities looked dull, I blackmailed Grandmother. I wheedled out the rupee or two tied up at the end of her pallu using a variety of methods. Once, it was because I was the reincarnation of her dead father, and not giving me the money would mean disrespecting his spirit. Another time, it was for a poor homeless man outside my school who hadn't eaten for three days. Sometimes it was for a puja I wanted to conduct in a nearby temple to get better marks. At other times it was a fee for touching her feet several times. The few paise I got from her added to the kitty.

Like a far-sighted farmer who cared about the water table, I returned to the treasure trove only after a suitable interval had elapsed. Never overdrawing – allowing nature to replenish the aquifer before drawing from it again. The cycle of pilferage, over-invoicing, arm-twisting and shady business deals continued undetected.

The funny thing was no one at home seemed to care that I was watching a heck of a lot of movies or wonder how in hell I was finding the money. They probably assumed I was so popular and my friends so rich that they were paying for my tickets.

It was just as well that I got the cut-off figure of five rupees from several sources and hence in loose change. A crisp five-rupee note would have posed several problems. Before I left for the theatre I divided my resources precisely. Two rupees and ninety paise for the movie ticket was kept in the shirt pocket. No room for the ticket-clerk to short change me of ten paise. A maximum of sixty paise for the to-and-fro bus fare, depending on which stop I'd get off at – in the rear pocket of my trousers. No irate bus-conductor to deal with that way. The balance amount of one-rupee-fifty-paise went into my side pocket. This gave me the power to purchase exactly one softy ice-cream/soft drink/cutlet/egg bonda in the intermission.

If the five-rupee note facilitated the experience, the destination was always Mount Road. Or, to be more specific, a three-kilometre corridor of it between the Gemini Flyover and India Silk House that housed practically every theatre that played English movies: the Safire trio, Anand and Little Anand, Devi and her three sister theatres and the venerable relic of the '40s, Casino. Slight detours off Mount Road gave you the spanking new Satyam complex, with Midland and Leo a little further away.

The first in line as soon as you descended the flyover were the three jewels of Madras entertainment: Safire, Emerald and Blue Diamond – three theatres showing three distinct genres of films in the same compound. The Veecumsee Complex (as in 'We-Come-See', I suppose) was a multiplex before the word was invented. Safire always had the big budget Hollywood blockbusters, and had been inaugurated in the '60s with what was then the most expensive film ever made in the world, Liz Taylor's *Cleopatra*. The first movie I ever saw in Madras was here. It was *The Sound of Music* along with my entire family during our homeless days.

Blue Diamond next door was a smaller theatre and showed smaller films and reissues of blockbusters. But it had just about the grooviest concept in film exhibition that there ever was. It had continuous shows. All you had to do was buy a ticket for two rupees and ninety paise, walk into the theatre and see the movie playing as many times as you wanted to. I saw *Roman Holiday* so many times I could tell you the exact number of water drops that had fallen from Audrey Hepburn's head after her swim.

But movies were the last thing on the minds of most people who went to Blue D. It was the default destination of couples with large libidos and small budgets. A majority of its patrons were young lovers with busy hands. The rest were randy little boys who did not have a Lanka Jhansi to guide them.

The third and smallest theatre in the Veecumsee Complex was Emerald and it showed only Hindi movies. Snob that I was, I never once went to Emerald.

The Veecumsee complex had several other firsts to its credit. The basement of the building housed one of India's first discotheques, Nine Gems. Very often, while I waited in the queue for a matinée, I would see Dodo stumble down its darkened stairs with Bliss in one hand and a bong in the other. One of my life's unfulfilled desires, second only to marrying Raquel Welch in an Arya Samaj ceremony conducted by Clint Eastwood, was visiting this place. But, alas, it was shut down years before my shimmying days began. Silversands, south India's first Caribbean-style beach resort in Mahabalipuram, was also a Veecumsee Enterprise. All movies shown in the Safire complex were preceded by an ad for Silversands. The concept: bikini-clad white women romp around the pristine sands of the Tamil coast, men drink gin out of tender coconuts, and they retire together to air-conditioned huts. The End.

Man, I couldn't wait to grow up.

EIGHTEEN

On the 14th of March 1913, when Subramanya Sarma looked at his newborn child, he was only aware of how beautiful she was. He wasn't aware that Ratnamma, for that was to be her name, was born with a severe birth defect. It was a mental disorder that affected a small percentage of people those days and has since, like smallpox, been very nearly eradicated.

The little girl was incurably good.

That the girl grew up to be Grandmother suited me fine. With incurable goodness comes irremediable naivety. This meant that when I got tired of exploiting Kavi, I didn't have to look far for an alternative. Over a period of time, I mastered a technique where I'd push Kavi to just short of breaking point and abruptly shift focus to Grandmother. This move had a dual benefit. For one, with me off Kavi's back, my thrashing stood postponed. Two, with Grandmother being targeted, a reward from Mother was imminent.

I understood the extent of Grandmother's innocence when I was very young. I had seen a film in which the drunken hero, all wobble and slur, comes home and passes out in front of his mortified mother. Fascinated, I re-enacted the scene in front of Grandmother. She ran screaming to Father to get him to call a doctor and hastily prepared a large glass of buttermilk to 'sober up' her seven-year-old grandson.

When Mother rewarded me with a toffee, I knew I was on to a good thing.

From then on, with minor variations, I played the same scene to Grandmother again and again. I was, at different times, an epileptic having a fit, a stab victim bleeding to death, a boy who'd lost his power of speech, finally (in what Father would have called 'no act at all'), a young man losing his mind – all with equal success. While these acts had Grandmother running in search of various specialists, Mother would be rolling on the floor.

This made me wonder about my true calling. Was I meant to be an artist or an artiste?

At about the time my roles began getting repetitive, Buster attained puberty. With all the humans around it being either prepubescent or asexual, the poor thing must have realized its chances of finding a mate were slim. In the manner of any self-respecting dog with limited opportunities, Buster began humping anything it could wrap its forelegs around.

Topping this list was the human leg, of which there was a perennial parade at Club Meghamala. Buster rode the hairy legs of dhoti-clad writers and the shapely calves of visiting dancers with equal ardour. Whether it was a Jnanpith awardee or the vegetable vendor, there was a time when there was no escaping our pet's pulsating pelvis. While this was embarrassing in itself for both victim and witness, Buster's chronic incontinence added a whole new dimension to the performance. As guests fought valiantly to disengage themselves from the canine's clinch, Buster bore on like a cross between a power drill and a fountain.

While we buried our heads in shame, Grandmother alone found the encounters terribly sweet.

'Look, look!' she would say, as Buster pounded away pointlessly. 'What a respectful dog! It is saying namaste to our guests.'

For some reason no one told her the truth. As for Mother, she was in her usual place – rolling on the floor. Mistaking the rest of her family's petrifaction for approval, Grandmother took the whole thing to the next level. On the rare occasion when Buster didn't smell a visitor, Grandmother began calling out to the poor thing. To the dog, a call meant the arrival of fresh meat. It would hastily drop the old shoe it was defiling and rush into the living room. Then Grandmother would request the guest to stick a leg out and invite the eager dog to 'respect' it. If the visitor politely declined, Grandmother would stick her own leg out and allow the dog to display its boundless reverence.

While Mother busied herself with the logistics of converting this into a travelling act, Father couldn't take it any more. He took Grandmother aside and, in a first-of-its-kind role reversal, son told mother about the birds and the bees. Poor Grandmother made a trip to Tirupati to atone for her sins and never looked Buster in the face till its death ten years later.

However, Grandmother's animal encounters were not quite over.

It was the wedding of Jacob Kurien, Father's racing buddy, and we were all invited. I was going for a specific reason. If the movies were right, after a church wedding, there would be unbridled kissing of the bride and I'd never seen live people kiss. However, at the end of the ceremony, there was no kissing – not even a peck. I wondered if it had anything to do with the bride's moustache. But things began to look up at the dining hall. Spread across the tables was the biggest buffet I'd ever seen.

The one thing Grandmother wasn't shy about was food. Before we knew it, she was first in the queue and had piled her plate up high. By the time our turn came, she was ready for Round Two and was being served choice delicacies by one of the groom's relatives. Grandmother didn't know a word of anything other than Telugu but from the look of it, was getting along fine with her new friend from Kerala. I wondered where Mother was. She was an equally adept trencherwoman and was not known to let Grandmother get the better of her. Inspection revealed Mother all by herself, at the furthest corner of the hall, bent over in discomfort. She didn't look good at all. Abandoning my hard-earned place in the queue, I ran up to her.

'Amma, are you okay?' I said.

Mother didn't reply. She looked like she was trying to dislodge something large stuck in her throat. Her face was red. By now I was alarmed and gestured wildly to Father.

'Amma, please say something!' I said.

Mother looked up. Her face looked worse than Saikumar's best recital face. It appeared as though she was trying to say something but couldn't. There were beads of sweat all over her contorted face. All at once, whatever it was that was choking her seemed to let go. Mother collapsed to the floor with a shriek so loud the buffet came to a standstill. It took us a second to realize it was mirth. Now that she had allowed the release, Mother began rolling on the floor, laughing hysterically. Five minutes and several relapses later, she was able to tell us why.

'Look...look at your grandmother,' she gasped weakly, pointing to Grandmother whose plate was full yet again, 'she's been hogging from the non-vegetarian section.'

The third mutton cutlet in Grandmother's mouth turned to mud. Among all of us she was the real vegetarian, eating even garlic only under duress.

With that, both Meghamala women were escorted to the ladies' room. While one went to check if she had soiled herself, the other went in the hope of turning her insides out to scrub them free of sin.

NINETEEN

It was the year that came to be known as The Year of the Madras Flood. Things had started off innocently enough, like most disasters. An MGM-style drizzle, ideal for a Gene Kelly outing, changed genre midway to turn into the Noah section of the Old Testament. The rain came down like a million pipes had burst with no plumber in sight and Madras looked like a giant cup overflowing with weak coffee.

Having exhausted my repertoire torturing Kavi, and with nowhere to go, this got me wondering. What if there was a new Ark? And CG was in charge of filling it up. Dr Sarathi and our neighbour, Old Stubble Butt, would have been dead certs. As for the female contingent, there would've been no avoiding Lanka Jhansi and Auntie Renu. And before you knew it, it would be *The Planet of the Apes* all over again.

The good thing was, with the city resembling the permanently clogged sink in the Banka home, schools downed their shutters like they had gone out of business. Rumour was our headmaster Amalraj, known never to waste a minute, had been sighted rowing away in a home-made boat, Ms Charlotte DeCosta in tow.

The bad thing was Mother decided to leave.

If you continue sharing a bedroom with your parents beyond the potty phase, two things are certain. One – the chances of your growing into a normal, well-adjusted adult are pretty nearly nil. Two – you'd know if things were amiss with the folks. But, on the fifth day of relentless rain, when Mother stood at the doorway with a packed suitcase and said, 'I'm leaving. Anyone wants to join me?' it came as a complete surprise – at least to me.

As a couple, my parents were hardly in the Savitri–Satyavan mould. I couldn't see Mother putting up more than a token resistance when the God of Death came for Father. If the muttered curses, the constant mockery of each other's habits and flying utensils were anything to go by, they had more of a Taylor–Burton thing going (without the budget, of course).

But *this* was unheard of.

Women didn't leave a Meghamala home.

Not unless they did it horizontally, wearing a garland (while the men went 'Gosh darn, who's going to make my coffee now?').

But, then again, this wasn't a Meghamala woman we were talking about.

It was Mother.

With Mother's announcement, Grandmother looked like she'd been asked to slaughter a goat, Lalli said 'Why?', Father continued drawing and CG was nowhere to be seen. Kavi alone ran to Mother and held her hand. I stayed put, wondering what to do.

Mother was an expressive woman. Happiness, anger,

disappointment or mischief – you could see her emotions clear as a children's illustration. What I saw on her face that day was calm. Something I'd never seen before. And that worried me. Maybe it was because the tiny, unexposed, adult core of my heart knew calm was often a mask for something else.

Something also told me that if there was a time to exercise the loyalty muscle, it was now. Mother and Kavi didn't look as good a team as Mother, Kavi *and* me. They needed a man. Besides, there was every chance of the rains abating, Amalraj returning from his dirty weekend, and it would be school all over again.

An hour after leaving, though drenched and homeless, the three of us were still less than two hundred metres from our house. Soosai the rickshawallah, Mother's charioteer for her weekly matinées, negotiated the flood waters the best he could but he was no Captain Nemo. The similar amount of arrack sloshing around inside of him didn't exactly help either.

'Where are we going?' said Kavi.

'Somewhere. Anywhere,' said Mother.

'But I didn't tell Pattu Miss. She'll scold me when I go back.'

Kavi knew how to spoil things. Here we were on an adventure of a lifetime and she had to bring in school.

Mother didn't reply, so I did.

'No more school for us, Kavi, from now on, we'll never *ever* go to school.'

Though I tried to sound sombre, Mother caught the repressed glee in my voice. I felt ashamed for a second. Then again, I didn't see the harm in my approach. After all, irons were struck while hot and hay was made while suns shone. Even when it was raining like tarnation. Kavi let out a wail.

'Make no mistake, Ramu. Wherever you are, whatever you do, both of you *will* go to school,' Mother said.

I wasn't overly worried. I knew that it would be some time before we were found admission in another school. That was good enough for the time being.

Soosai, who had managed to progress five feet in the last ten minutes, came to.

'Engey, ma? Where do you want to go?' he said.

'Central Station,' said Mother, prompting him to take a hefty swig from his 'water' bottle.

The earlier instruction to Soosai had been, 'Move!' which could've meant anything. Now it was obvious Mother meant business. We *were* leaving.

From Pandari Bai to Nirupa Roy, mothers had been doing this for years. Heading out into a cruel world, children in tow, on account of a drunken, dysfunctional or defunct husband. Though Father didn't quite fit these categories, it was pretty clear what fate had in store for us.

First, Mother would buy a sewing machine. When that didn't cover rent, she'd reluctantly send me to break stones in a quarry while Kavi went to school. As Mother pedalled away tailoring a fat woman's blouse, a moneylender would try to outrage her modesty. I would save her in the nick of time by stabbing him with her scissors. He would die. I'd go to jail. Meanwhile, an earthquake would separate Mother and Kavi.

I'd return fifteen years later, the most glamorous smuggler in all of south India, save everyone, forgive my penitent father, marry the police commissioner's daughter and we'd pose for the group photograph. The End.

The part I liked best – I wouldn't have to go to school.

Faithful charioteers had their limits, too. Ten minutes and five feet later, Soosai stopped the rickshaw. I could understand why. While the external water level had risen by half a foot, the level in his bottle had dropped to near-empty.

'Can't, ma,' he said.

'What do you mean, "can't"?' said Mother.

We were in the middle of G.N. Chetty Road, waist-deep in water. Central Station could have been on another planet. A handful of people (who'd probably decided to abandon their families as well) were visible chest-upwards wading through the muck. The body of a dead cat floated by.

'Can't means can't,' said Soosai. He picked up the floating feline by its tail, examined it and, finding no immediate use for it, threw it back in the water.

'Come, get off,' said Mother.

She had decided to leave. It was going to take more than a drunken rickshawman and the worst natural disaster Madras had seen (if you didn't count the Bankas, that is) to stop her.

Having got off, we realized we had a problem when Kavi tried to wail and went 'Glub!' instead. All we could see of her above the water was the top of her head and a pair of round eyes. Mother handed me our lone box of belongings and picked Kavi up. Barring her eyes and forehead, she was an even shade of brown. She spat out a jet of what looked like dilute Bournvita and let out her wail.

Soosai took stock of the situation. One destitute woman with a mad glint in her eye, one sewage-coated little girl, one emaciated boy teetering with an overstuffed suitcase, one dead cat floating away in the direction of Dr Sarathi's clinic, and his arrack-sodden heart gave.

'Why, ma?' he said. By now the country liquour had breached its barriers and was coming out of his eyes in little fountains. 'Why are you leaving? Who'll I take to Rajakumari on Sunday afternoons now?'

An hour later we were in Mount Road. The rain had stopped but the water showed no signs of subsiding. Yet Soosai persevered. His bottle was empty, his spindly legs were on autopilot and he was singing an unrecognizable version of an MGR hit that spoke of living like a free bird. Mother couldn't take it any more.

'Stop, for God's sake,' she said.

If we had planned it we couldn't have done it better. We were outside Anand Theatre and it was three o' clock and *Mr Majestyk* was on. *A Charles Bronson movie.* Unless the projectionist didn't know how to swim, we were in. The three of us, suitcase and all, walked in for the matinée show like it had been our plan all along.

He didn't want to be a hero until the day they pushed him too far...said the poster. It had Bronson kicking a guy's face in, a minimum of four guns pointed at the viewer and a bus being blown to matchwood. The state may have been reeling under the fury of the rains but for at least two people it hadn't turned out all bad: Mr Amalraj and me.

Bronson delivered as he usually did. Other than the mayhem promised on the poster, there was a scene where an entire crop of water-melons was blasted to bits. It was the bloodiest massacre scene in movie history.

I wandered around in the intermission checking out the coming attractions. The publicity stills had tons of guns and even more cleavage. Maybe leaving Madras wasn't *such* a good idea. After all, Father always said English movies were first released here. I wondered whether the rain had stopped, what Lalli was up to and if anyone was missing us.

I didn't enjoy the second half of the movie as much as the first. Bronson wasn't to blame. He continued his squint-eyed brand of bedlam but I just couldn't focus. I noticed Kavi was asleep and Mother was staring sightlessly at the screen. Maybe, for her sake, we should've gone to the Hindi film in Little Anand instead. I also had a funny feeling in my stomach. I wondered how much it had to do with the two packets of popcorn I'd eaten.

I'd always hated it when a movie ended. While the rest of the audience ran out like it was a prison break, I would be the only one in the auditorium seated till the last of the credits had rolled up. I had done it so often I had begun recognizing names of gaffers, continuity girls and best boy grips without having the faintest idea of what they did. That day, Mother and Kavi remained seated with me.

Outside, that unmistakable air unique to theatre exteriors hit me as it had a hundred times before. It was an equal parts mixture of stale popcorn, male piss, smoke and reality.

'Can we go home now, Ma?' said Kavi. She was not yet fully awake but from the look of it she was done.

Mother didn't reply.

'We can leave tomorrow if you want,' she said.

Mother still didn't say anything. I could see why.

CG was standing just outside the main door.

He had a dripping umbrella over his head and the headlights of a car had turned the drops to diamonds and his hair into optic fibres.

The four of us stood around awkwardly for a moment. I caught sight of a thoroughly drenched Saikumar in the background. He made big eyes at me and I shrugged.

Thaatha wrote something on his scribbling pad. Mother read it and began to cry. We all stood that way for some more time. Saikumar took the suitcase out of Mother's hands and put it in the boot of a white Amby I didn't recognize. Mother didn't protest.

On our way back, Kavi sat with CG in the front seat. I looked at Mother. She looked calm. I wondered if it was a different calm. From the rear windscreen I could see the sky had cleared.

TWENTY

It's the final scene in *Butch Cassidy and the Sundance Kid*. Paul Newman and Robert Redford are trapped. The Bolivian army has surrounded their hideout. They look at each other one last time and charge out guns blazing into a fusillade of bullets.

When you reach a certain age, it's the same with the subject of sex. There's no escaping it.

For Lalli, its introduction came through the joint efforts of Lanka Jhansi and Kerala's nascent adult entertainment industry. That hardcore experience shook my sister up so badly that for years she immersed herself in the gentler works of Louisa May Alcott. But it was like re-enrolling in primary school after completing a master's degree. She never did manage to unlearn anything.

For me, too, the subject of sex arrived in many ways, and through some unlikely messengers – like the First Citizen of the Indian Republic, for instance.

Ask any boy who went to school in the mid-'70s and he'll tell you that no leader of this country or, for that matter any other, has helped free speech more than this man. His very name made him the most popular leader we had – at least where schoolboys across the country were concerned. Classmates who'd mumble something unintelligible when asked our president's name in civics class were now referring to him, unasked and out of context, in maths class, the school corridor, the playground and the toilet.

> *Maths Teacher*: What's the square root of 144?
> *Student who has no clue*: **FAAARK....**
> *Maths Teacher*: What?!
> *Student*: Nothing, sir. Fakhruddin Ali Ahmed, sir. Apparently, maths was his favourite subject, sir.
> *Maths Teacher*: Really? How nice. It's good to be inspired by our leaders.

When you got hit in Holly Golly, when you were goosed, when you had forgotten to do your homework – suddenly everything was a reason to invoke the president, with undue emphasis on the first syllable of his name.

The constant references to our president had me rushing to the dictionary to find out what the fuss was about. Sure, I had a rough idea of what the word meant. After all, Father's exchanges with salesmen and security guards had kept me in the loop. But rough wasn't good enough any more. I wanted precise answers with illustrations if possible. But the dictionary was disappointing: 'have sexual intercourse with' is what it said. Big deal, I knew that. But what did *that* mean? What did who have and where did what go when? And why?

As my leave letters had already proved, the authorities at Vidya Vihar were quite naive. It took our headmaster a couple of months to realize that it wasn't precocious political awareness that was making the president's name pop up all the time. So, in a manner befitting the time, he clamped down on our free speech.

'No one will refer to our president's name out of turn,' said the notice board one day, to our horror.

Fear of having our bottoms turn the navy blue of our uniforms at the hands of our headmaster Amalraj kept us from saying the president's name in vain from that day on. One day, we were playing a particularly violent game of Holly Golly. It was more gory than usual probably because of the suppressed rage of censorship. In the heat of the game, Rusty Mistry unintentionally intercepted a scorcher of a throw from a freakishly large classmate with his testicles.

Holding his groin with both hands he screamed, **'FAAAARK…'**

Unfortunately for him, the headmaster was walking by at that time. Mistry, red in the face, with the remains of his genitals still in his hands, stared at Amalraj. The headmaster stared right back – challenging him. Mistry had to come up with something – and he did.

'I mean…V.V. Giri.'

As it happened, I needn't have worried for long about my lack of knowledge because the Class Six Rosebud Reader came to our assistance quite inadvertently. One of the lessons in our English textbook was about how films were made. Halfway into the lesson one thing became obvious to the entire class. *This* was a case for Meghamala Gopal. Who better at combining films with cutting school?

'Ma'am,' I offered my English teacher unsolicited, 'I can arrange for the class to watch a film shooting. It will help us understand the lesson better.'

Our English teacher thought it was a wonderful idea. Instantly I became the most popular boy in class. Grandfather was more than willing to get us the required permission. He had a couple of calls made and gave me a letter. All I had to do was show it to the security guard at Vennela Gardens (the most exotic studio in Madras where the brightest of Telugu and Tamil filmdom walked around in pancaked glory) and we would be given the Deluxe Tour.

On Excursion Day, forty schoolboys and Mrs Madiman, our English teacher, arrived in the school bus at the hallowed gates of Vennela Gardens in Vadapalani. The guard looked impassively at our letter and called someone on the intercom. His reaction wasn't what I'd expected. Whenever we had gone to the studio with Grandfather, we had always been waved in with a salute. A couple of minutes later, a man came to the gates and read the letter. The driver of our bus kept the engine running. After what seemed an eternity, the man addressed Mrs Madiman.

'Madam,' he said, 'the film industry is on strike. It was sudden. So, all the…most…shootings have been cancelled.'

Mrs Madiman looked at the disappointed faces of the boys. Through the corner of my eye I caught T.V. Suresh and Ashok Malwani cracking their knuckles. I knew that violent death awaited me at school.

'Is there no shooting at all?' asked Mrs Madiman, giving it

a last shot. 'Anything will do. The boys can't take another day off…'

The man looked at us. Forty boys and a teacher on the verge of tears. He relented.

'There is *one* shooting, Madam,' he said, looking over his shoulder, 'it's on Floor 8. Go quietly, see it for a few minutes and leave quietly. And…also…er…please don't tell anyone I sent you.'

So saying, the man disappeared behind a giant head of Lord Shiva with crescent moon and a fountain Ganga spouting out of his dreadlocks into a nearby pond.

Thirty-nine schoolboys swaggered into the studio. One slunk in wiping his brow, relieved that death had been postponed.

On Floor 8, a reluctant production assistant read our letter, shrugged, and let us in.

'Keep quiet!' he warned us.

The tiny door within the giant door closed and we were in a high-ceilinged, asbestos-roofed room bustling with silent activity. Wooden planks suspended on ropes hung from the ceiling. Precariously perched light boys held giant arc lights in place, lighting up the centre of the floor. The camera and some more lights stood perched among miles of wire crisscrossing the studio floor. It was hot as hell. On a foldable metal chair in the middle of the room, as artificially coloured as cotton candy, sat the heart-throb of south India, Devisri. For some reason, she was wrapped in a giant towel. A little further away, shaking his legs to a silent rhythm, a cigarette dangling from his lips, sat the dreaded Kommineni, that actor whose very appearance in a film meant that all wouldn't be well. No Krishna or Sobhan Babu anywhere in sight, just the heroine and the villain. That was odd. What were they going to shoot?

The director looked through the camera and made some final changes. Devisri walked into the frame and threw off her towel like a boxer throws off his cloak. Underneath, the poor woman was attired in a most unheroinely fashion. She was wearing a torn blouse, a petticoat and nothing else. The make-up man brightened the livid scars on Devisri's back. The director yelled 'Action!' and Devisri ran round and round the set while Kommineni chased her enthusiastically, trying to scratch her. All the while Devisri kept yelling 'Don't!' and 'Scoundrel!' in Telugu while Kommineni responded by laughing. Forty schoolboys and a petrified English teacher watched the proceedings transfixed. The director yelled 'Cut!', Devisri stopped running, her assistant covered her with the towel and Kommineni retreated to a corner to continue squeezing an imaginary coconut between his legs. When the director yelled 'Action!' again, the running, screaming and scratching restarted. This went on for about twenty times. Strangely, though all the hard work was being done by Devisri and Kommineni, it was Mrs Madiman who passed out. That marked our exit from the closed set. As Mrs Madiman recouped with a tender coconut supplied by the production assistant, we were allowed to do as we pleased on the endless grounds of Vennela Gardens. Taking a cue from the actors we'd just seen, we ran all over the place.

Along toy bridges going across artificial streams. Through palm-lined avenues. By man-made ponds with real lotuses. Down cobbled pathways running under flimsy plaster-of-Paris arches. From Jaishankar to Jayalalitha, from Krishna to Kanchana, no path traversed by the lead pairs of the times was left unexplored by schoolboys pumped up by their first viewing of non-consensual sex.

We were yanked back to reality by the sound of a tremendous crack. Inspection revealed that the sound was caused, not surprisingly, by Rusty Mistry. He was found lying on his back, trying to wriggle out from under the crescent moon that he had somehow managed to dislodge from Lord Shiva's head. Very quickly and very silently all forty-one of us climbed back into the bus and retreated before Shiva opened his third eye.

Unlike on most other excursions, we were not asked by our English teacher to write an essay on 'My Experiences at a Film Studio'. That year, for some reason, Mrs Madiman left Vidya Vihar.

Thanks to our president, we knew the F-word and thanks to our Rosebud Reader we had experienced rape firsthand, the next logical step in our search for the meaning of sex was via the favourite sport of boys – and by that I don't mean Holly Golly.

You can't study in a boys' school and not hear of masturbation. That's like studying in a girls' school and not knowing what an Alice Band is. Of course, no one called it masturbation. 'Shagging' was the term of choice. There was a lot of shagging, or talk of a lot of shagging going on in our school. Every time T.V. Suresh, Ashok Malwani or any of the more hirsute members of our class mentioned it, the rest of us wimps who didn't have the faintest idea of what it meant or how it was done laughed knowingly.

One day, Suresh was boasting, 'My brother does it *every* day!'

All of us laughed. Sendhil helpfully added, 'Big shagger, your brother.'

We all laughed uproariously.

'What do you know about shagging, da?' Suresh challenged Sendhil, the mouse who'd been unsuccessfully trying to break into the 'in' crowd. 'You only have an elder sister. Does she shag?'

There was more uproarious laughter from a bunch of guys who had absolutely no idea what was going on. From the nebulous subject involving doing something with one's own privates, Suresh had moved into the realm of the unknown – *women* – doing god-knows-what-heaven-knows-where.

'No...but...' the creaky levers in Sendhil's head moved, '... but...I have a father...'

There was dead silence from everybody. Now, *this* was unknown territory even for the shavers. Sendhil looked around. He realized he was on to a good thing. Even the venerable T.V. Suresh had his mouth open. This called for a clincher of a closing line.

'And...and he does it five times a day!'

A while later Sendhil was hospitalized during the course of his summer vacation. Not, as you might think, because

T.V. Suresh found out that he didn't have the faintest idea what shagging was. Quite the contrary, actually. In the following months Sendhil had not just managed to find out what it meant but had become a seasoned practitioner of the art that still remained elusive to most of his classmates. That summer, with a lot of time on one hand, and his penis in the other, Sendhil attempted to shatter his father's fictitious record for fifteen consecutive days, after which he was admitted in hospital for 'exhaustion and dehydration'. With no statistical data available on past cases of a similar nature, all the doctors could do was come up with something that would minimize the chances of a relapse. This they did by putting Sendhil's hands in casts for the rest of the summer.

Sendhil was probably the first guy in recorded history who'd been hospitalized for shagging. His classmates were not going to let Sendhil go unfelicitated, so they poured in every day, making the authorities of the obscure clinic wonder if they had a celebrity in their midst. Simultaneously, a think-tank of seniors was working hard on coming up with a name for Sendhil that did justice to his summer feat. Bruce Lee provided the inspiration and Sendhil was named 'Fist of Fury'. His experience has served as a cautionary tale for generations of Vidya Viharites on the verge of puberty.

But it was Prasad, a non-Vidya Viharite, who finally cleared any doubts I might have had about sex. Just as the tree-climbing skills of Pandu & Co. were beginning to pall, Prasad came into our lives. Or, to be more specific, crashed into it. Prasad was a year older than me and had been trying to catch our attention for a couple of months. He skated up and down Ramalingam Street to break into our Ice Boys gang because, creepy as it might sound, he had a crush on my ten-year-old younger sister. Two months and three pairs of skates later, with no signs of a formal invitation, he literally ran over me one day as Kavi and I were off to buy our Sunday treat of 007 bubble gum.

On Day One itself, Prasad took on the designation of senior statesman in our gang. His credentials were impeccable. For starters, he had the beginnings of a moustache. Secondly, his father was a film producer and his older sister was an actress – so this pretty much gave him the incontrovertibility of a research scholar on the subject of sex.

Prasad saved us the embarrassment of asking. One evening, having got rid of Kavi, Chanti, and the other juniors, he gave Pandu and me our first and most unforgettable lesson on how it was done.

'What do you chaps know about sex?'

Pandu and I mumbled something about knowing a little, quickly adding that we were open to learning some more.

'I have a girlfriend, you know,' said Prasad.

'Did you do it?' Pandu burst out, inadvertently indicating the nature of his future sex life.

'All the time.'

'How, da? Tell us, no,' we chorussed.

'*First*, you've got to know when a girl's ready to do it.'

'How do you find out?'

'Well...you put your hand *there*...'

'Where??' Both Pandu and I were exasperated. Why was everyone talking like we knew? We needed specifics. Illustrations with arrows and captions if possible.

'Here,' sighed Prasad wearily, pointing between his legs.

'Then?'

'If she's ready, you'll feel hot air coming out.'

'What??' Pandu and I were expecting the unknown – *but currents of warm air from between the legs of girls*?

'Bastard, you're pulling our leg,' said Pandu.

'Swear, da!' said Prasad, putting his hand on his head in the local equivalent of a Scout's honour. He couldn't be lying.

'Won't your hand get burnt?' Pandu didn't want his tree-climbing skills compromised in any way.

'You're a real idiot, da. What do you think? They have a pressure cooker *there*! It will be hot – but not burning hot, okay?'

'What if the air that's coming out is cold?'

'Good question. Then you squeeze the balls.'

This was getting insane. How could squeezing *your* balls get *her* hot?

'My balls?' I had to ask.

'No you idiot! *Her* balls.'

'Girls have *balls*!?' exclaimed Pandu. Even he knew that couldn't be true.

Prasad was just short of thumping us. He poked either side of his chest with his forefingers. 'What the fuck are these?'

'I think tits or boobs is the preferred term...' I volunteered. My James Hadley Chase hadn't gone totally to waste.

'Tits, balls – all same, da! They look like balls, no? So balls is what *we* call them!' said Prasad, dismissing my fastidiousness for terminology.

'Then, what?' Pandu wanted to get on with it.

'Well, you keep on squeezing the balls till hot air comes out of *there*.'

'I get it. You keep squeezing the air out of the balls till it goes down there, right?' said Pandu, happy that he could identify the chain of scientific logic in the whole operation. Prasad stared at him. Pandu thought for a while and realized the flaw in his theory.

'I guess that's really not it, right?'

'And why is that?' asked Prasad. His tone was alarmingly similar to our science teacher's, who loved making students admit they were wrong.

'Because...then *these*,' I jumped in, ever-ready to show up a friend, pointing to my chest, 'will become flat!'

Prasad gave me a pat on my back and flicked Pandu's ear.

'It's not that simple. You squeeze in one place. It gets hot in another. That's all.'

Pandu rubbed his bruised ear. 'Okay...then what?'

'Well, then you take off your clothes and do it.'

'Do what?'

'*It*, you fuckers!' said Prasad. He couldn't have been more wrong. If we didn't know what *it* was, how could we be fuckers?

'How do you do it? Be specific, or admit that you are a big dhapper!'

'Well, you take off your clothes and you hug and *it* goes in.' This time Prasad was specific, pointing exactly where *it* was.

'And…'

'That's it!'

'*That's it?*'

'Yeah, what else did you expect?'

Pandu was not satisfied.

'Okay, where do kids come from?'

'From here, of course,' said Prasad, pointing to his behind and concluding the first and most significant sex education class of our lives. 'You guys don't know fuck.'

Years later, when Pandu's wife left him after just six months of marriage to elope with the driver and my life went a certain way, I couldn't help but wonder whether I should have got a second opinion.

TWENTY-ONE

If there's someone in a family who spends most of his life on a dais, one thing's a certainty – haemorrhoids. Not, as you might think, for the celebrity, because stage chairs are usually well-cushioned, but for the rest of the family forced to spend an equal amount of time squirming on unyielding seats in raggedy auditoriums.

As kids, if one F-word, popularized by an unfortunate president, brought immediate joy, there were two others that sent shivers up our spines: 'function' and 'felicitation'. At home, all three words were extensively used and quite often in combination. The first word usually as a response, muttered under our breath, to any mention of the other two.

It was a big bore that CG was the grand old man of Telugu culture in Madras. It was as if all of T. Nagar (short for Thyagaraya Nagar, not Telugu Nagar as it might well have been named) had put its collective pride into a filigreed wooden chest and handed it over to Grandfather. This made him the automatic chief guest for all celebrations Andhra. It could be a new author's book release, it could be the Sankranti celebrations of the IIT Andhras' Association or it could be the coming-of-age festivities of a film producer's hapless daughter. 'Let's call Meghamala' seemed to be the consensus.

While this was just another day at the office for Grandfather, it was an opportunity to bring out the Conjeevaram silks for the women. On such days Father seemed to have access to an invisible escape hatch that invariably led to the Madras Race Club. Without fail, after having lulled us kids into a sense of false security ('It'll be fun. There'll be soft drinks and light music'), Father would disappear at the last minute, handing over the reins of the excursion to a driver procured on a temporary basis. While he put his feet up in the bicentenary stand losing *my* movie ticket money, the three of us listened to speeches that sounded like 78 rpms being played at $33^1/_3$ speed. For some reason, on such days, being left alone at home with a book didn't seem to be an option at all.

Though the majority of such functions made you wish you owned a Smith & Wesson, it wasn't as if they were completely joyless. When there is a stage, sooner or later, things are bound to go wrong.

It was at such a time that Kurnool Krishnamraju, super-rich merchant of oilcake (just a polite word for cattle feed), stumbled upon us. One day, as he sat in his office in Tondiarpet, that smoke-laden northern corner of Madras that no culturally inclined Telugu would dare venture into, something struck him. He had three cars and eleven telephones but, other than cattle merchants, no one knew who he was. He did not have fame.

Raju realized that he could correct this shortcoming in two ways. One way would be to do something so spectacular that the world and its press agent noticed. Now, what was it that he could do in his chosen field that would catapult him into the front pages? Not having met our Dr Sarathi, that accelerator of anabolism, the idea of inventing cattle feed that would jet propel cows over the moon did not occur to him. So he decided to take Route Two. Become famous by courting someone famous.

The answer to the question 'Which famous Telugu person could a fodder manufacturer of limited contacts woo easily?' proved to be an easy one and before long Krishnamraju turned up at Ramalingam Street.

For a man who made what became dung, Raju seemed to possess slightly more culture than our average Andhra import. He was soft-spoken and at the second meeting itself brought gifts for everybody from his recent trip to Singapore: a lockable scribbling pad with a built-in pen for CG, water-soluble colour pencils for Father, a synthetic sari for Mother, a little glass box with lights to put a tiny god in for Grandmother, and assorted chocolates for us. The guy had done his homework. We were hooked. It didn't occur to us that he could have just as easily bought these at Burma Bazaar on his way home from Tondiarpet.

Goodies aside, Raju also presented to us for the first time a sartorial choice no less insane in Madras than my Lal Imli bell-bottoms of a couple of years ago – the safari suit. Dressed in a variety of resplendent monochromes, sweating like Rusty at a maths test, he landed up at home almost every day, dangling custom-made carrots for everyone. For Grandfather it was a meal prepared exactly the way he liked or a special screening of a b/w oldie at a preview theatre with guests of his choice; for the ladies, it would be a chauffeur-driven trip to a suburban temple with his rotund, gold-encrusted wife for company; for Father, a biography of Lester Piggot; and unlimited chocolates for us. The long, unsupervised hours at home when he took the adults away was a bonus.

It was a good time for all.

But all good things come to an end. One day, Krishnamraju came up with the mother of all schemes, one that guaranteed to put us all on inflatable pile seats for the rest of our lives: the Ultimate Felicitation (that mother of all 'f' words) for Grandfather. A function so grand, with a guest list so distinguished and an entertainment programme...well, so entertaining that the applause would be heard in Delhi, prompting the powers-that-be to fall over each other trying to confer a Padma Bhushan or a Padma Vibhushan on Grandfather. There would be singing, dancing and a felicitation committee comprising the 'Who's Who' of Telugu literature. Father's escape route was cut off by putting him on the committee. Just as we were about to kiss our asses goodbye came the pièce de résistance – Krishnamraju proposed a purse of one lakh rupees to CG on the occasion. I couldn't speak for my sisters, but as far as I was concerned, that changed *everything*. Permanent rectal damage was a small price to pay for my share, which I estimated at a conservative five thousand smackeroos. Loosely translated, it was a thousand films.

Within a day of his proposal, it became obvious that I wasn't the only one with an eye on the cookie jar. Auntie Renu turned up with a sheaf of foolscap paper tucked under her arm and a lone tear dangling from her kohled eyelashes. What surprised us wasn't her arrival, because everyone knew

Auntie Renu could smell a deal if she was in a coma. It was her response time. Maybe Grandmother was sending smoke signals from our terrace.

'Babai,' she said, showing CG what looked like a hastily chalked-out plan, 'you know it's been my lifelong dream to start a dance school for Niranjan, don't you?'

I couldn't see her plan but if Dad's bookies were anywhere in sight, I would have placed a quick bet on her outlay being in the region of a lakh. That way I would have recovered a portion of my five thousand which seemed to be dissolving right before my eyes.

'Really?' scribbled the old man, putting aside the *Madras Mail* crossword for a minute, 'I was under the impression it was wangling a Padmashri for yourself.'

Auntie Renu promptly burst into tears. Mother, on the other hand, clasped her hands together behind her back to prevent herself from strangling Auntie Renu. It was a scene that had played out several times at home with minor variations.

'Thank god...(sob)...my father is not alive,' Auntie Renu gave it all she had. 'Otherwise...(sob)...he would have known that all that talk of me being your daughter was just talk... (sob)!'

At the mention of his long-dead writer friend, CG softened. He scribbled something on his pad and showed it to his 'daughter'. I couldn't see what it was but it was clear now that the purse would turn up at home considerably diminished because Auntie Renu jumped up and down and hugged CG.

Mother bit her knuckles till they bled.

I wasn't overly perturbed. I'd got used to relying on more than one revenue stream. If it wasn't the purse, it would be something else.

Mother, however, didn't look like she would let it go.

'How can she do that?' she asked Father as he tried to duck behind his little pink book. 'We don't own a house, there's nothing set aside for the kids...and the bloody woman wants *our* money for her homo son's dance school!'

Father quickly shushed her. He knew, his interludes with salesmen notwithstanding, our ears weren't equipped for Mother on song.

'Relax,' he said, 'nothing's happened yet. It's a long way off.'

Mother wasn't convinced. She went into the kitchen and burnt the potato fry to a cinder.

CG probably wasn't the person to rely on when it came to doing what was best for us but when it came to mixing it up there was no one better. Instead of calling the big guns of the Telugu film industry who were a phone call away to participate, CG insisted on digging into the vast pool of idiot performers who had traipsed through Club Meghamala at one time or another. This meant Saikumar and Lanka Jhansi, which in turn meant strangulation and sequins, with every possibility of sickle-wielding rowdies making an appearance. So what if I lost my share, things were looking up.

Within a month of its birth in Tondiarpet, feeding off of CG's goodwill, Krishnamraju's idea grew like a rampant tumour. Famous singers, actors, dancers – everyone wanted in. Soon there was a waiting list for the programme sheet.

With fame breathing down his neck, the first thing Krishnamraju did was order a dozen new safari suits. While his collection was already nothing short of what Vidya Viharites referred to as 'jaal', the new suits bordered on phosphorescent. They were made of material I'd never seen before. It was as if a million sequins were ground to dust and interwoven with terene. It wasn't hard to imagine Krishnamraju in a dark, windowless room, fine-tuning the programme sheet in the glow of his suit.

I couldn't wait to see his outfit for the big day.

Predictably, Jhansi and Saikumar appeared at Ramalingam Street in a stop-block with the accompanying 'ping'. CG averted war by quickly informing them that they would both get equal stage time. An empty house across the road was fixed for the three-month-long rehearsals, with the iridescent Krishnamraju overseeing things. Kavi and I literally dropped out of school and spent all our time watching the rehearsals.

Soon, it was evident that among the various items on the programme, Krishnamraju's real interest lay in singing. He seemed to spend most of his time hovering around the music troupe in general and Lanka Jhansi in particular. This unfair attention made Saikumar go the purple he aspired for *without* asphyxiation. It could've been my imagination, but in the combined glow of Jhansi and Krishnamraju's sequins, Saikumar's face appeared doubly lurid.

On the day of the 'do', there were the usual reporters from Telugu newspapers. It was no surprise, they would have covered CG's bowel movements, given the opportunity. But there was representation from the English papers as well, and a camera crew from the Films Division. Obviously, the manufacturer of oilcake knew how to lubricate the system.

Krishnamraju had put ads in the local papers welcoming all and followed it up by distributing invites with impunity for a month preceding the event. The five-hundred-seater Rani Mahal resembled his waistband – ready to burst any minute.

Some idiot had decided it would be grand if CG made an entry into the auditorium on a palanquin borne by writers and poets. So, about a furlong away from the venue, a reluctant CG was stuffed into the flower-bedecked monstrosity designed for the occasion. Looking at him staring helplessly from its innards like some trapped animal I wondered how someone could love and hate the same thing for so long. For the first time in my life, I prayed for things to go *right* at a function, at least for the time being.

Snaking through the petrified peak-hour traffic, with a dozen writers taking turns as bearers, CG reached the auditorium in one piece. There, Krishnamraju made a big show of receiving him with garlands and sandalwood paste. A bunch of priests chanted without punctuation while a band played '*Come September*'. As the erstwhile baker of oilcake chewed up the scenery in a safari suit that appeared green from the left, maroon from the right and a dusty gold head on, I felt bad that the Films Division newsreels were made in black-and-white.

Thanks to the organizational skills of Krishnamraju, the programme unfolded without a wrinkle. Speakers spoke, dancers danced and actors acted. An hour into the programme, I yearned for the time when gun laws in India would change.

The only thing that kept me from yanking out my wobbly armrest and clubbing the bald head in front of me to a purée was my share of the purse. Post-Auntie Renu's requisition I'd lowered my expectations to an attainable thousand.

Then it was time for light music. I was hoping Saikumar would go first. It would be interesting to see how he'd maintain the baritone in front of a large audience. Maybe he'd have an assistant walking up to him every couple of minutes to discreetly strangle him. To my disappointment, it was Lanka Jhansi who came on first, in flaming-red sequinned nylex. The emcee announced that she would start off with one of CG's evergreen hits. I resigned myself to watching her glittering bosom heave.

Jhansi took the mike and cleared her throat and, instead of singing, began to speak. 'Respected Thaathagaru, ladies and gentlemen,' she said. I could have sworn she was blushing. 'I would like to make an announcement. Standing in front of all of you, it wouldn't be right if I kept the happy news to myself. What I mean to say is…I am about to become a mother.'

There was a brief silence, followed by polite applause, obviously from a section of the audience that didn't know Jhansi personally. Thanks to the collective efforts of Prasad, Devisri, Kommineni and the President of the Republic, *I* knew something was amiss. To the best of my knowledge, in her progress from single girl to expectant mother, Jhansi had skipped a vital step. She'd got herself a double promotion, except it wasn't good.

'And the father of my baby,' she continued, rubbing her glittering belly, 'is my ootchie-cootchie-piggy-wiggy, sitting right there!' Jhansi pointed to the front row. A thousand eyes and the Films Division camera followed the singer's finger and came to rest on Kurnool Krishnamraju squirming in the halo of his suit.

In order of importance, the events that followed:

I got nothing because there was no purse.

T. Nagar witnessed what looked like its own Gold Rush. In reality, it was a sparkling Krishnamraju and a glistening Lanka Jhansi just one step behind being chased by his bejewelled wife with the Films Division Team tagging along.

Auntie Renu's idea of a dance school was dropped.

A few months later, Lanka Jhansi gave birth to a baby boy. She mailed us a photo of him wearing a safari-collared bib and sequinned nappy.

Krishnamraju attained the fame he had sought. His wife blitzed the papers with ads with his face on them, offering a reward to anyone who had info on his whereabouts. The sum was, not surprisingly, one lakh.

And, though it had nothing to do with any of this, CG got a Padma Vibhushan.

TWENTY-TWO

On a dark and stormy night sometime in the mid-nineteenth century, a fifteen-year-old Niyogi Brahmin girl of exceptional beauty stole out of her agraharam and ran towards the docks. She didn't care that her husband would cut her head off with his sword (the one he'd been presented by His Excellency, the Yuvaraja of Masulipatam, for exceptional service in the revenue department) if he found out. All she cared about was that the *Peking Duck* had berthed a few hours ago and her beloved Chow Yun Chan was on board. She didn't have to run very far because the equally lovelorn Chinese sailor was waiting near the burial ground, his pigtail flapping furiously in the wind. The young couple embraced passionately and collapsed on the wet grass and made wordless love. Maybe it had something to do with Chan not knowing any Telugu and the girl being similarly impaired in Cantonese. Nine months later, the girl gave birth to a baby boy whose first words were 'ginseng'. The baby grew up to become my great-great-grandfather and this, in my mind, accounts for why my sisters and I, and our mother before us, looked ridiculously Chinese. Either that or there's a secret society operating in the nursing homes of Hyderabad dedicated to replacing babies from random families with infants from China. Whatever the reason, the three of us had chopstick-straight hair, narrow slanted eyes with the tell-tale epicanthic overhang, and skin the colour of a recovering hepatitic.

Most of our childhood was spent brushing aside unimaginative nicknames that alluded to our incongruous far easternness. It started with 'Suzie', an uncle's nickname for Lalli as a tribute to the movie, *The World of Suzie Wong*. Naturally, no one at home thought it was inappropriate for a child to be named after a fictional prostitute from Hong Kong. In later years, bitchy classmates, unable to match her grades, asked her to give them a haircut or a pedicure. I was Bruce and Cato at different stages in my life. That was okay with me. It didn't hurt when people wondered if the skinny kid actually knew some Kung-Fu.

But when someone hollered, 'Hey, Chou En-Lai, what's new?' as you surreptitiously tapped an old tyre down your street trying to generate a little revenue, it definitely cramped your style. Friends got even with me whenever I gave them a bit too much sass by offering me the job of watchman in their house.

My kid sister, with her big fat grin, was the only one who got off easy.

'See the little dear,' guests would pipe up as she played mercilessly to the galleries, 'looks just like the airhostess in the Singapore Airlines ad!'

However, the highpoint of our career as T. Nagar's sole representatives of the Exotic Orient was achieved at Auntie Renu's. One day, Dodo and his band, having inhaled bales of grass, were jamming together to the usual audience of stoned American flower children. A few minutes after Kavi and I walked in, I noticed that the focus of the hippies had slowly drifted from the song to us. When the entire bunch of redolent rock fans began whispering among themselves and staring at us alternately, my bladder threatened to go the way of Buster's. But nothing prepared me for what followed. Without preamble, the entire group of hippies rushed at us and knelt at our feet! Kavi let out a howl. Atomic Lingam stopped '*Purple Haze*' mid-scream.

'Please forgive us for what we've done to your country,' said the leader of the exodus, his hands folded, tears pouring out of his dilated eyes.

'We'd like to pay for the horrible crimes our country has perpetrated on your people,' sobbed a stringy blonde in a dirty kurta. 'Please ask for anything. One of us will give our life if you so wish. In fact, you can kill him,' she said, pointing to a shirtless young man in a headband.

'Yeahhh! Groovy, man!' said the would-be martyr, giving me the peace sign.

Kavi and I thought for a bit. The matter was settled with two chocobars for me and a bead necklace for Kavi. It was a pity though that history would never acknowledge that, in a suburb in south Madras, Vietnam had been avenged.

Other than the fact the three of us looked like we belonged to the family that ran The Southern Chinese Restaurant in Mount Road, we didn't have a single other similarity. Maybe it had to do with the sequence in which we were born or the times my family was going through at each birth. Or maybe no two siblings in the world have anything in common at all.

Lalli was the studious one. She began wearing glasses by the time she was ten to prove it. If she'd asked CG to get 24-carat gold frames for her spectacles, he'd have got them for her and put in a solitaire on either side for good measure. She was his golden child. Being Grandfather's favourite in my house had several advantages. It meant being Grandmother's, too, because she didn't know any other way. Father didn't want to go against the tide and behaved in a way that could be interpreted as her being *his* favourite as well. Mother, as always, bucked the trend and was never partial towards any one of us. She didn't fool me. I was her favourite.

If Lalli's early behaviour was any indication, she was the one who was going to follow in CG's literary footsteps. She topped her class without trying and was surrounded by books. She would read Somerset Maugham for an hour and switch to *Vyavaharika Andhra Mahabharatam* in Telugu seamlessly. She was the favourite student of both her English and Telugu teachers. She could do no wrong – at least up until the day she told Father she didn't want to go to school any more.

It was in the middle of an academic year. Father reacted in his customary manner – going from non-committal to hysterical in five seconds. He did a headstand in the living room. Angry speech bubbles with upside-down swear words popped out of his mouth. When that had no effect on his daughter, he referred the problem to CG, who sat Lalli down and attempted to get to the bottom of things.

'Why don't you want to go to school?' he wrote on his scribbling pad.

'This school is low-class, Thaatha. I want to go to St Anne's. The uniforms are much smarter.'

The very next week, powered by Grandfather's connections and her own impeccable academic record, Lalli walked into St Anne's, wearing their smart green-and-cream pinafore and a toothy grin.

That evening Lalli returned – the uniform intact but no matching grin.

'What's the matter?' said Father, who'd spent so much time in the last week in and around a convent that he had begun greeting people absently with a 'Bless you, my child.'

'I don't like this school. The girls are all snooty. I'm not going from tomorrow,' announced his first-born.

Father considered his course of action, scratching his chin. Then he calmly got up and went downstairs. A minute later he returned, armed with Raghavan's step-ladder. Without much ado, he climbed on to it, tied a dhoti to the ceiling fan and the other end around his neck and stood on one foot, poised for afterlife. Grandmother ran to stop him, tripped over Buster who was attempting congress with the willing ladder, and nearly succeeded in tipping Father over. The rest of us knew he was bluffing. There was a big event at the Race Club the following day. There was no way he was going to miss *that*.

Matters reverted yet again to the old man. Grandfather and Lalli sat in his room and discussed the course of action. An hour later they came out, each sporting a self-satisfied smile. It looked like things had been sorted out, after all. They had been, in a manner of speaking. CG and Lalli had jointly decided that she would sit a year out at home and ponder over which school she'd like to go to the following year. This time, Mother did the headstand.

For a whole year Lalli sat at home and read everything in Grandfather's library. The following year, her old, uncool school took her back as if nothing had happened – *with a promotion*. The same year she also got herself a National Talent Search scholarship. I wondered why I hadn't thought of that.

Lalli did not give Father any more opportunities to do headstands or attempt suicide for some time. Except for the Lanka Jhansi episode, and the baritone she sported due to the ingestion of veterinary-strength steroids, Lalli posed no problems at all. Kavi and I were too young to rustle up anything more serious than a grazed knee or chipped tooth. For some time things went swimmingly for Father.

Then Lalli discovered love.

If you look at it, the change in her reading taste should have been an indication for any discerning parent: from Maugham, Steinbeck, Nannayya and Thikkana to Mills & Boon and Yeddanapudi Sulochanarani, that grand dame of Telugu romance. Overnight, Lalli abandoned Grandfather's collection and began foraging around in Books Paradise, our neighbourhood circulating library, for romantic fuel. Lying on her bed, sighing every now and then, she devoured two to three books a week.

Lalli borrowed the M & Bs by the kilo from the neighbourhood library. The authors, with names like Veronica Windchime and Crystal Snowpeake, wrote of demure heroines whose bosoms heaved every time they came in contact with the male hardness or, on occasion, the hard maleness of a hero named Cord or Rip. I wondered how my sister would have felt if she'd known these books were actually written by middle-aged men from small-town America stroking their beer guts and belching loudly as they clacked away on their Underwoods.

I don't know if the boy preceded the books or was their result – but he arrived in Lalli's life with the predictability of a pubescent pimple. His name was Bhaskar. At sixteen, he was six feet tall, pencil-thin, had the beginnings of a moustache and was togged in the widest bell-bottoms you'd ever seen. Like everything else in our life, he was a product of the film industry. His father was a twice-married film-maker with two official mistresses. Bhaskar was the youngest son of the second wife, and his oldest brother was roughly Father's age. My father didn't know it then but his Malayalam nightmare was on the verge of turning into reality.

Once Lalli – sitting on our balcony all silky-haired and intense, pretending to read a book – was locked into his radar, Bhaskar took the most time-tested of all routes to get to her: through the kid brother.

One day, as Pandu and I sat on the culvert outside our gate listening to one of Prasad's patently impossible claims on the subject of girls, Bhaskar walked up to us and introduced himself.

'You know,' he said, addressing me, 'I've been watching you for some time and you speak English very well for a guy your age.'

Prasad and Pandu watched the newcomer suspiciously as I crackled with pride. Then, ignoring the other two boys completely, for the next hour Bhaskar spoke only to me, complimenting me on my maturity, my sense of humour, my great hair. The only reason I didn't see Lalli furtively watching the proceedings from the balcony was because my head had got so bloated that I couldn't turn it around. When Bhaskar finally said 'bye' and left, I turned to Prasad and Pandu to see if they shared my view of my wonderful new friend. I was surprised to find that I was alone.

Soon, from the culvert in Ramalingam Street, imperceptible as an oil spill, Bhaskar made his entrance into our house. At home, true to form, no one found anything suspicious about a sixteen-year-old boy choosing a twelve-year-old to be his best friend and welcomed him. That is, everyone other than Grandfather who had a hunch that, in the vein of the boy's father's productions, this one would be a stinker, too. It must have been the protective instinct for his favourite grandchild kicking in. One day, looking at Bhaskar and Prasad arguing about something, CG called me over and showed me what he'd written on his pad: the words seerabuddi-kalam ('pen and ink' in Telugu). I didn't quite get it. When I looked at him, a question mark on my face, he pointed to my two feuding pals – one long and thin with a pointy head and the other inky, rotund and free of a neck. They did look remarkably like an animated pen and bottle of Camel 99.

Grandfather showed me his pad again. On it was written, 'You can surely do better than this.'

However, I didn't take his advice and hung out with my mature new friend. The two of us saw several movies together, all sponsored by him. This was terrific for me; it meant the cache of saleable junk in the oven room at the top of the stairs would replenish itself. It wasn't so terrific for Pandu and Prasad because Bhaskar didn't want to increase his overheads any more than he could help and paid only for me.

If my parents had bothered to look they'd have noticed that my teenage sister had turned highly spiritual. Every evening at six o'clock, Lalli, whose interest in the gods had been purely academic so far, was now toddling off to the Agastya temple looking as pious as she could in a pair of bell-bottoms with jasmine in her hair. The ever-present Bhaskar would also find an excuse to tear himself away from my scintillating company at about the same time, but not before giving me my daily goody of 007 bubble gum or Triple Taste Toffee.

After three whole months of Lalli's precision-timed daily pilgrimages, come rain or shine, Father finally figured out that there might be more than god at play. The late-blooming Savyasachi wondered if Bhaskar's house being right across the temple had anything to do with his daughter's new-found spirituality. One day, he shadowed Lalli in the tradition of the trench-coated leading men of the film noir of his youth. The neighbourhood folk wondered what had come over the quiet man from Ramalingam Street – hiding behind trees, diving under parked cars and ducking behind garbage bins on his evening walk. Father needn't have bothered, really. He'd have made it undetected to the temple even if he had dressed himself as a matador and danced down the streets, waving a cape and yelling *'Toro! Hey, toro!'* because Lalli was blind as a bat.

At the temple it looked like Father's worst nightmare had come true. His little girl was circumambulating an idol with

Bhaskar one infatuated step behind her. To Father it looked like a dress rehearsal of their wedding. Breaking into the kind of language that had been last used before god only by Sisupala, he ran behind the young lovebirds, brandishing a folded *Madras Mail* like a club. The large crowd of devotees, ignorant of the fact that the diminutive man's ire was directed at only one of them, took it personally. The pious pace of the pradakshanam took on the frenzy of a hundred-metre dash. After about the fifth lap around the idol, those who'd been overtaken by Father realized that he wasn't after them and dropped out, one by one, to replenish their body salts. The race finally narrowed down to just three people: Bhaskar with flapping bell-bottoms in the lead, Lalli with flying jasmine a close second and a rapidly tiring forty-five-year-old with a rolled-up newspaper in third position. After about the tenth lap, Bhaskar changed course and ran out of the temple gates to the safety of his house. Lalli, too, committed a foul and followed suit – but in the opposite direction towards Ramalingam Street. Father by now had gone past the long-distance runner's wall and continued to run around the idol – the only man in the race. The crowd chanted '*Baa-loo! Baa-loo!*' No one could stop him now. It was mind over matter. In reality, it was Father hallucinating due to the lack of oxygen in his brain. After about twenty-five laps, the novelty of watching a strange little man running with a glazed look and a rolled-up newspaper wore off and people began trickling back home. At about closing time, a straggler took pity on the freelance cartoonist who came from a decent family running around in circles by himself.

'Your daughter left about half an hour ago,' he yelled out as Father ran his twenty-sixth lap around the idol.

'What?' said Father as he went past the man the following lap.

A few laps later Father got the picture. The man bought Father a soft drink and helped him to a cycle rickshaw. Father returned home, far too exhausted to remember why he'd been trying to break the record at T. Nagar's first-ever devotional marathon.

The next day, he recovered after the regulation dose of magic medicine from Dr Sarathi, and grounded Lalli. My sister's temple visits and, more importantly, my own junkets, came to an end. But, overall, Father did little damage. His own visits to the Race Club every weekend left a gaping hole in the curfew through which Lalli and Bhaskar continued to hold hands. As it turned out, Father needn't have bothered at all. A year or so later the relationship came to an end naturally. Lalli caught Bhaskar with another girl, willing to hold far more than his hand at that bargain basement bastion of bawdy pursuits, Blue Diamond. Lalli realized that the young man was following in his father's polygamous footsteps, dropped him and returned to her academic pursuits. Father, for his part, was happy at not being called upon again to bludgeon horny young men to death on temple premises with nothing more than rolled-up newsprint.

TWENTY-THREE

If Kavi was born in the US, she'd have been the quintessential dumb blonde. But back east in Madras, she worked out her own dark-haired, prepubescent variation of the theme. To begin with, like all dumb blondes, she was far from dumb. Though she didn't get the steady top-notch results of Lalli or follow my own erratic academic pattern of dismal failures punctuated with one or two astounding successes, she had a keen mind ticking in her perfectly round head. At a very young age she had figured that her chubby cheeks, silky blunt-cut hair and crooked smile would do more for her than all my convoluted plans or Lalli's swotting.

Lalli might have been CG's pet, but with her Bessie Bunter glasses and hunted air, not to mention her occasional baritone, was far from the audience favourite. The same went for her skinny, long-haired, smart-aleck brother who spent far too much time in the oven room and could talk of nothing but movies. This left the field wide open for Kavi to work the large audience that was forever available at Club Meghamala.

While Lalli and I gave my parents constant grief, me with my tendency to being just one step ahead of the law and Lalli with the school switches, Kavi was pure gold. She skipped through life with a big grin on her face, never asking them for anything, never causing trouble. Old uncles, writers, artists, freaks from Andhra, Father's racing buddies, why even Lalli's classmates – everyone loved Kavi.

An early memory I have of Kavi's all-encompassing popularity was of her sitting on the floor, her chubby little legs outstretched onto the lap of a sixty-year-old award-winning writer, saying, 'No, no. A little to the right. Yeah, that's it!' as he patiently massaged them. In later life, too, several young men would be willing to occupy a similar position.

Unlike the general populace and in the tradition of all the male protagonists of Enid Blyton, I found my younger sister very annoying. Maybe because we were born just a year and a half apart and that made her far too close for comfort. Lalli was a good four years older, we occupied different universes. It would've been ideal if Kavi was as many years younger. But my father, going through the most prolific period of his career then, obviously had other plans. He extended his fertility to his connubial life and inconsiderately came up with Kavi a little too quickly for my liking. (Mother, on the other hand, took matters into her hands and along with her doctor made sure that the assembly line production of Meghamalas came to a halt.)

This chronological proximity made Kavi think that everything that was mine was hers and everywhere I went, she followed. If I wanted the upper berth, she wanted it, too. When I climbed a tree, she followed, and like all girls with the exception of the super-cool Padma, would either fall off or get stuck in the branches – both resulting in a bawl fest. A ride on a hire-cycle would mean her on the pillion. Going to Rishi's house would have her tailing me. All this togetherness, which most definitely was not of my doing, made CG go all Telugu on us and insist that I call Kavi 'chelli', and Lalli 'akka'. I managed not to throw up only because I had made a loop of my favourite words for sisters and ran it in my head twenty-four frames per second: *'morons-cretins-pests-girls-morons-cretins-pests-girls-morons-cretins-pests-girls…'*

The truth was I tolerated my kid sister's peskiness for a reason. When I was completely jobless I could fool her easily and bully her into doing unpleasant chores assigned to me. There was a brief time in our lives when we got into drinking a cold Fanta every day, courtesy Mother. On one occasion I used my arch-villain technique to get back at Kavi.

'Hey, Kavi,' I said, 'let's have a competition.'

'Sure, whatever it is, I'll beat you!'

'Okay, let's see who'll drink the Fanta faster, you or me…' and before she could say yes or no, I went, 'one, two, three…'

At the sound of the countdown, like Pavlov's dog, Kavi jumped headlong into the game, eager to beat me at something. She downed the aerated drink in slurps so big that she had bubbles coming out of her nose. In her hurry to finish she didn't notice that I hadn't taken even a sip.

Stoically ignoring the brain freeze, with an orange trickle running down her nose she waved the empty bottle at me triumphantly. 'I…(choke)…won. You…(gulp)…lost.'

At that point, I cruelly changed the rules of the game. 'But I still have a full bottle of Fanta and you have nothing.' I then proceeded to drink my Fanta in delicate little sips and made it last an hour. Kavi, to my glee, went bawling to Mother.

One day, Kavi got into the habit of humming the same tune that I was humming. Under normal circumstances that would have been okay but she began every time I did and sang in another key. It was the musical version of the annoying game where one kid repeats whatever the other says without break. I wasn't going to take that. My favourite tune was Ennio Morricone's theme from *For a Few Dollars More*. As soon as I began humming while copying one of Father's drawings or as I bounced a ball against the balcony wall, Kavi would join in. She sounded like a hinge that needed oiling. I tried to tell her to stop but she just wouldn't listen. I pinched her hard once and paid a hefty price to Mother.

Threats and violence didn't work, so I did what any self-respecting artiste does for protection: brought in the copyright act. (One of the advantages of coming from my family was a familiarity with intellectual property rights.) I listed out all my favourite tunes on a piece of paper. These included two of Morricone's spaghetti western themes, '*Baby Elephant Walk*', '*Popcorn*' and other carefully picked evergreen gems. On another piece of paper, I made a list for Kavi, a far bigger one comprising tunes I couldn't stand, like '*Chopsticks*', the Sangu Mark lungi radio jingle and a host of requisitional songs favoured by blind or crippled beggars on the electric train. I first sweetened her with a toffee I'd been saving for exactly such an occasion and put forth my proposal. Why not share the world's music in the manner I had envisaged? Kavi was completely taken in by the size of her list. She thought I was a fool to hand over the rights to so many songs while I'd kept so few for myself. We shook hands and she signed on the dotted line before the toffee in her mouth had even begun to melt.

From that day onwards, my concerts remained solo. In the beginning Kavi absently strayed into my domain but I would whip out the contract that was permanently in my pocket and shush her. But that didn't flummox her at all. Dipping into her massive tune base, she'd instantly shift to that all-time beggar favourite, triumph writ all over her small face.

Loosely translated, the Tamil lyrics went:

> *A li'l orphan girl, I beg*
> *For my daily share of food.*
> *Not meat or chicken leg.*
> *Just old rice would be good.*

The fun of listening to Kavi sing the most heart-rending songs with a deliriously joyful lilt lasted only for a while, though. She completely stopped humming 'my' songs. Kavi just had to take the fun out of everything. Who could believe a ten-year-old fulfilling her contractual obligations? Here I was, prepared for a long-drawn legal battle, my imaginary robes swishing around with Lalli serving as judge hoping to mete out a terrible sentence and Kavi refused to break the law. So I began following her and lurked about hoping to catch her violating my copyright. On a couple of occasions when she was all alone wondering whether she could get away with a transgression, she heard a voice from the shadows saying, 'Hey…don't you dare!'

One summer vacation, CG noticed we had far too much time on our hands and feared that he might lose all three grandchildren to boredom-induced fratricide. He came up with a proposal that the three of us write a story each in Telugu and English every day, for thirty days. The reward – a hundred rupees each. That translated into *twenty* movies. For that amount I would have gladly shaved my neighbour's ancient buttocks. My request for a twenty-five per cent advance was however turned down.

'Sixty stories. Thirty in Telugu. Thirty in English. Payment on Delivery!' Grandfather wrote on his pad. He'd never got an advance from his producers. He saw no reason why we should. However, he did get us six 120-page Wisdom notebooks to fill up.

With the hundred-rupee note floating above my head in a thought bubble, I wrote story after convoluted story for five straight days. Such was my speed that my pen left skid marks. There were detectives, horsemen, giants and murderers. There was blood, gore, betrayal and retribution. I revisited the territory of my leave letters. On the sixth day, when I tried to churn out another miniature potboiler, my pen felt like it had the handbrake on. I couldn't write a single word in either Telugu or English. My muse had taken off surreptitiously, like Father on a weekend afternoon. I looked at Lalli. She was plodding on, not once raising her head. That didn't surprise me. She was known for getting the job done.

The revelation was Kavi. With her tongue stuck out, she was writing away furiously. To my horror, as I struggled to write one line every day at the designated time, she sat and wrote like a seasoned stenographer, finishing both her stories in record time with a satisfied 'Ammayya!'

This was ridiculous. How could *she* write when I couldn't? My attempts to sneak a peek were dealt with by a blood-curdling howl from her followed by swift corporal retribution from Available Parent. After five days of empty pages, I decided to take the time-tested route of deadline-facing hacks – plagiarism. Altering names of well-known folk heroes from around the world, incorporating my own twists and changing the MacGuffins whenever necessary, I cleared the backlog and managed to write sixty stories that wouldn't have stood up to a copyright test.

On the thirtieth day, all three of us presented our notebooks to CG. He read our efforts and gave us each a hundred-rupee note and a pat on our backs. The competition was over. Now we were allowed to look at each other's work. I grabbed Kavi's books first. I just had to know how she'd written sixty stories with such ease. Given below are samples of her prose.

THE TRANSISTOR

```
Two radios got married. They gave birth
to a transistor. They lived happily ever
after.
```

THE PIG

```
Once upon a time, there was a pig. It
crossed the road. A car hit it and it
died. They lived happily ever after.
```

While Lalli and I had slaved over our stories, dealt with writer's block and contemplated suicide from time to time, Kavi proved that she was the smartest dumb blonde far-eastern Telugu Brahmin brunette that ever lived in Tamil Nadu.

TWENTY-FOUR

Maybe he was inspired by Mother's daring exploits in fields as diverse as doll-making and cookery or maybe there was a bit of his grandfather in him, the freedom fighter-cum-part-time inventor who wrote a book on how to build a fully operational plane with household items. Or maybe he had panel fever from filling box upon box with pictures every day for twenty years and accepting small change as remuneration from tight-fisted editors. Whatever the reason, Father was bitten by the business bug. He had, after all, been a successful publisher of children's books earlier. There was no reason why he couldn't come up with something that society was in dire need of that involved his artistic skills.

One day, just like that, Father came up with his idea: customized greeting cards and calendars for any business you could think of. *That's* what he'd make. What started off as doodles at his easel between assignments caught fire and, before we knew it, he'd prepared mock-ups for a whole range of businesses.

The template for all of them was the same: a simple two-sided foldable desktop calendar that had six months on each side. Only the illustration and caption would change to suit the business. Fashionably dressed men and women for garment retailers saying 'We shop only at Akash Dress Emporium'. Sickly car with bloodshot headlight eyes on one side saying: 'Oh, God! I feel terrible'. Shiny-coated, fully 'cured' car, suspended half a foot above the road saying: 'Thanks to Cartech Auto Aids, I feel brand-new!' A sweaty Aladdin asking the genie for a Simla Table Fan on Side A. A sticky Alibaba discovering a cave full of Simla Ceiling Fans on Side B.

Even our baby photos were not spared. Three-year-old Kavi on one side and me during my drag queen phase on the other. Father thought it would be ideal for a children's tonic. Sure – if you wanted your kids to turn Chinese.

There were similar ideas for fertilizers, chemicals, shaving blades, cosmetics and any business that you could think of with the exception of haemorrhoid cream. Not that he couldn't come up with a concept; it would've been a cinch for him if he'd put his mind to it. Cowboy on one side, sore from all the riding, saying with a pained expression: 'I think my days on the saddle are over'. Same cowboy, sporting a huge grin – riding bareback, declaring: 'Who needs a saddle when you have Ban-O-Pile Haemorrhoid Cream!'

For the greeting cards, it was women with lamps, women doing the kolattam, the boom boom ox man of Pongal, street dancers and scenes of festivity. For the religiously inclined there was Ganesha, Buddha, Rama & Co., Jesus and Durga, blank on the inside with butter-paper inserts of 'Happy Deepavali', 'Happy Pongal', 'Happy New Year' or plain old 'Season's Greetings'.

He had it pretty much covered. There was only one hitch. Who was going to sell them?

As if on cue, from the vast unutilized talent pool at Udipi Sri Shanta Bhavan, the perfect man for the job appeared at our doorstep. He was a leathery-faced chain-smoking sales rep type called Santhanam. Over a masala dosai, Father and he had discovered they were a match made in heaven. One was all ideas and the other's enthusiasm to sell made you wonder if he was consulting Dr Sarathi. Added to this was Santhanam's original turn-of-phrase.

'The words "cannot able to" do not exist in my dictionary,' he told my fascinated father.

Santhanam was full of stuff that you couldn't find in any dictionary. The day Father proudly presented his discovery at home for the first time, only Lalli and I were home.

'I thought Baloo had three childrens,' he said, looking around for a third kid.

I succumbed to the disease that was to become a lifelong affliction. 'That's right. He also has two stepwives,' I said with a straight face.

'I see,' said Santhanam, wondering what the significance of that was.

Lalli pissed her bell-bottoms.

Father was not happy. He was quite taken by his new friend's zeal and seemed to be far more forgiving of his unique way with words. He took us aside and said, 'I've never been to school. Maybe some show-offs like you two are laughing at the way I speak English.'

We were temporarily silenced.

The next day, Santhanam turned up at home and gave Father news that confirmed that he was on a daily dosage of not less than 500 mg of the magic medicine.

'Partner, I've quitted my job,' he announced, sticking out his hand, 'from today I'm going to sold our products full time.'

In the family album there is one photo of Father carrying Lalli when she was a baby. To my memory, it is the sole evidence of his ever having bodily contact with any of his offspring. The expression on Father's face in that photo was unforgettable. It didn't need a speech bubble.

Father produced the exact same expression at Santhanam's declaration. But he made polite noises and they worked out an agreement. Father would invest the money required for block-making, paper and printing. Santhanam would sell the products and receive a fifteen per cent commission on sales.

Based on Santhanam's projections, Father decided to have an initial print-run of a thousand copies of each design ready. The name and slogan of the clients would be printed in later in the allotted space. According to their estimate, Father would make a profit of twenty thousand rupees in the first year itself. Santhanam's own share would be in the region of ten thousand rupees. They were going to be rich. Which meant that I could see as many films as I wanted to.

Santhanam believed in being prepared. He wanted all the samples ready by August to facilitate canvassing on a war footing. By end-July, Father, the master of deadlines, was done. He was richer by several thousand greeting cards and calendars, all neatly packed and occupying every square inch of space in our house other than the bathroom, and poorer by about twelve thousand rupees.

Santhanam and he met every day and chalked out a marketing plan. When I was present at every one of their meetings, Santhanam mistook my interest for admiration. The truth was I was just waiting for fresh bloomers to repeat to my friends, among whom he had already become something of a god. Santhanam didn't disappoint.

Patting me on the back, he said, 'Always remember, Gopi, "well done is half begun."'

Lalli, who strayed in at that moment, turned a Saikumar red trying to control herself. But this was gold. I couldn't let it go.

'Yes…and many drops make the mighty oak,' I said solemnly.

Lalli's lungs and her bladder gave up simultaneously. Santhanam put away my wisdom in a corner for later use on prospective clients.

August was a flurry of activity. Armed with two albums, one each for calendars and greeting cards, Santhanam left no client unturned from Tondiarpet to Thiruvanmiyur. By September, the verdict was out.

Santhanam was an idiot. For all his sales talk peppered with Wren & Martinisms, he could not have sold a toupée to a Telugu hero.

Looking at ten thousand numbers of a product that would expire on the thirty-first of December, Father took the extreme step. He decided to sell the calendars himself. But sales and Father? This was the man who dealt with sales reps the way Grandfather dealt with dogs, swearing like a multilingual sailor and waving a blunt instrument.

Seeing Father jump off the deep end, we were seized by a rare sympathy for the poor man, and Kavi and I volunteered to join his sales force. Father wasn't very happy putting his kids to work but it seemed he had no choice.

'Don't worry, Nannaa. We'll sell the cards,' I said, giving him a pat, 'and I'll take only ten per cent.'

I had sold fake jeans, bald tyres and old newspapers. Father's cards would be a cinch. I also had Kavi with her infantile wiles tagging along as a trump card. I would make a killing. Then it was going to be the simple matter of cheating Kavi of her share. Safire-Casino-Devi, here I come. As we got all set to tackle prospective buyers, door to door, my father spoilt everything by saying, 'Shivakumar will come along with you.'

Shivakumar was a buck-toothed idiot relative from Grandmother's side. He was a guest member of the Meghamala Club of Freaks and hung around our house from time to time. Shivakumar was a man of many talents. To begin with, he had a distinct body odour that preceded his arrival by a good five minutes and lingered on for a couple of days after he left.

Shivakumar was also an adept and compulsive thief. He'd have stolen stuff off of Raghavan and Sachu if they had married and put their collective loot in a Chubb safe with burglar-proof combination lock and six-inch steel door. I somehow didn't see the merit in his being our co-rep. But Father didn't want to see us sold off as child labour in Sivakasi while we were out on the streets. So Shivakumar it was going to be.

Our efforts bore results right from Day One. Kavi and I managed to sell a few cards on our street itself. They were pretty, cheap, and being sold by a couple of kids. Our neighbours looked at the cards, took a few and paid us instantly. In some places we even managed to get lemonade or toffees. Shivakumar didn't contribute much – he just stood behind us and smelled. I held on to the money and the merchandise very carefully and I could see this was pissing off the guy. Watching us sell the merchandise card by painful card, Shivakumar put in a petition.

'You'll never sell volumes this way, Gopi. And we need to sell volumes. I know a rich businessman who'll buy a hundred cards in one shot,' he said, 'but when we're there, both of you'll have to just nod and not contradict anything I say, okay?'

Having run through our immediate neighbourhood, we agreed.

Soon we were outside a palatial house a couple of streets away. The building looked vaguely familiar. Shivakumar whispered something to the watchman, who gave us a look that bordered on sympathetic and let us in. We were shown into a living room with plush velvet-covered sofas. Who knew, maybe our redolent relative was on to a good thing. In a short while, a distinguished-looking gentleman came and sat down with us. He seemed to know Shivakumar and he smiled politely at us. Shivakumar handed the cards to him as Kavi and I looked around, slightly embarrassed.

'Sir,' said Shivakumar, launching into his sales pitch, 'these two children are my relatives. Their father is an impoverished artist and their mother is on her deathbed…'

What the hell was the fellow saying? I tried to stop Shivakumar who shushed me with a violent pinch of my thigh. I stifled a scream of agony.

Shivakumar continued, tears flowing down his cheeks by now, '…they come from a good family, sir. They have fallen on bad times. Their grandfather is Meghamala…'

'Oh, the great poet,' the man said, shaking his head sadly, 'I didn't know they were in such a bad way…'

I didn't hear the rest of the conversation. It didn't matter. When you find out your mother is on her deathbed, nothing really matters. With no interruptions, Shivakumar found his rhythm and began narrating a Dickensian tale starring my entire family. It had deprivation, squalor and grand tragedy. In fact, it featured everything other than the unwanted pregnancy of my teenage sister. As the epic unfolded, the venerable businessman was slowly transformed into a babbling wreck. A harrowing quarter of an hour later, he begged Shivakumar to stop and gave us a tear-stained cheque with smudged figures. It was for an exorbitant sum of money, courtesy Shivakumar, who had jumped up the rates at the last minute. We gave a large stash of greeting cards to the man in return. He barely looked at them.

'You poor, *poor* kids,' he said, patting us with barely controlled emotion.

I had never been this humiliated in my life before. I was going to strangle Shivakumar to death if it meant losing my olfactory senses. At that exact instant, Kavi who had been silent all along, maybe inspired by all the pleading and weeping, absently broke into Verse Two of her favourite song:

> *I wander here and there*
> *Barefoot, 'lone and smelly*
> *Hoping for some fare*
> *That'll fill my concave belly*

The businessman took this as a cue to collapse on the floor and begin hyperventilating. This was the worst, most horrible, moment of my life. Nothing could top this.

As always, I was wrong. The noise and drama, enough to wake the dead, stirred the businessman's family and they charged into the living room en masse. First out was the businessman's son, a bewildered-looking boy of about my size.

It was my snooty classmate Sridhar.

No wonder the house had looked familiar. Sridhar had waved at me one day as I'd walked past. Had I been the heroine of an epic, this would have been the moment Mother Earth would have come to my rescue with a tailor-made fault.

'Gopal...?' said my classmate, wondering what I was doing in his house and, more importantly, what that had to do with his father writhing on the floor.

'You know this boy?' the prostrate businessman said between sobs.

'Yes,' said the boy reluctantly, 'he's my classmate.'

'The horror, the horror!' wept the man.

With great difficulty the businessman tearfully repeated Shivakumar's saga to my classmate, stopping now and then to hold back racking sobs and blow his nose. At the end of the story, he extracted a promise from his stricken son: 'Promise me that you'll never tell a soul about this at school.'

When we walked out, I couldn't help admitting that, in spite of the humiliation, Shivakumar's method had worked out quite terrifically. This was the fellow Santhanam should've been taking lessons from. I put aside my urge to kill him temporarily and congratulated him.

'Not bad, Shivakumar,' I said looking at the cheque, 'not bad at all.'

'You don't know the half of it,' said Shivakumar, pulling out a wallet from his back pocket and waving it at me. It was the businessman's. My estimate was that he'd have made a lot more than Father in this deal.

Needless to say, I quit the greeting card business and my classmate Sridhar never spoke to me ever again.

Father, for his part, didn't do too badly. For a non-salesman, he sold his entire stock and even got orders for reprints. He continued the greeting card and calendar business quite profitably for a couple of years.

Shivakumar joined the police force and retired as a senior official with the Department of Vigilance and Anti-Corruption.

My classmate's father gave up the shaky world of business and opted for the stability of insanity.

Mother, fortunately, made it.

Poor Santhanam didn't, though. The cigarettes got him. Apparently, his last words were: 'Cannot able to'.

TWENTY-FIVE

There are two distinct categories of friends: home friends and school friends. A home friend is the product of geography. A boy lives next door, he owns a ping-pong table and you're Siamese twins before you know it. A kid walks along your street, thinks the trees at your place are Ice Boys-ready, and soon you are giving away your dad's vintage comic books to him.

Home friends drop in unannounced and see you in your rattiest shorts – and that's okay. With home friends you don't pretend that your parents are actually retarded relatives staying with you because your elegant mother and your debonair father, currently holidaying in France, have taken pity on them. The very nature of such a friendship is that you are okay revealing who you are – a runny-nosed misfit putting up with less-than-perfect parents while plotting to slit the throats of insufferable siblings. And, in turn, the home friend gives you an entry pass into the hell-hole he calls home and is quite okay letting on that his dad's an out-of-work alcoholic and his sister's eloped with the milkman.

A home friend understands that it is a 'You Against Parent' situation for all kids. Sometimes you cover for him and he takes the rap for you at others. Home friends are a self-help group fighting for a common cause. A spontaneous Parent Haters Anonymous. That is its strength.

A classroom, on the other hand, is not the best place for friendships. By job description, you are already classmates, meaning competitors: competitors for the same rank, for the teacher's favours, for the best desk in class. Unlike a home friendship, a true friendship in school takes time to evolve. The impression a classmate has of you is one based on the picture you paint of yourself between 9.30 a.m. and 3.45 p.m. Like a cutout-style drawing, it is devoid of a background. He has absolutely no idea where you live, what your home looks like, how many siblings you have and what your parents do. And you want to keep it that way.

When I joined Vidya Vihar, I didn't want my classmates to know that Father was an artist who'd never been to school or that my mother was, well, plump. And I sure as hell didn't want them to know I performed my daily ablutions squatting in a five-by-five cubicle designed by a sadist. In fact, the image I tried to project was of an English boy in Indian skin who had jumped out of an Enid Blyton book, blazer and all, and walked into Vidya Vihar to give it some class. In two days flat, everyone knew I was a fraud and christened me 'thagarai-dabba'. It meant 'tin can' in Tamil.

Gulab Chand and Rusty Mistry were my earliest allies in class. One sat next to me because our class teacher said so and the other I sought for his inexhaustible supply of boo-boos. For a while, I had hung out with Sendhil, too. But that ended after his hospitalization. I had humoured T.V. Suresh and Ashok Malwani on occasion to minimize PT goosings and Holly Golly decapitation. But I didn't find myself inviting any of these guys back home for Ice Boys. I made my first real friends at Vidya Vihar only much later. It wasn't by any grand plan. There was no carefully written-up list from which I picked out the most charming prospects.

Why 'Ramki' Ramakrishnan, Debashish De and I became friends and revealed to each other the sordid lives we led while out of uniform was a complete mystery because it didn't look like we had much in common.

Debashish De was a bow-legged kid with a penchant for delivering doomsday predictions with a blinkless stare. He joined Vidya Vihar in '76 fresh out of Calcutta. Debashish didn't know a word of the local lingo, and the Tamil boys ragged the impassive Bengali mercilessly, if predictably, about Kali Mata. Debashish retaliated in a unique manner.

'Do you know that Kali devotees know black magic? I could make your testicles shrivel up by performing a small puja at home.'

The boys of Vidya Vihar, their loins already under the constant threat of Holly Golly, decided not to test the veracity of the Bengali's claims and laid off.

Nonetheless, an informal, if secret, committee was set up to come up with a suitably cruel nickname for the Bong. As we struggled to produce one that didn't involve Rabindra Sangeet or rasagollas, our class teacher, Alagappan, inadvertently came to our assistance. One day, while taking attendance, Alagappan's seamless recital came to an abrupt halt. The problem was the new boy from Bengal. Alagappan, who'd never been further east than Marina Beach, didn't know how to pronounce his name. It had more 'sh's than a ham playing a drunk. But the gentleman from Salem wasn't about to admit defeat. He cleared his throat, took a deep breath and grappled manfully. 'Deba...er...Desa...Debsh...I mean...Deshbush!' he finished triumphantly.

The boys who had waiting to get a rise out of the Calcuttan jumped on it.

'DESHBUSH! DESHBUSH!' screamed the entire class in agreement.

From that day on, Deshbush it became and remained so forever. The pity was Deshbush, as was his wont, didn't seem to give a rat's ass. In fact, Deshbush rarely showed any affect. He received centums in maths and beatings from his Hindi teacher for his accent with the same inscrutability. Deshbush also had theories on sexual activity in the afterlife and the untapped hydro-electric power of public urinals which he wrote down painstakingly in a little book he kept for the purpose.

One day, ten minutes into lunch break, I wondered aloud to no one in particular why my tiffin carrier hadn't arrived. Tucking into his daily lunch of fish and rice, Deshbush paused mid-morsel and said, 'Maybe your maid is late because she's mixing Tic-20 in your curd rice,' and continued eating.

'Ramki' Ramakrishnan joined Vidya Vihar the same time as Deshbush De, returning to his family after having concluded a three-year stint in a boarding school. Surprisingly, Ramki displayed none of the bravado of a former boarder. There was not one story of midnight meetings, initiation rituals or homosexual wardens. In fact, he spoke only when spoken to and replied in monosyllables. After much questioning, all he revealed was, 'I was expelled while in Class Three from my school and my dad decided to send me to boarding school for discipline.'

It seemed his dad's plan had worked. Ramki had about as much personality as an octogenarian paralysed neck downwards. The only time he exhibited any signs of life was in the cricket nets, and how! The sombre boy smashed the ball to all corners of our playground with a maniacal gleam in his hooded eyes. Maybe boarding school hadn't wiped out his spirit entirely.

If I had to pick a time and say *that*'s when our friendship began, it would be the day we went on a trip to Pondicherry to coincide with a history lesson. Ramki, Deshbush and I found ourselves sitting next to each other on the bus. For some reason, on this trip there seemed to be a larger than usual number of teachers, all enthusiastic about joining us. The thirty kids in all who would have been accompanied by a couple of teachers at best were chaperoned by eight adults. This all-male assemblage included a hakoba-shirted PT master and the septuagenarian Anglo-Indian office clerk, Mr Daley. Grapevine had it that the other history teacher in our school, Mrs Singh, was keen on coming too, but for some reason had been discouraged.

The journey began with a soporific lecture followed by a breakfast of cold idlis at our history teacher's house and then we were off. After a tail-bone crushing four hours, we were in Pondy. Thirty sore-bottomed kids and eight surprisingly chirpy men disembarked on the pencil-straight Goubert Avenue running along the Pondicherry coast on a cloudless day. Not having paid the slightest attention in class or the recent lecture, we had absolutely no idea what the connection was between our history lesson and Pondy.

'Boys...,' said our history master as we prepared ourselves for the next instalment of the torture saga, '...er...here's the thing. I want you all to walk around Pondy and return to the bus at three o' clock...'

'Four-thirty might be better,' interrupted Mr Daley, looking anxiously at his watch, 'we'll, you know, need...'

The history teacher shushed Mr Daley and the eight men went into a huddle. There was frantic whispering. A minute passed. The history master addressed us again: 'Well, it's decided then, report back to the bus at four. We have certain official duties to attend to. Enjoy Pondy. Don't get into any trouble, okay?'

Before any of us could react, the eight men did a perfectly coordinated about-turn and disappeared into a by-lane with the resolve of a sheriff's posse. For one moment, thirty kids stood silently, not an adult in sight, as the wild Pondy waves crashed against the concrete barriers. Then a cheer so loud went up that the crows lining the parapet took off in fright.

Who can describe the joy of a group of boys at an unsupervised outing in a strange new place – that, too, when they're least expecting it? Picture my father – he wakes up one day and finds out the three of us and my mother were just a nightmare, then he stretches, looks out of his window and he sees the racecourse instead of our octogenarian neighbour having his rear sheared.

That day in Pondy, what we felt was the same thing – only a hundred times over. Soon, thirty schoolboys of varying depravity had broken into smaller hunting parties to explore Pondy independently. Ramki, Deshbush and I hired cycles at forty-five paise an hour and rode around the French quarter of the town. Neat blue-grey houses unfettered by compound walls and joined at the hip lined narrow streets with open drains. Blond pyjama-clad men and scantily dressed women with unshaven armpits cycled past. They looked and smelt so much like the audience of Atomic Lingam that I kept my eyes open for Dodo. A few waved at us with a cheery 'allo'. Deshbush maintained his rigor mortis look, and me, my fake smile.

It was the normally taciturn Ramki who was the revelation, wishing everyone back ebulliently, if inappropriately, with 'Bon voyage!' or 'Bon appetit!' and, finally, having run out of greeting words from our *Elementary French Reader*, greeting one flummoxed cyclist with a 'Bon Vita! Cadbury's Bournvita!' Where was Sachu when you needed her?

Pretty soon, we'd explored every little orifice of the incongruous Gallic township in coastal Tamil Nadu and Ramki had exhausted every French word he could come up with. He was now waving at passers-by with 'Hey, Jean-Paul Belmondo!' and 'Je ne sais pas!' When their polite 'allos' turned into glares and finally culminated in the finger, two things became apparent. One, maybe Ramki's parents weren't totally off the mark sending him to boarding school. Two, certain things meant the same the world over.

When a French couple who'd been 'greeted' three times by Ramki in ten minutes began to chase us, we migrated at high speed, at my behest, to the Tamil side of Pondy. Stiff-thighed and hungry, we had two hours to kill before our teachers returned from their official work. The prospect of eating the sour curd rice in my aluminium tiffin carrier was nauseating. A Fanta and a bun-butter-jam would hit the spot. My pockets yielded three-rupees-and-seventy-paise and Deshbush produced a fiver, so the buns and the soft drinks seemed attainable. If Ramki added to the kitty we could just about manage it and pay for our bikes. Ramki, that master of revelations, dug deep into his pocket and lazily produced a crumpled fifty-rupee note. Ah, the joy of having a businessman father.

Without wasting a second, Deshbush moved our lunch into fourth gear. 'We should have lunch at Hameedia's. They have *the* best biriyani in Pondicherry.'

'Really? Who told you?' I said, amazed yet again at the information that the Bengali had at his disposal.

Deshbush pointed to a spot behind me deadpan.

I turned and there was a nameplate. It said:

> **HAMEEDIA'S**
> *For the Best Biriyani in Pondicherry*

The chicken biriyani at Hameedia's was as good as their slogan claimed. We washed it down with ice-cold Fantas. The bill was well under fifty rupees. Ramki picked up the bill and gestured to me to wait outside.

'We need to go to the loo. We'll join you in a minute.'

I ambled out of the hotel, full of the chicken of human kindness. Life looked good. No teachers, a French revolution quashed in the nick of time, and a rich new friend who could sponsor god-knows-what in the future. I sat on my bike and stretched out in preparation for the ride back to the bus. The next couple of days were holidays. Maybe I could invite the guys over for Ice Boys. My future plans were cut short by a yell.

'Rascals. Pudra andha pasangale!'

I turned around and found Ramki and Deshbush charging out of Hameedia's.

'Run, you bugger! Run!' screamed Ramki.

Of all the words in the English language that are obeyed unquestioningly, 'Run!' tops the list. I turned my bike around and was off like a hare on Dr Sarathi's pills. An auto screeched to a halt to avoid me as I cut across the main road. A flurry of Tamil cuss words followed. I didn't stop. I pumped away with a fury that would have left the legendary Sendhil open-mouthed. I didn't know what my buddies were up to behind me and I didn't dare look. But the symphony of screeches, yells and Tamil expletives gave me some indication. I zoomed through the maze-like French quarter, cornering into the right-angled turns without the slightest deceleration. Several unbathers jumped out of my way. After what seemed like an eternity of wrong turns and double-backs, I reached our bus. Ramki and Deshbush were already there, panting like Buster.

'*What the...(pant)...fuckin'...hell...happened?*'

'The waiters were...(pant)...chasing us,' said Ramki,

grinning. For an affectless guy, he'd been doing a lot of that of late.

'What the...(huff)...heck for?'

'They wanted us to pay up,' said Deshbush.

I was genuinely puzzled. 'Pay up what?

'The bill, I suppose,' said Deshbush. Then they both burst out laughing. I didn't get the humour.

'So why didn't you? You had the fifty bucks, didn't you?' I was annoyed.

'Let's presume you are the owner of Hameedia's,' said Deshbush, getting professorial on me as Ramki squirmed with bladder-busting mirth, 'would you accept *this* note?'

He handed me the fifty-rupee note that Ramki had pulled out of his pocket.

I looked at it and realized that they had a point. Even in a Tamil-speaking Union Territory where he was second only to god, a fifty-rupee note with a picture of MGR wouldn't be considered legal tender.

Never in my life, filled though it might have been with minor extortions and petty theft, could I have come up with a plan as audacious as this. Eat – Don't Pay – Run. What if we'd been caught? So *that* was why I was asked by the guys to hang around outside. They didn't want the gang's greenhorn botching up the plan. I looked at the panting, grinning duo and a film clip of what the future held for us played out in my head. Fifteen years hence, Deshbush, by now addicted to cocaine, would come up with an elaborate plan for a bank heist. Ramki, an incurable alcoholic, would fund the operation and bludgeon a couple of cops to death when things went horribly wrong; I would drive the getaway car over a cliff in slow motion to escape not so much the fusillade of bullets as my closet gayness.

A half-hour later, sure that the hotel authorities had given up their search, I, too, began seeing the humour in the situation. Deshbush, Ramki and I sat on the foot-high wall running along the sea wondering where our guardians were as classmates trickled back from their own adventures. At about four-thirty, our teachers returned through the same lane that they had made their determined exit. But the similarity ended there. The entry had none of the straight-backed heroism of their departure a few hours earlier. While the eight of them had left as one man, goose-stepping to some inaudible marching tune, they returned in units of two and three, with the air of those soundly thrashed by an enemy far more powerful than themselves. First out was the PT master, wearing only a banian, being half pushed and half dragged, like luggage with faulty casters, by our Tamil master. Mr Daley, our history master and the biology master followed with their arms around each other, singing:

> *Charlotte, the harlot,*
> *Is the girl we adore,*
> *The pride of the teachers,*
> *The headmaster's whore.*
>
> *She's dirty, she's vulgar, she spits in the street,*
> *Whenever you see her, she's always in heat.*
> *She'll lay for a rupee, take less or take more,*
> *The pride of the teachers, the headmaster's whore.*

The lilt of the ditty was somewhat spoilt by Mr Daley abruptly bursting into tears though the other two continued the rendition undaunted. Then came the chemistry and physics teachers. The former walked normally, if a tad unsteadily, but the latter was bent over, walking backwards in quick, short steps. It looked like he was dragging something heavy. Inspection revealed it to be a dried-up coconut frond atop which was the final member of our school staff – our Hindi teacher, whooping wildly and twirling an imaginary lasso.

It took us a while, but with the help of T.V. Suresh, we did actually crack 'The Case of the Tottering Teachers', piecing together the clues. The initial enthusiasm of such a large group to accompany us, followed by the reluctance to allow a female member to join in, the hurried exit that facilitated our unsupervised mayhem and their final dissolute re-entry – it all fell in place. It was a simple matter of eight thirsty men, two governments, one that imposed Prohibition and one that didn't.

On the way back, their heads stuck out of opposing windows, Mr Daley and the Hindi teacher sprayed unsuspecting travellers with an inexhaustible supply of vomit. The others snored at different pitches, emitting a cocktail of odours. We used the opportunity to scream out every obscenity we knew in a variety of languages. The more daring ones poked and pulled at the hair of their unconscious teachers and scurried back to their seats giggling. The driver kept his gaze glued to the uneven road.

It was the best excursion of our lives. Also, in what was becoming the norm with our class outings, no one asked us to write an essay on the trip.

Maybe it was our penchant for crime or maybe each recognized that the other was an outsider like himself, but after Pondy, Deshbush sealed our friendship with the ultimate act of faith: calling us over.

'Why don't you drop by for lunch? I'll ask Bansilal to make some fish.'

'What's the occasion?' I said.

'Oh, nothing in particular. My dad's out of town – that's all,' said Deshbush.

That Saturday, Deshbush gave us the Deluxe Package. To begin with, after polite 'hello's, his mother and sister disappeared to reappear only when we left that evening. I didn't know what the situation was in Ramki's place but without a restraining order that was an impossibility at my place. Then there was fried fish, Bengali style – courtesy Bansilal. Like solar-topeed sahibs back from hunting big game, the three of us stuffed ourselves silly with Bansilal hovering over us and choosing choice fillets for his young master. Chilled Limcas hurriedly fetched by Bansilal from a neighbouring shop followed. After all, a good meal required washing down. The rest of the afternoon we spent in Deshbush's room that he didn't share with a sister, feet up, listening to $33^{1}/_{3}$ rpms, sipping tea provided by Bansilal. Deshbush was living the dream. No dad, his own room and a twenty-four-hour slave.

TWENTY-SIX

It had to happen, it was only a matter of time. The malodorous spectacle our teachers had made of themselves, combined with the danger of circumventing Prohibition, made it clear that alcohol was the next logical step for us.

One Sunday afternoon, Ramki, Deshbush and I sat on the compound wall of Ramakrishna Ground pretending to watch a cricket match. All of a sudden, I began, 'It's time…' Deshbush continued, 'we had…' and Ramki concluded with a resounding thwack on Deshbush's thigh, '…a drink!'

It was a Huey, Dewey and Louie moment unlikely to appear in a Donald Duck comic. The secret desire scorching our virgin livers since our Pondicherry trip had finally erupted in concert. Which was a good thing because, ten years on, repenting at an AA meeting, it would be impossible for any one of us to blame the other. While other boys our age were content coughing out a Gold Flake Filter at street corners, we had decided to give ourselves a double promotion. Now all that remained was the simple matter of procuring the booze. We looked skywards for ideas.

'Maybe we should distil some from potatoes like in *The Great Escape*…ouch!'

Ramki thwacked Deshbush again, aborting further discussion in this direction. Unlike the scientific-minded Bengali, the local boy favoured the direct route.

It was this same uncomplicated approach that had led to his earlier expulsion. He had fancied a classmate's geometry box and figured the natural way of having the ownership transferred was by hitting him repeatedly on the head with a duster.

He offered a simple solution: 'We'll just have to find someone whose father drinks.'

Very often, the answers to all of life's pressing questions are obtained from the same source. For some people, it is the Gita. For my family, it was the film industry. In our case, it turned out to be Prasad.

Prasad came into our collective consciousness by appearing on the balcony of his house, which happened to be right across the ground, and waving sullenly to us. Dear old Prasad, who had taught the neighbourhood children everything they needed to know about sex and the very real dangers it posed to the hands of its practitioners. It was common knowledge that Prasad's father, a film producer, possessed, among other things, a liquor permit.

Before the next ball was bowled, the three of us were ringing his doorbell.

'We want booze,' said Ramki, by way of greeting. He understood the phrase 'cutting to the chase' better than any Hollywood film editor.

If Ramki was direct, Prasad was equally good at recognizing business opportunities when he saw them.

'Fifty bucks. I'll get you a quarter. Plus, I get one drink.'

Ramki put his hands into his pocket, hesitating for a split-second. I knew that look.

'Forget the MGR note, da. I don't think he'll buy it.'

Reluctantly, Ramki produced a real note. As was his wont, he doubled the scale of operations without preamble.

'Here's a hundred. Make it a half. You still get only one drink.'

'Two,' said Prasad.

'One and a half.' It wasn't for nothing that Ramki came from a business family.

'Sold.'

Even if Prasad were to replace his dad's missing booze, which was unlikely, he would come out fifty bucks richer.

Before long, sitting in Prasad's living room conveniently devoid of adults, we were in possession of half a bottle of Bullet XXX Rum wrapped in two layers of *Andhra Prabha*. Well, nearly half a bottle anyway. Prasad brought a peg measure and poured out his share of 90 ml into an empty shampoo bottle without spilling a drop. The air was redolent with promise. Deshbush let out an uncharacteristic giggle.

'How are we to… ahem…drink it?' said Ramki.

'With Campa Cola or 77.'

'Can we use your place?' It was Ramki again, taking the initiative. After all, what was the harm in looking for end-to-end solutions from the same vendor?

'For a hundred,' said Prasad.

The calculator in Ramki's head whirred. He was down a hundred bucks. Chips and soft drinks would set him back further. Deshbush and I, as our expressions indicated, weren't good for a cent. He made a decision.

'No, thanks, we'll drink at Gopi's place.'

So that was that. Ramki had paid and I apparently was in charge of providing the venue. I glowered at Deshbush who was staring at the ceiling. It wasn't fair. What the hell was he bringing to the party?

The plan I came up with was simple like all my other plans, unmindful of the fact that several of them had failed magnificently. Each of us would say we were sleeping over at the other's. The reason: preparing for the selection round of the Bournvita Quiz Contest which was around the corner. We would congregate at my place, armed with reference books. After dark, we would bid innocent goodbye to whoever was in the living room. (The booze, chips and soft drinks would be distributed among our three pockets and waistbands.) Instead of walking down the staircase, we would sidle off upstairs to the terrace. We would drink, eat our chips and sneak back into our respective homes in the dead of the night. We would sleep the odour off and continue life, reputation and hide intact.

Part One of the plan went gloriously well. The Meghamalas could be counted on to believe anything. If I'd told them we would be crawling the IIT woods in search of a herbal cure for cancer, they would have been okay with it. However, Ramki, in his debut performance, cast against type as innocent guy, nearly messed up everything.

'Auntie, we will be up the whole night studying,' he said to Mother, who hadn't asked us a thing, '...right, Deshbush?' He tapped on the reference book in case she didn't get it.

'In fact...' he continued. I silenced him with a pinch. Before long we were on the terrace, the contraband spread neatly across our reference books. We had half-a-bottle of rum, two 77s and a packet of Rajaratnam Potato Wafers.

'Pour the drinks, Deshbush,' said Ramki, leaning wearily against the outer wall of the oven room. He had the air of a hard-working executive who relaxed with a drink each evening.

'Into what?' said Deshbush.

'The fucking glasses, you idiot!'

Ramki was right. Deshbush was an idiot. As were the two of us. In our meticulously thought-out plan, like my mother who had forgotten the cocoa powder for her chocolate burfi, we had forgotten to include glasses.

After three minutes of pinching, kicking and cursing each other in the dark, we settled down. Ramki turned his ire to the soft drink and yanked its cap off with his teeth. The warm cola gushed out with a hiss.

'Ass!' said Deshbush to Ramki.

'Idiot!' I said to Deshbush.

'Cretin!' said Ramki to me.

We had an open bottle of rum and an open bottle of cola and nothing to mix it in. Then, just like that, the Bengali, whose contribution so far had been deadpan stares, came up with an idea, proving beyond doubt that India's genuine intelligentsia came from the banks of the Hooghly.

'Let's mix it in our mouths!'

The mouth was, after all, a container. A swig of rum, a swig of cola, gargle them together and swallow. It was brilliant. If Deshbush could see us in the dark, he wouldn't have missed the pride in our eyes. No wonder we were a team. Our roles were so well defined. Ramki was the sponsor, I was the planner and Deshbush gave us the vital breaks whenever we came to a dead end.

Having provided the venue, I was given first dibs. I took a sip of the rum, held it in my mouth, took a sip of the soft drink and swirled it around in my mouth and gulped it down. It smelt like kerosene, tasted like Waterbury's Compound and went down like fire. It was fantastic.

Under the starlit sky, with our Bournvita Quiz books playing mute witness, the bottles were relayed wordlessly from boy to boy. Sip, sip, swirl and gulp. In under half an hour the bottles were empty and we were men.

Supporting myself against the wall of the oven room, I stood up. I felt perfectly steady. I hadn't needed the wall after all. Maybe, like a Mickey Spillane hero, I was one of those guys who could hold his booze. I went for a stroll, testing my legs. They felt good. I wondered why I was wearing six-inch clogs though. I looked at my feet. Still had my ratty Quo Vadises on. I looked around to see if anything else had changed. Someone had fiddled with the regulator. The sky, which had been stationary so far, was rotating on Speed Three. What an idiot I was. So that's what England Dan meant by *'there's a whirlwind blowing the stars around...'*

Suddenly, an Arctic Wolf let out a long howl followed by a series of snorts. It wasn't a dog, it wasn't any old wolf – it was the unmistakable howl of a male Arctic Wolf in heat. I knew from the documentary we had seen in school. I wondered how it could have wandered so far off its habitat. But I wasn't scared. With my new height of nearly six feet, I was invincible. I looked around to see where it was coming from.

It was coming from Ramki, who for some reason was on all fours. His upturned profile, rim-lit by the moon, looked somewhat prehistoric. I could have sworn there was a globule of spit hanging from his lower lip.

'*Owwwwwuwwwwwwwwwwowwww! Grunt, gurgle, snort!*' he went.

Buster howled in response. Ramki had the packet of chips gripped between his teeth and was violently shaking it this way and that way. I didn't see the point, we had eaten the chips long ago.

I looked up. Someone had moved the regulator to Five.

Suddenly there was a knock on the door. Who the hell could *that* be?

I saw Ramki taking in a long breath in preparation for an encore. I dived at him and clamped his mouth shut just in time. He let out a stifled growl. I scratched him under the chin.

'There, there!' I whispered. Ramki calmed down a little. I took my hand off his mouth and he let out a whimper, giving my hand an even coat of 80 proof saliva with a surprisingly rough tongue.

The knocking continued, this time louder.

Someone was calling out my name. I was dead.

What the hell was I going to do? There was more knocking, this time even more insistent. For a second I considered shinnying down the pipe leaving the two. Not possible. I looked at the door wondering what to do. Standing there, like a lone ear of corn oscillating in a gentle breeze, was Deshbush. There was another burst of knocking. Before I could do anything, Deshbush opened the door. I braced myself for the assault.

It was Kavi.

How in hell did she know? And if we hadn't fooled *her*, chances are the entire neighbourhood knew and was filming our orgy with a Super 8 camera.

Holding her nose, she took her time doing a 180-degree survey of the scene. It yielded three empty bottles, a couple of bottle caps with tooth marks, a small pile of rum-stained books, one revolting boy on all fours with a plastic cover clenched between his teeth, and another she held by the pant loops in the hope of keeping him vertical. Best of all, there was me, older brother, torturer, know-it-all and resident pain-in-the-ass, standing there quip-free and sans bravado for the first time in her thirteen-year life.

I could see her savouring the moment.

'Do you know how many times Deshbush's father has called?'

We obviously didn't.

'Fourteen times in the last half-hour!'

'Why?'

'Apparently your friend here hasn't got permission to stay out the night.'

Deshbush, still dangling from Kavi's forefinger at 30 degrees, gave her a serene smile. He then followed it up with a yelp. Ramki, still in Arctic Wolf mode, had bitten him, taking a small chunk of flesh out of Deshbush's thigh. Having sated his bloodlust temporarily, he turned his attention to Kavi. His wolf eyes turned Labrador-soft for a second.

'Kavi, I want to tell you something,' he said, enunciating each word with care. 'If Gopi dies, please don't worry, because I'm also your brother.'

Before Kavi could respond, the vulpine glint returned to his eyes and he took another bite out of Deshbush whose scream of agony was strangled by my death grip.

We needed a plan. If Deshbush's dad landed up at home, it would mean the end of civilization as we knew it. That was, of course, if Ramki didn't beat him to it.

What the hell was I going to do?

'Who knows about this?' I asked Kavi.

'For the time being, no one other than me.'

'How did you find out?'

'I saw the bottle sticking out of Ramki's pocket. You're such idiots.'

'Will you do me a favour?'

'Depends…'

I dropped whatever dignity I had left on the floor and ground it to dust.

'Please, I beg of you…' I said, my hands clasped.

'Okay, but…'

'I promise, I swear I'll make it up to you.'

'We'll see…'

'Please ring up Deshbush's place and tell his dad that we are all sleeping over at T.V. Suresh's place…'

'What good will that do?'

'T.V. Suresh doesn't have a phone and no one knows where he lives.'

'But what about tomorrow when he goes home?'

'Ask me if I care.'

Kavi began to see my point.

'What are you going to do with these drunkards *now*?'

'I'll think of something.'

When Kavi left, I realized my six-inch heels had somehow gone back to being sandals. The sky, too, had come to a standstill, proving that, in my case, fear was stronger than rum. Meanwhile, Ramki and Deshbush had apparently worked out their differences. They were leaning side by side against the parapet in what looked like an intense discussion. Maybe they had a plan, maybe it wouldn't be that bad. Closer inspection revealed that their new-found camaraderie had nothing to do with helping me out. They were vomiting in unison.

A little later, aided by a music session going on at home, I managed to get Ramki and Deshbush into the street undetected. An operation that should have taken a minute took fifteen. Deshbush refused to budge and Ramki alternately cried, growled and reassured me that he would take care of Kavi's wedding expenses in the event of my premature demise, which was evidently a certainty.

I seated my friends on the culvert outside our gate. They promptly keeled over and came to rest on each other's shoulders like bookends holding up too few books. It looked like Ramki's blood-lust had finally weakened. He nibbled harmlessly at Deshbush's ear.

It was a Sunday night and the street was dark, empty except for a lone lorry parked near the Dikshits'. I sat on the other culvert wondering what to do. It was impossible to send my friends home in their current avatars. There was no way I was taking them back upstairs. What was I to do with them the whole night?

Maybe a walk would clear the residual rum and give me some ideas. I got up and wandered off towards the main road. A moment later I heard a muffled thump, and then another. I turned around. It was the sound of Ramki and Deshbush falling off their perch. From the look of it, they were fast asleep by the side of the road. It was, after all, past their bedtime.

'Good evening, saab.'

The greeting startled me. It was Bahadur, the Dikshits' watchman, standing by the lorry.

'Oh, good evening, Bahadur.'

'Your friends okay, saab?'

'Not really.' I made a drinking gesture with my thumb and little finger. 'Too much.'

'And what about you, saab?'

I measured a small peg with my thumb and forefinger to indicate that I was okay.

'Wondering what to do with them, Bahadur.' I thought there was no harm in asking my new friend. 'Any ideas?'

Bahadur thought for a minute. 'You can put them in the back of the lorry, saab. It belongs to Dikshit saab,' he said. 'They can sleep there and leave in the morning. That way, they won't be bitten by the street dogs.'

The way I saw it, it was the dogs that needed protection.

I looked up at the sky that had stopped swirling a long time ago. The pain of being ragged all these years for looking Chinese/Japanese/Korean/Thai/Vietnamese, depending on which nationality was in the headlines at that time, all of it disappeared that instant. That day I knew why god had created me with poker-straight hair and eyes one size too small. It was so that a Nepalese gentleman would look upon me as a brother on the most difficult day of my life and save me from a fate worse than death.

Ha, rag me now, suckers!

Resisting the urge to prostate myself at Bahadur's feet, I ran back to my house before he changed his mind. Ramki and Deshbush were settled in comfortably by now. They were lying on their bed of mud, with their heads on a mound of garbage. Ramki's leg was casually thrown over Deshbush. Flies buzzing around their vomit-scented faces completed the picture of domestic bliss.

Before long, the unconscious duo was deposited in the back of the Dikshit lorry with the help of my north-eastern saviour, a mission expedited by the eight rupees foraged from our pockets. I was thankful for the two-inch layer of sand on the lorry's floor. It would take the sting off the damage caused in transit. After all, how efficient could a thirty-five kg runt and a small-boned Nepali carrying two totally prone, vomit-coated bodies be? As I thanked Bahadur one last time and headed home, Ramki bade me farewell with a snore. It still had a vulpine edge.

The next morning, I woke up earlier than usual, sporting a pounding headache and a tongue that smelt of old sock. I figured it was my first hangover. I kept my distance from everyone at home, skipped breakfast and spent all morning with giant gob of toothpaste lodged inside my mouth. Kavi's laser gaze didn't leave me for a second, not even when I threw up quietly.

On the way to school there was no sign of either the lorry or Bahadur. When the bell rang at school and there was no sign of either Ramki or Deshbush I began to worry. What could have happened? Had they died of an alcohol overdose? Had Deshbush's father beaten him to death? Worse still, had they ratted on me?

The truth, I found out the following day, was a little different.

Apparently, the lorry driver had arrived at 4.00 a.m. sharp, taken his keys from Bahadur's empty cabin (the watchman had gone off for a quick tea), and driven the Dikshit lorry at high speed to their new factory site in Tada on the Andhra–Tamil Nadu border. At the back of his vehicle, he had found two foul-smelling underage passengers who were unable to explain why they were there. The out-of-towners, funded by sympathetic passers-by, had rung up their disbelieving parents, then partly walked, partly hitched a ride on a tempo carrying chickens, and finally taken a bus to arrive home at around noon, after which they had been thoroughly hosed down on their lawns. Then they were given a hiding.

More importantly, I found out *'I really love to see you tonight'* didn't actually go *'…there's a whirlwind blowing the stars around…'* as I'd thought that night. It went *'there's a warm wind blowing, the stars are out…'* proving that, with the right amount of rum, I was a better songwriter than England Dan.

Net result:

Deshbush and Ramki swore to their parents in front of Kali Mata and Lord Shiva respectively that they would never again talk to T.V. Suresh.

I tore up the contract Kavi and I had made up sharing the world's music in exchange for her silence. She celebrated her victory by humming *'For a Few Dollars More'* for three straight days.

Without his father's knowledge, Deshbush took fourteen injections around his navel on account of the mysterious bite marks all over his body.

The three of us never spoke of this again.

TWENTY-SEVEN

How does a young man know he has attained puberty? For me it was something as simple as which side of the road I was on. Literally. One day, if a girl walked towards me, I was looking down and crossing the road. The next day, I was crossing the road to be on the same side as her.

I'd felt an unnamed sadness watching Audrey Hepburn in *Roman Holiday*. But that wasn't *my* puberty. What was the chance of that when my testicles hadn't even begun their descent? It was just the bizarre case of a son re-visiting his father's puberty, what with the woman in question now being roughly Grandmother's age.

In real life, I had been rendered breathless by Lanka Jhansi's fore and Kanika Krishnan's aft, but that was prepubescent too. Had it really been puberty, would I have been more interested in the bottom line than *her* bottom line or, for that matter, would I have been relieved to see a do-it-yourself erection kit like Lanka Jhansi leave Club Meghamala?

The unmistakable sign of puberty is when you notice girls your own age and, for the first time, don't feel the need to club them to death. For me, these came in the form of the students of Sacred Souls Anglo-Indian School. Legend had it that at least three generations of young men from T. Nagar before me had discovered first love among the alumni of this hallowed institution.

It wasn't as if these girls materialized en masse one day on a perfectly empty road to catch my attention. Madras was small, and T. Nagar even smaller, so I must have walked past some of these girls every single day for the last six years. But, that summer, it felt like someone had adjusted the focus on my camera, brought them into clear view, tapped me on the head and said, 'Hey, look!'

There were so many of them. All wearing identically dowdy uniforms of green skirts and white shirts, yet each one unique. The first thing to change on the appearance of these girls was my attendance. I found myself going to school *every day*. Word in the staff room was that poor M. Gopal had made a miraculous turnaround with his fragile health and might actually make it into his twenties. The fact was I still hated school. Just the walk to school and back home made me put up with the murderous boredom of maths, chemistry and physics. Little did I realize that, each day, it was these very subjects that I was putting into practice on my walk.

In the past, with films, comic books and my other pursuits, I had figured out that my mind was incapable of spreading itself too thin. Now I found I could not scatter myself among nearly fifty candidates and decided to narrow down the possibilities to a number that I could wrap my head around.

In the first month itself, with mathematical precision, I commenced the process of elimination based on physical compatibility and that unknown something called chemistry.

I began by ruling out any girl who'd have a weight advantage of more than five kg over me. I didn't see the point in giving her hand a romantic squeeze and having my carpal bones broken in response. Runt that I was, that instantly erased about fifty per cent of the girls right off my list. As for the rest, there were a couple of girls who were actually thinner than me. This meant that in certain angles you couldn't see them at all. I knew that I didn't have the wherewithal to nurture such girls to normalcy. Moreover, it did not make sense to be widowed early. So that ruled them out.

One day, I was on my way to school, and a bunch of girls giggled as they went past. Was this chemistry at work? Soon after, I felt a draft, looked down and found that it was actually physics. My fly was open. So that lot had to go, too. Every day the list got smaller. Oily plaits were a no-no. So were soda bottle glasses and hairy legs. I couldn't get close enough to any of them to see if they had BO. Finally, I was left with two girls, both equally gorgeous – and the complete opposite of each other.

One was tall. Maybe even an inch taller than me. But I wasn't going to test that and break my heart. She'd have to do even if she was. The option of reconsidering some of the ones struck off the list just didn't arise. Real men didn't do that. In fact, the tall one would have to stay even if her breath smelt of garlic. If there was one thing I'd learnt from Father, it was that you always hedge your bets. You never played on just one horse in a race.

Tall Girl rode a BSA *SLR* with no front bar. Luckily for me, she was joined by a friend halfway through her journey. So she walked the rest of the way to school, wheeling her maroon cycle instead of whizzing past me. She had a carefree air, an open face and the biggest smile I'd ever seen. She seemed to break into uncontrollable laughter every now and then, making me wonder if my renegade fly was open yet again. It didn't occur to me that maybe she didn't know I existed and laughed because she was happy.

Candidate Two was petite. She walked with the self-possession of a much older person and was the first and probably only dignified thirteen-year-old I'd ever seen in my life. It was strange. My hormones were playing such havoc with me that, first, I was going to school regularly and now, I found decorum attractive?

By some quirk of fate, I also found out that we would cross each other at the exact same spot every day if I left my house at 8.27 a.m.

Two months after I'd noticed the girls, I had my routine pretty much figured out. I'd leave home at 8.27 whether my lunch was ready or not, pass the petite one first, hope for a smile which never came, and, a little further along, cross the tall one wheeling her cycle accompanied by her friend, acknowledgement due. If I didn't see either of them, I'd spend the entire day in school wondering if they had moved, fallen terribly ill, been forced into a child marriage with a lecherous octogenarian to repay a family debt or plumb died on me. Even Rusty Mistry's choicest boo-boos failed to jolly me out of my blues on these days. I was hell at recess. Holly Golly saw me red-eyed and deathly calm. I aimed to kill and nearly succeeded on a couple of occasions. Every evening, at 3.45, at the first clang of the bell, I shot out of class like Father on Derby Day. My day wasn't complete without crossing the Sacred Souls in the exact same sequence. I thanked the time-keepers in heaven for coordinating the clocks of the two schools to facilitate this crossing.

Three full months of this made one thing very clear to me. I had as much hope meeting these girls, leave alone holding their hands, as knowing Audrey Hepburn. What the hell was I going to do? The enterprise that I had shown towards endeavours criminal seemed to be sorely missing in the area of girls. Maybe I was just a sap like the rest of the men in my family, after all. Maybe I'd die old, miserable and single with several unanswered questions. What would it have been like to have a girlfriend? Was any of the stuff Prasad had said about girls actually true? And, most importantly, what exactly was it that Sendhil did to get himself in hospital?

Sometimes, god tosses random debris from heaven and one of the fragments ends up being not only the exact piece missing from your jigsaw but also lands in the precise spot left open for it, completing the picture when you've all but given up hope.

My divine debris came in the form of Rishi, for the youngest of the Bankas had just made the transition from school to the big, bad world of pre-university. The guy who'd been playing Ice Boys with us till yesterday now hung out with boys who had a razor blade allowance. His shabby red schoolbag had now been replaced by a multicoloured elastic band that held three books. He now took a train to distant Tambaram, dressed in cool civvies. Unless he was incarcerated or opted for a career in domestic security, his days of wearing a uniform were over. In a way, I could understand his reluctance to hang out with a drill-wearer like me.

One evening, after what seemed like an enormous gap, Rishi landed up at home.

'Hey, I'm off to a friend's place. Want to come?' he said.

Was he kidding?

The thought of meeting a college guy was both exciting and scary. On the one hand I could get a close-up view of how college buddies behaved but on the other – what if his friend ragged me? I decided I was quite up to handling a college boy by myself, with Rishi's support. But that didn't mean I was going unarmed. I asked Rishi to wait, went into my room and put on my widest bell-bottoms. Then, with an eyebrow pencil I'd secreted away for precisely such an occasion, I darkened my philtrum, adding what I thought would be a couple of advantageous years to my visage. I looked into the mirror and tried hard to imagine myself on the verge of college. I blew imaginary smoke from one side of my mouth and went 'Nah, I prefer Benson & Hedges' a couple of times in my best baritone. When I began to sound like Saikumar, I knew I was ready.

The guy we were going to meet was Rishi's new best friend, 'Lucky' Lakshmanan. Listening to Rishi go on about him it was obvious that this guy was a cross between John Travolta and Mahatma Gandhi. That was as ideal a combination as you could get in a man. *Saturday Night Fever* and *Grease* had just come out. Macho young men who'd beat up a guy just for being in the vicinity of Kalakshetra were now wearing white suits and doing something called the Hustle. And, if

Rishi was to be believed, Lucky was the greatest exponent of disco dancing in south India. That wasn't all. Apparently his parents were okay with him having dance parties at home. For someone like me who came from a family where sexual deviants were welcome but Western dancing was a no-no, that put him right up there with Bapu.

I was so caught up listening to Rishi's new and wonderful college exploits, I didn't notice we were approaching a large group of menacing-looking men. There was raucous laughter and the sound of backs being thumped. I could almost smell the man-sweat and see the fronds of disgusting chest hair sticking out of their unbuttoned shirts. Like most boys, I had a fear of any male with body hair. From time immemorial, young men have somehow been under the impression that it's hilarious to cause bodily harm to their juniors. As I tried crossing over surreptitiously to the other side of the road, Rishi stopped me.

'Where are you going?' he said. He pointed to the large gang of evil-looking men. 'That's Lucky's house. Those are my classmates.'

I had come prepared for one college boy. This was a lynch mob.

I gulped and wiped the sweat off my face. To my horror, my fingers came out looking like an engine driver's, all sooty from my last-minute makeover. I was sure the instant moustache running down either side of my mouth made me look like an underfed Mongolian despot. It looked like 70 mm humiliation was a moment away. I yanked out my hanky and rubbed my face so vigorously that it burned. Then there I was in the middle of ten college boys. Rishi introduced them one by one but I didn't hear a single name because of a deafening hum in my ears. I was sure my face was a multicoloured collage of eyebrow pencil, laceration and embarrassment. I saw Rishi's lips moving and the boys laugh and shout. But it was like watching TV with the sound turned off. Sweat poured from my armpits which I'd thankfully not touched up with an eyebrow pencil. After what seemed like an eternity, my ears began to work again. I hadn't been thumped to death after all. The burly boys seemed harmless enough and were totally caught up with matters collegiate. In fact, one of them absently leaned on my shoulder and asked me where I was studying. Before I could reply, a girl's voice called out from the staircase. 'Luckieee!'

The boy who must have been Lucky absently shouted back, 'Whaaat?'

A girl padded down the steps and stood on the bottom step of the unlit staircase, arms akimbo.

'What do you mean "what"? Mom wants you.' The tone reeked of younger sister. A couple of boys called out to her: 'Hey, Lata!' 'What's up, Lata!' The girl came out and stood illuminated under the streetlight. Immediately, my hearing failed again. Lucky's little sister Lata was 8.27 – the smaller of the Sacred Souls. Wearing a pair of maroon shorts and a strappy top, she looked nothing like the demure little girl I saw every day on the way to school.

Lucky ran upstairs and Lata took his place in the crowd of college boys. She chatted away, perfectly comfortable in a group of scary men towering over her. I tried to blend into the trunk of the nearest tree. Perhaps if I hid behind the tree first and slunk away no one would notice…

'Hey, Lata, I want you to meet someone,' said Rishi, pointing to me at the exact moment when it looked like I was rubbing myself obscenely against the tree.

'That's my little friend, Gopal…we call him Go-pee,' he said, unnecessarily elongating the second syllable of my name.

In my hurry to dispel any doubts whatsoever that I was some kind of tree-raping pervert, I pushed myself off the trunk so fast that I didn't see a stone behind me. I tripped over it and fell backwards. I was saved from having my skull cracked open only because a college boy caught me mid-fall and casually put me back on my feet like I was made of balsa wood. There I stood, a five-foot-five-inch runt, with a red-and-black polka-dotted face and the remains of a fake moustache about to meet the girl of my dreams for the first time.

'Hi, Gopi…' she said, and after a moment, 'don't I see you every day? You go to that school with the navy blue uniform, right?'

Before I could answer, the boy who was beyond doubt the guy called Lucky came back and joined the group. He looked at me with narrowed eyes.

'Oh, you know Lata? You didn't tell me?'

Never in my chequered academic career had I faced a more challenging set of questions. How was I going to answer them? If I admitted that I did, indeed, see Lata every day, would she think I was a stalker of some sort? On the other hand, if I pretended not to have noticed her, would I be considered a snob or, worse still, a liar? Further, what was my answer to Lucky's second question? Why hadn't I told him I knew Lata? The answer, of course, was: I didn't because I hadn't known that she was his sister until a minute ago. But how was I going to tell a hairy college boy who happened to be the older brother of one of the two most important girls in my life that without sounding sassy? And that, too, in front of ten senior citizens and a puzzled Rishi?

People crib about there being far too many gods in the Hindu pantheon, but I'm not one of them. Because, as I stood there with my mouth open, an empty speech bubble hovering over my head, it was one of these underutilized deities that dot the Vedic heavens that came to my rescue.

The head of a woman popped out of an upstairs window and yelled, 'Lucky, Lata! Please come on up. Dinner's getting cold,' rendering my reply redundant.

That night I dreamt of the scene where reporter and princess, both soaking wet, kiss each other in *Roman Holiday*. Only, in my version, instead of Audrey Hepburn and Gregory Peck, it was Lata and me.

TWENTY-EIGHT

From then on, my relationship with Rishi, which had been in cold storage for some time, found itself on high flame. Ramki and Deshbush were dismissed without notice. It made sense. I had, after all, moved on from wine to women. I was at Rishi's place almost every day and tagged along wherever he went, which was mostly to Lucky's place. After a few visits, it turned out the college boys, Pramod, Vincent & Co., were neither as hairy nor as scary as I'd first believed. Maybe they didn't receive me with open arms but I was grateful they didn't seem interested in examining my orifices either. I was even more grateful to be able to see Lata. Just a month ago, even saying hello to her seemed about as probable as CG breaking into song. Yet here I was, in the same room as her. Talking to her, if only in monosyllables, in the day. And dreaming of her, in black-and-white, at night. I walked about with a contextless grin. This was exactly the way I wanted things. They couldn't get any better.

However, it turned out the scriptwriter of my life was ambitious. Instead of keeping it simple, where I marry Lata next, have four kids by the year-end and live happily funded forever after by CG, he decided to explore a subplot that could just as easily have been edited out.

You've seen it a hundred times: the hero's wife dies in a plane crash, her body is never found, he is inconsolable. Aided by the love of an equally beautiful woman, he slowly recovers. They decide to marry. It's the day of their wedding, the hero is about to say 'I do', a voice says 'Stop!'

Cut to close-up of dead wife *very much alive*.

Interval.

My 'interval point' came on a Sunday as I walked up Lucky's staircase a respectful step behind Rishi's college-boy stride. Sitting in the living room, right next to Lata, was my other Sacred Soul – the tall one. I'd all but forgotten her in the recent high drama. And there she was, surrounded by boys. She was dressed in civvies but the big old grin that had got me in the first place was still there, plastered symmetrically between her ears. She was wearing Wranglers with a 'W' and a pink T-shirt, and in her hands was a sketch pad which she turned page by page to the 'oohing' and 'aahing' audience.

This really complicated my marriage plans.

While Rishi joined his friends seamlessly, I stood a safe three feet away and tried peering in. Lata beamed at me from her moda, completely oblivious to my oscillating heart. I managed an awkward display of teeth in reply.

The sketches were all landscapes in charcoal. They were really good. My first feeling was one of jealousy. I hated anyone my age who could draw well. What if they were better than me? I noticed that the sketch pad was similar to the unaffordable imported one I had been eyeing in Perumal Chetty & Sons for years.

I didn't know where to look – at the drawings, at Lata or at the tall one. Why did my dreams have to change genre? What ought to have been a crime story with a happy ending was about to become a triangular love story. And triangular love stories almost always end unhappily. I understood how Father felt at the bookie's when he had to choose between the horse that had popped up in his calculation and the *Madras Mail*'s Tip of the Day.

For the time being, I was happy that everyone else was occupied. It made transitions easy. By the time they were done with the sketches, I would have managed to blend into the furniture. But I hadn't factored in Rishi.

'Hey, Gopi,' he said, 'look at these drawings. Are yours better than these?'

My tenure in the comfortably shadowy area, just beyond the perimeter of the spotlight, ended instantly. The lightman in the sky, spurred by Rishi's unnecessary directorial cue, turned the Super Trouper on me. Ten college boys and two grinning Sacred Souls turned along with it. I tried to say something. But it is difficult to form words when your mouth is open. All I could come up with was a strangled Saikumar-like croak.

'C'mon, da!' said Rishi, now just taunting me. 'You're showing off all the time about what a great artist you are. Are you better than Vini?'

So *that* was her name. I tried to think of a clever retort as everyone continued staring at me. I was sure they could see the cavities in my upper molars caused by the Nutrine sweets. Where was the famed wit that had always got the better of Kavi?

It was Vini who came to my rescue.

'Leave the guy alone. I'm sure he's better than me.'

This was really unfair. Not only was she absolutely gorgeous, she was sweet, too. Now, I had to marry *her* as well. How was I going to manage that on CG's income, my treasure trove of junk notwithstanding?

Vini may have created long-term problems for me but she did solve the minor one at hand. The boys decided to leave me alone. A little later the gang broke up into smaller groups and I found myself with Vini and Lata. My stomach had quietened down and I was considering saying something when Vini spoke.

'Hey, aren't you the guy who walks past us every day?'

Before I could reply, Lata said, 'That's him!'

The girls went into a giggling fit. I held my breath. What were they giggling about? Were they on to my precision-timed departures at 8.27? Had they seen me with my fly open? Worse still, what if the college guys wanted to know why they were laughing? What if they beat a confession out of me and found out that I was a bigamously inclined stalker of schoolgirls?

I decided to change the subject.

'Your sketches...' I said in my most professorial tone, 'have you learnt how to do them from the Walter Foster books?'

'No! I took a summer class. You know, I've been trying to get those for ages but Higginbotham's just doesn't seem to have them!'

Now we were talking. Vini may have had the genuine Wranglers and the imported sketch pad – but *I* had the Walter

Fosters. They were a gift to Father from one of Grandfather's admirers who lived in the US. I had spent many afternoons with them in the oven room between the cleavage watching.

'Oh,' I said, trying to sound as nonchalant as I could, 'I have a few. I could…you know…lend them to you.'

Vini had a look on her face that reminded me of Father's the day he thought he had won the jackpot. (That he didn't and replaced it with an indelible double-strength scowl is another story.)

'You serious?' she said. 'You mean I could actually borrow them?'

'Of course,' I said. She could have had CG's Padma Vibhushan if she wished.

'Oh, good! Where's your place? I could pick them up on the way back from school.'

Great opportunities followed by insurmountable obstacles – the story of my life. Why would I want this incredibly posh, Wrangler-wearing dream woman to see the nuts I lived with? And what if she had a weak bladder? I shuddered at the thought of having to direct her to the torture chamber at home that passed for a loo.

'Actually,' I said, '*I* could drop them off…if you tell me where your place is.'

'Would you? That's so sweet,' she said.

To my horror, she then tore out the corner of a page from her sketch pad and scrawled her address and phone number on it. Lata smiled. If only she knew I was two-timing her even before I had begun to one-time.

That night I didn't dream at all. That was because I didn't sleep a wink.

A couple of days later, it was evening and I was on my way to Vini's house. I had called her and told her I'd drop by. Our conversation, my first telephonic one with a girl, was short and awkward.

On my way to her place, I couldn't help but wonder at my meteoric rise. A month ago, I didn't know a single girl. Yet, here I was, Walter Fosters under my arm, going off to a place even the college boys hadn't ventured into – a girl's house. Somehow, going to Lata's didn't count because it was under the guise of seeing Lucky. This was different, there was no middleman. I was in the big league. I wondered what Ramki and Deshbush, whom I'd been ignoring of late, would think if they knew. The half-bottle of rum was kid stuff.

Vini's house was a creaky bungalow of similar vintage to ours. But, unlike ours, I was told it was the family home. It was nestled in a gloomy corner of a large compound full of trees.

'Don't forget, it's upstairs,' she had said on the phone, 'our tenants live on the ground floor.'

I walked up the narrow staircase and stood at the door. I was glad I'd decided against thickening my moustache, because I was sweating like a hog on account of walking a kilometre in high-heeled boots one size too small, carrying a bunch of books. I took five deep breaths, checked to see if my fly was closed, and rang the bell.

The door was opened by a tall, stern-looking woman with short hair. She looked at me, her lips pursed. I noticed they were a bright red.

'Yes?' she said. I could smell her strong perfume. My legs felt wobbly. The one thing that scared me more than college boys was parents. This had to be Vini's mother.

'I'm Vini's friend,' I croaked. It seemed as though that was my primary mode of communication these days. I realized I wasn't being entirely truthful. I had met Vini once. That didn't constitute a friendship.

I showed her the books. 'I came to drop these off.'

'Okay,' said the woman, 'I'll tell her.'

Before I knew what was happening, the woman took the books from my outstretched hands, gave me a cold smile and closed the door. I stood staring at the door for a couple of minutes. This was it? My high-heeled boots, my vintage Walter Fosters, the hours I'd spent combing my hair – all so I could have an unfettered view of Vini's ageing teak door? I had, after all, risen like a meteor. It was unfair of me to expect a parachute for my fall. I hobbled down the staircase and slunk off towards the gate like Buster on its way out from the vet. The boots I'd borrowed from Rishi pinched like hell.

'Hey, Gopi, where are you running off to?' I turned around. It was Vini standing on the balcony, holding my books. 'C'mon up.'

I ran up the stairs and was back at the door. This time Vini let me in. The tall lady, who was definitely her mother, was there, too.

'What do you mean, giving the books and running off like that?' Vini sounded cross.

'I didn't…er…actually, I thought Auntie…' How was I going to tell Vini that her mother had slammed the door in my face?

'I told you to wait,' said the lady. There was a forced smile on her face. 'But you seemed to be in such a hurry.'

Like a million kids before me, instead of contradicting an errant adult, I went along.

'Sorry, Auntie…'

A man in tight Levi's and a white shirt joined us, cutting short my excuse. I was amazed. First her Wranglers, now his Levi's. What else did they have in their wardrobes? They must have been among the very few two-jean families in Madras.

The man was tall and slim. A cigarette dangled from his mouth which was framed by a dyed French beard. Other than the tobacco, I detected base notes of cologne *and* booze. After our Pondy trip and our bar night I knew my odours.

'Ready?' he addressed the woman before turning around to look at me.

'And what have we here?' he said, exhaling a long straight plume of smoke from the corner of his mouth. I knew it was 555 from the unmistakable yellow-and-gold pack that was visible through his transparent shirt pocket.

'Dad, this is Gopi…Gopal,' said Vini. 'He's come to drop off some…'

'Awright, you guys have fun,' he said, cutting Vini mid-sentence with a peck on her cheek. Then he gave me a handshake that rendered my hand useless for at least a week. From the corner of my eye, I caught Vini rubbing the kiss off her cheek with the back of her hand. What she was trying to erase – the prickle of his beard, the odours or her dad in his entirety?

'Be good,' he said to no one in particular. With the current state of my hand nothing else was possible anyway. Before I knew it, the couple was off, leaving a confusion of fragrances in their wake.

It was just Vini and me. I had never been alone with a girl before and didn't know what to say. I had a minute to think of something clever because she was totally engrossed, poring over the books I'd brought.

I was happy that I was in Vini's house and not the other way round. I imagined introducing her to my folks. Mother would have pinched her cheeks, looked at me and said, 'She's so cute, ra!' and run off to get my baby pictures in drag. Father would have remained his inscrutable self. As for my sisters, they were best forgotten.

'Your folks…they're pretty cool,' I said.

'They're okay,' she said, shrugging her shoulders. She didn't look up from the book.

I rubbed my hand, still smarting from Vini's dad's death grip. I smelt it discreetly. Equal parts Old Monk, Jovan Sex Appeal and 555.

'I'm sorry about my mom, though…' said Vini. I quickly stopped smelling my hand as she closed the book and returned it to the pile on the table.

'What do you mean?' I played innocent.

'She can be rude…but don't take it personally. It's just that she and Dad are having, you know…kind of…problems.' She shrugged again.

I didn't get it. When my folks had problems, it involved swearing, the flight of blunt instruments and a first-aid kit, in that order. Apparently, the posh people did it differently. They put on make-up, slugged back a couple and left for a party – together.

With the wealth of knowledge I had gleaned from the *Picturegoers* and James Hadley Chase, I attempted to console Vini.

'It can't be that bad. I'm sure it'll be okay soon.'

'They're getting a divorce,' she said simply.

I looked at the girl who sported the happiest grin I'd ever seen every morning. She didn't look all that happy now.

'Hey,' she said. The grin was back. 'How come most of these books are on caricatures, animation and cartoons? No watercolours, oils? Aren't you interested in fine art?'

'Actually, I want to be a cartoonist, like my dad…and cartooning is a fine art, too.' I came off sounding a bit short.

'I'm sorry, sweetie. I'm sure it is,' she said, giving my shoulder a squeeze.

Sweetie? I had been called sweetie by Mother and a couple of aunts I had managed to con from time to time. It sounded different coming from her. We sat on the floor and talked about art, parents, school, books and music. We talked like we had been friends all our lives and it didn't matter I was a boy and she was a girl.

I found out her father was a pilot, her mother ran a beauty salon and that she was an only child. When the divorce came through, she would either have to stay in Madras with her mother or go to Dubai with her father. She told me of their love marriage and how they had come to want different things. When I looked at my watch it was ten o'clock. Death awaited me at home but I didn't care.

When I finally got up to go, Vini gave me an impulsive hug. I was taken by surprise. This had been a day of so many 'firsts'. My hands hovered uselessly over her shoulders like an uncoordinated ape's.

'Drop by again soon,' she said.

As I walked home I didn't feel the shoe bite at all. I was delirious with joy. I could still smell her shampoo from our micro-hug. The road was empty except for me and a lungi-clad man who was leaning thoughtfully against a lamp-post. He had a beedi in his mouth while a forefinger examined his anus. I felt like telling him, 'Hey, buddy! Guess what? I just got called 'sweetie' and then I got a hug from a girl who wears Wranglers. And I'm only fifteen. Top *that*!'

But I had another feeling, too, which was quite the opposite of joy. Of all things, it most resembled foreboding. It was like a split-screen film clip was playing in my head. One half of it showed an upbeat montage featuring Vini, Lata, films, hanging out with college boys and the great big party my life was. The clip running on the other side was out of focus. Though I squinted hard, it was impossible to see the detail. But even through its blurriness there was one thing I could tell. It sure as hell wasn't a happy film.

TWENTY-NINE

Lucky had finally delivered. There *was* going to be a dance party at his place. It was fixed for late February and it was going to be hep. There would be college boys and girls, Lucky's cousins, the Sacred Souls *and* me. To accommodate some of the guests who were under age, the party was scheduled to begin at one in the afternoon. Though it was a couple of weeks away, I was buzzing like I'd had Mother's 'chocolate' burfi.

While the rest of my class prepared for the school finals, I was wondering what I would wear to the party. One day, Father, who had watched my past transgressions with the detached eye of an uncle once removed, abruptly altered course.

'What the hell is wrong with you?' he yelled. I was practising John Travolta's moves to a borrowed LP of *Saturday Night Fever* and the last thing I expected was Father bursting in. It was a weekend and it would have taken nothing less than a country-made bomb placed under his chair to dislodge him from his racing sheet.

I froze like Travolta on the LP jacket, my legs apart, right forefinger pointed towards the ceiling, my left thumb pointed towards my trouser pocket.

Father wasn't known for outbursts. His method of intimidation was the disgust-filled stare that turned humans into dung beetles in five seconds flat. I was looking at a different man that day. He stood there all white-knuckled, expelling toxic fumes from his large ears. In my fifteen-year existence, Father had evoked several emotions in me – admiration, disgust, hate, anger – even sympathy. This was the first time I felt fear.

'What's the big deal?' I brazened it out.

'What's the big deal! You ask me what's the *big deal!*' I could hear the timer on his detonating device being activated. 'You fool, you're throwing your whole life away, that's what's the big deal!'

'What do you mean…I was dancing…'

'Dancing! Dancing, you say!' The tick-tick had grown louder. 'Who the hell do you think you are, *Gene Kelly*?'

Good god, no. Was my dancing so off the mark that it came out more soft-shoe shuffle than the Hustle?

'Not Gene Kelly, John Travolta…' I said, ignoring the timer, which was growing louder every second.

tick, Tick, TICK, **TICK**…

Now I was insulting the '50s? His effeminate voice turned guttural with rage: 'And you have *girls* phoning you! You're not yet fifteen, is this any age for such bloody nonsense? You've got your finals less than a month away and moreover Thaatha's not well and here you are going…'

Words failed him at this point. So he launched into a violent impression of my moves. They would have probably been hilarious under different circumstances. At that exact moment my sisters walked in and saw their dhoti-clad old man having what looked like an epileptic fit to musical accompaniment and pissed their pants.

Red-hot anger replaced my fear. Who was this man who had never been to school, worshipped the MGM song-and-dance routines, and went to the races every week to talk about responsibility? And how dare he mock me! I crossed the invisible line that I had flirted with from the time I was about ten.

'What the hell do you know about school?' I yelled. 'How the fuck does it matter whether I pass or fail? Did it ever make a difference to you when I stood first in class…?'

I was screaming so loudly, my face so contorted with rage that I didn't see him going off.

Pha-tack.

It was a back-handed slap that stopped me dead, mid-tirade. For a second, I stared at Father trembling with rage. His hand was still hovering in the air. In the background '*How Deep is Your Love*' continued playing.

If you're a boy and have managed to make it to fifteen, that you've taken a few knocks is a given. Teachers, older boys, bigger boys, parents, sisters – everyone's had a go at you. The taps on the head to show who's boss, the whack on the bum to restore peace, the ear flicks, the punches, the pinches – you've pretty much experienced all the variations. You're bruised, you cry, you hit back or slink away depending on who the perpetrator is, and you carry on with life.

But this was different. I could sense there was a lot more than Father's five fingers behind that slap. There was the fury of disappointment, the venom of long-time enmity, and the finality of an obituary. This was a declaration of war. Carrying on with life was not an option any more. In an instant I turned from son to wild animal.

I caught my father by the collar and yanked him up. I was a couple of inches taller than him and lifted him enough to look him in the eye. He stared at me, sickened.

'Don't you *ever* fucking touch me again!' I hissed between clenched teeth.

Suddenly it was the climax of *Enter the Dragon*, a thousand men against Bruce Lee. My sisters, Mother and CG, who had walked in by now – everyone was hitting me or pulling me away from Father. Only Grandmother watched from behind a door.

'No, Gopi! No, Baloo! Please stop!' she said over and over again.

I let go of him and pushed everyone away. The verdict was out. *I* was the bad guy. Before anyone could say anything, I turned around and ran out of the house. I rushed up the staircase and into the oven room and silently bolted the door shut. Downstairs I heard Mother yelling out my name. Then I heard Father.

'Bloody fool!' I heard him say, his voice deathly cold. 'Where'll he go! He'll come back with his tail between his legs.'

I sat down and waited for my heart to stop pounding. Tears stung my cheek – I was literally putting salt on my wounds.

It was just me and my treasure trove of junk. I tapped around a pile of newspapers with my foot, the same ones that had funded many movies. If only there were a couple of gold coins among them, I could walk out and live on my own. I would quit school and practise drawing every day. Within a year I'd be so good that a magazine would hire me and I'd earn my own money and live like a king. That would show them.

I wondered what I had done that was so wrong or different. How could they expect school to be the most important thing in my life? It was not like I was failing. I'd pass my finals, probably get a first class by the skin of my teeth. That ought to have been enough. Why didn't Father get it? Moreover, it wasn't as if I'd got my idea of what life ought to be from Bhaskar or Prasad. Everything I knew, I had learnt right here in the oven room – reading and re-reading *his* books, looking at *his* drawings and obsessing over *his* films. Why was I expected to behave like Raghavan's son Sekhar all of a sudden, who had barely come out for oxygen the last couple of months, preparing for the IIT entrance exam?

I felt like calling up Vini. She would understand. Just a few days ago hadn't she borne similar ignominy on her cheek? Her dad's rum-spiked kiss would have stung no less than the slap I'd got. Or maybe I could go to Lata, of the perfect family, welcoming parents and open house. Wherever I went, the one place I wasn't going was back. The oven room had always been hot. But it was ablaze now with the searing hatred of my entire family which had turned against me in that fraction of a second when I held Father by his collar.

I knew I would remember this day forever.

As I sat there thumbing through a stray *Picturegoer*, life downstairs hadn't come to a standstill as I'd hoped. Father's racing buddy honked – the unmistakable sign that it was one o' clock on a weekend. I heard the heavy-duty latch on our gate squeak open. Then the familiar, conclusive ka-thunk indicating that the gate and everything else for Father was shut till Monday. A little later, through the dining-room windows, I could hear the clink of stainless steel. Everyone was having lunch. Then there was silence. No search party of anguished sisters. No distraught phone calls to friends and relations to ascertain my whereabouts. Everyone was asleep.

An hour later, face suitably dry and heart back in the rib-cage, I went down. Mother was sitting in the living room, pretending to read a magazine. She didn't fool me. She was waiting for me. I ignored her, went into Father's studio and was rummaging around for a pen and paper when I felt her hands on my shoulder. I felt like bursting into tears again.

'Ramu,' she said, calling me by the name reserved for special occasions. 'Please eat.' I was hungry as hell and could smell my favourite fried potato. But I knew I couldn't give in. I pushed her hand away roughly and went back to the oven room. For the next two hours I wrote.

I didn't eat anything the whole day and slept exhausted. All through the night, I could feel the dying embers of Father's slap.

When I woke up the next day, I whistled as I drank my coffee and stared brazenly at Father, making him uncomfortable. I felt surprisingly light. It didn't take long for me to figure out why.

In any story, it's the hero's path that's never smooth. Every few pages, just as he's about to kiss the girl or stumble upon treasure, circumstances play dirty. It comes with the territory. A hero's job is to keep the plot alive, and this he does by facing obstacles. Add to this the poor fellow's contractual obligation to the public to always do the right thing and you realize his life isn't much fun. And he gets to live happily ever after only in the final page.

A villain's job, on the other hand, is much easier. And fun, too. He does whatever he wants, gleefully free of guilt, for a hundred-and-ninety-nine pages out of two-hundred. He doesn't give a rat's ass about public opinion. His is obviously the better deal.

As of yesterday, having been anointed the heavy in my own life, I was liberated. For instance, if I wished, I could now sip rum and cola buck naked in our living room while my neighbour's barber shaved my bum. That I first needed to have some fuzz on my bum was a mere technicality.

Instead of outstaring Father or blaring my borrowed music, I decided to put my new-found powers of villainy into the party around the corner. I was glad there wouldn't have to be any tippytoeing. I would go to the party, dance my heart out and carry out the Grand Secret Plan I had devised. I dared anyone to stop me.

I chose to ignore the fact that villains are usually handcuffed and taken away to Sing Sing in the last page. I was fifteen. I figured my last page was a long way off.

THIRTY

I guess time flies for the bad because the party day came at me like a fighter jet, its high-octane wake blurring the rest of the world. While classmates grappled with physics and maths, I grappled with the Hustle in my new pin-striped trousers and matching vest. The jacket, which would have completed Travolta's three-piece suit look, had to be abandoned due to budgetary constraints. At school, Ramki and Deshbush hardly took their heads out of their books, partly out of fear of the approaching finals but mostly because they couldn't bear to see my smug-ugly face. Meanwhile, at home, Dr Sarathi made a couple of rare visits to see Grandfather.

'Just a touch of the flu – no cause for worry,' he said.

But I *was* worried, though not so much about CG. He'd seen a lot of action, I knew he'd be back to dodging the overtures of composers pretty soon. My fears were about the party. How would the Dance Room be kept dark enough to accommodate slow dancing during the day? What if there was an earthquake on the day of the party? Luckily for me, the college boys were equally concerned and came up with an idea. Unlike Deshbush, who would have addressed the prevention of unforeseen seismic activity first, they dealt with the problem of superfluous light. They would pack all the windows with several layers of newspaper to make the room grope-friendly.

Finally, it was party day. Time, which had been careering at breakneck speed towards me, coughed, sputtered, shifted gears and came to a turtle crawl that morning. I was up at five and didn't know what to do with myself. By six, I was bathed and ready to try on, yet again, the new duds I'd had made for the occasion.

Now that I had the freedom to do exactly as I pleased, I realized I wasn't all that cut out for the role of villain. The desire to shock the family with a variety of show-stopping acts had waned and I was back to being the unobtrusive supporting actor.

My pulling back had more than a little to do with CG not feeling his best. Somehow, it didn't seem entirely appropriate traipsing around in party wear when the old man was down. So I put on my new clothes in the secrecy of the cramped oven room and practised a few moves to the '*Stayin' Alive*' playing in my head, all the while sweating like Raghavan in front of a vigilance inspector.

Despite my best efforts, the rubber band of anticipation twanged me to Lucky's gate a good hour before commencement of festivities. I couldn't really be blamed. This was the day I had been waiting for since puberty. This was the day for which I had alienated my entire family, not to mention Ramki and Deshbush. This was the day for which I'd paid with my cheek. This was my Indian equivalent of the Prom, where I was going to dance with Lata and Vini and, if Hollywood movies of the '50s were to be believed, have my first kiss.

As I hung around on G.N. Chetty Road, waiting for the first guests to arrive, I had a feeling that passers-by were staring at me. An emaciated teenage boy, dressed like a waiter in a five-star hotel, peering out from behind a tree at noon wasn't a common sight in Madras.

It was just as well that there weren't many passers-by later that day. Had there been, they would have seen the same boy sitting in the dark on the sidewalk, near the same tree, not exactly the Prom King he'd hoped to be.

For starters, my vest was missing and the spotless white shirt of a few hours ago was brown with dirt and torn in a couple of places. And, if the blurred vision of my left eye was any indication, I was also sporting an enormous shiner.

How had the journey that had begun a few months ago, when I'd gone to Lucky's house for the first time, ended like this?

Though I remember the events of that day pretty clearly, I am unable to recall them in sequence. Life had been confusing enough with that damn fool Time moving alternately like a water lorry without brakes and an arthritic snail. It had been playing tricks on me for the last month. But on that day, somewhere along the way, it abandoned all pretence of linearity and decided to lurch about like our teachers on the Pondy trip.

* * *

Lata and I walked down the stairs. We had run out of paper cups and there were some in the storeroom downstairs. Meanwhile, guests, dehydrated by the frenzied dancing in an airless room, were already drinking the lime juice right out of the tap on the steel drum. The five-page letter that I'd written in one sitting in the oven room after the slap singed my shirt pocket. As Lata knelt on the floor, rummaging around in the cardboard boxes, I had an aerial view of her and was glad that the contents of my letter were more Anthony Hope than James Hadley Chase. Even the back of her perfect little head was dignified.

'Ah, there they are,' she said. She'd found the wretched cups. Now we would go back upstairs and that would be it. I considered the things I'd done in the recent past. I'd drunk myself silly, I'd held Father by his collar, I'd skipped the Maths Model Exam. Handing over a love letter to a Sacred Soul didn't seem that radical an addition to my repertoire.

Lata picked up a stack of cups and handed them to me. She was pushing the box back into place when I tapped her gently on her shoulder.

'What?' she said, turning around. There was a streak of dirt running on one side of her face. It didn't make her the slightest bit less attractive.

'I have something for you,' I said. Surprisingly, my voice didn't come out Saikumar.

'What...what is it?'

'Oh, nothing, just a letter,' I said, shrugging. I felt calm.

'A letter?' she said. She didn't sound surprised. She didn't sound ecstatic either, just matter-of-fact. I wondered whether she'd be as self-possessed after reading it. We stood there staring at each other in the dusty storeroom.

'Hey, Lata!' It was Lucky from the top of the stairs. He sounded exasperated. 'Where are the cups, man?'

'Yeah, coming!' she yelled out without taking her eyes off me.

'Here,' I said, pulling out the letter, adding uselessly, 'this is for you.'

Lata took the letter from me, folded it once more and put it in the little bag slung on her shoulder. She turned around wordlessly and walked up the stairs.

I remained right where I was, staring at the boxes. It was done. If nothing else, my gargantuan writing effort in the oven room hadn't gone to waste.

'Where's Gopal?' I heard Lucky ask.

'He's putting the boxes back,' I heard her reply.

* * *

I realized soon enough that the insurmountable hour looming over me could only be conquered elsewhere. Then there was also the probability of being sighted by Lata or, worse still, her parents. So I decided to move myself, waistcoat and nerves, to the nearby park. It was a warm summer day and the unkempt Jeeva Park, the after-dark mating point of T. Nagar's homosexuals, was empty except for a lone beggar sleeping on a bench. I chose the furthest one from him and sat down, but not before checking to see if it was clean. I figured my moves on the dance floor wouldn't have the desired effect on my twin loves if I had crow shit stuck to the seat of my pants. With the better part of an hour at my disposal I did what any young man on the threshold of his first slow dance would do. I wondered about my life.

The split-screen film clip, the same one I'd seen on my way back from Vini's place, came on for a re-run. One half of it showed the familiar cheery medley featuring the Sacred Souls, college boys and the great big party my life was. The clip running on the other side, the one that I had a feeling was far from feel-good, still remained out of focus.

One o' clock finally came and I walked back to Lucky's place. The Travoltan spring that I'd had difficulty suppressing the last month gave out – *minutes before the party*. It was the damn film clip. I sidled in, a cross between Buster and Deshbush, hoping to enter undetected. People were already there in the large living room that had been cleared to make room for the dance floor. The only furniture in the successfully darkened room was the two rows of chairs lined up facing one another and a table that had the National Panasonic Two-in-One and Vincent's Sansui amplifier. On either side of the table were the Arphi speakers, the property of another college boy, blaring out Abba's greatest hits. However, the girls were sitting in one row and the boys were sitting along the other and no one was dancing.

* * *

I gently touched the area just below my left eye. It hurt like hell. I couldn't see myself but I was sure I looked like a one-eyed raccoon. I bruised easily – something to do with low haemoglobin, Dr Sarathi had said. Even my Holly Golly injuries usually took weeks to fade. This one would probably last into my middle age – if I lived that long. My sisters would no doubt find this hilarious. Maybe I'd have to write my finals with dark glasses on. I could always say I had Madras Eye. I wondered where my vest was, not that I wanted to wear it ever again. It was just that it would help cover my torn, muddy shirt when I went home.

'Hey, Gopi, there you are!' the voice startled me. The road had been empty for some time. It was Saikumar, of all people. I was glad that the streetlights weren't working.

I covered the bruised side of my face as casually as I could. 'Hey, Saikumar, what's up?' I said.

'You'd better come home quick,' he said, all serious.

'Or else what?'

It was a cheap trick on Father's part, sending one of CG's flunkies to strong-arm me.

Maybe Saikumar had a memory of his septum being brutalized by my errant arrow but his tone softened.

'No, no…not like that. It's just that Thaathagaru's not well. It might be good for you to get back,' he said.

* * *

'You want to lead or you want to be led?' She was grinning as usual.

'Lead, I suppose,' I said.

I'd seen *Top Hat* and *An American in Paris*, yet I was doing something wrong.

'Then stick out your left hand…not the right…out – *like this!*' she said. The schoolmarmish tone was back. I did as I was told. She held my left hand in her right. It was soft, warm and surprisingly small for someone her height. She then took my right hand and placed it around her waist. '*More Than a Woman*' played in the background. I could look right into her eyes. She was grinning.

'What's so funny?' I said. It would have been easy to find her annoying if I wasn't crazy about her.

'We aren't just going to stand here, are we? Lead, big boy!'

Big boy? This girl wasn't reading Mills & Boon, that was for sure.

I took a deep breath. I could smell her shampoo or perfume or whatever it is that girls used, the same giddying scent of our hug at her place. I closed my eyes and decided to keep it simple. No point crushing her feet with the Cuban heel of my borrowed boots. One-two, one-two, one-two, one-two.

'Not bad,' she said. 'Not bad at all for a Tamil Brahmin boy.'

'*Telugu* Brahmin,' I said without opening my eyes.

'You'd lead much better if your grip on my waist was firmer,' she said. She somehow always seemed to have the last word.

'How come you know everything?' I came out sounding short.

She giggled.

'That's coz my dad taught me to dance when I was ten.'

'Well, I'm not your dad.'

'Thank god for that, my li'l artist friend...my *angry* li'l artist friend,' she said. I found her tone patronizing.

Before I could come up with an insult she took her hand off my shoulder, made me tighten the grip on her waist and put her hand back. I was now three centimetres from her grinning face. I could feel her girl breasts press softly against my chest. It didn't feel anything like my facial encounter with Lanka Jhansi's. I felt a twinge of guilt. I looked at her to see if she'd figured out that I was just a dirty old man in the making. She didn't seem to notice and was looking over my shoulder past the groping couples, beyond the dance floor at some calm, soothing place she'd found, probably a place her mother and father couldn't fight in. Or, better still, couldn't get to. Her own little oven room.

I leaned forward and kissed her. I'd seen enough films to know I had to tilt my head so our noses wouldn't get squashed. She didn't turn away. Her mouth smelt like the imported Bell Boy I'd buy when I had extra cash. Only in her case it wasn't artificial flavouring. It was her. For a second we danced that way – one-two, one-two – my petrified lips against her undecided ones. Then she pressed her mouth right back, at first softly and then harder, till our teeth collided. I pulled out first for breath.

I looked at her, not knowing what to say.

All I could come up with was, 'Thanks.'

'You're an idiot,' she said, hugging me tight.

* * *

The college boys stood around me in a circle. Lucky, Pramod, Vincent and the rest. The last of the streetlights flickered weakly in the background just seconds away from its death. It made Rishi, who was just outside the group, appear and disappear. I found it funny. It was like the strobe light we couldn't afford for the party.

'So, you think you're a big pista, do you?' It was Pramod, the thinnest among the bunch, doing the talking. At just an inch over me, he was an apology for a college boy. I wasn't particularly afraid. I had a rough idea of what it was all about.

'Personally, I think of myself as an almond but pista's okay, too, I guess,' I said.

Pramod looked bewildered. For a second he thought I didn't know what 'pista' meant and was about to go into an elaborate explanation. I spoilt everything by snorting.

Crack!

It was the sound of his fist against my face. I didn't see it coming but I should've guessed I had it coming. Pramod might've been puny but I was punier. His punch lifted me right off my feet. I reeled out of control and thudded against a tree – the same one that had seen so much drama.

Pramod had chosen the wrong day to mess with me. A couple of months ago I'd have dealt with him the Meghamala way – by turning tail, running home screaming choice obscenities in three languages and following it up with a consultation with Pistol Rangarao on retaliatory methods. But this was the new me – the guy who had nothing to lose. With a wild scream I charged at Pramod, taking him completely by surprise. Mid-flight, I grabbed his neck with both my hands in a grip that Saikumar would have envied, and brought him down with a thud. I squeezed with intent to kill. It took four college boys to separate us. Two to lift me off the ground with a gurgling Pramod attached to my hands and two to break my clasp of his neck, which was beginning to turn blue. Then it was a Holly Golly of punches. None of them had the venom of Pramod's opening punch. But, coming from four to five guys who were a foot taller, twenty kilos heavier and a lot hairier than me, they managed to injure a bit more than just my pride. I fought back the best I could with the weapons at hand – my nails, teeth, knees and vocabulary. Judging from the one effeminate yelp that popped up among all the manly growls, my knee had connected with at least one pair of squishy testicles.

But what hurt more than Pramod's punch or the backhanded swipes of college boys who were merely toying with me was Rishi. He stood in the background, hands in his pockets, his face devoid of expression, and did nothing to stop them.

Finally, one of them said, 'Stop, da. The runt'll die.'

As I lay there, vestless and temporarily one-eyed, the boys turned around and walked off. Rishi was the first to leave.

I heard someone say, 'That'll teach the little pisser to write love letters.'

I wondered if my beating would have been twice as bad if they'd known I'd done a little more than that.

* * *

There was a mess of slippers before our front door. It could mean only one thing. I ran into CG's room. Through the sea of familiar heads I could see him lying on his bed, eyes closed, his breath coming out in shallow rasps. I pushed past Kavi, Grandmother and Auntie Renu to get a closer look. CG tried to smile. I noticed his lovely white hair. It radiated on the pale pink pillowcase in straight lines, making his head look like a child's drawing of the setting sun. Father was sitting by his side, looking blank. I looked around. That seemed to be the expression on everyone's face. Only Saikumar looked like he was about to burst a blood vessel. But this time it didn't look like it was to sing. I felt my hand being clutched. It was Dodo. He stared at me sadly with his stoned eyes.

CG coughed a couple of times and died.

'It's over, man, Gopi,' Dodo said unnecessarily before walking off to the balcony to roll another joint. Grandmother held Auntie Renu and began to cry. Father turned away from CG and stood up. He stared at me. I became aware of my blackened eye and dishevelled hair. For the first time in my life, I looked away first. His thoughts couldn't have been clearer if they were in a spiky speech bubble in all caps: I wish it had been you instead of my father.

THIRTY-ONE

One day, the nuts stopped coming, just like that. It was as if the Andhra Pradesh government had gone on a clean-up drive and torn off those wall posters inviting everyone over to Club Meghamala for a good time. Or maybe the Glacier of Freaks had finally melted into a muddy puddle and dried up. At about the same time, the writers, musicians, artists and the powerful began disappearing, too. The once perennial river of visitors that had cascaded through our living room ever since I could remember now resembled the output of a Madras tap in summer. There was a calm in Ramalingam Street – but it wasn't a happy calm.

When CG died, he was eighty-four. He had to die sometime. But if you looked at Father that wasn't what you'd think. He sat there looking like he'd forgotten how to draw.

On the day of the funeral, a strange man walked up to me and patted me on the back. 'Your grandfather's no more. Now you are the man of the house,' he said.

I nodded blankly. At fifteen you don't know what to say in such situations. Maybe you never do. It was the first time I'd seen anyone die. I envied Dodo who could deal with it with a quickly rolled-up joint.

Another man, a writer friend of CG's, put his hand on my shoulders. 'You must take good care of your father. You have to be strong!'

After a couple more such condolences, I knew it wasn't a coincidence. I *was* being singled out. From the time I was born, Grandfather had been the man of the house. After his death, it seemed obvious to everyone that it was my turn. Like some diseases, evidently, responsibility skipped a generation in our family.

I looked at Father and I, too, saw what all the others could see so clearly. It was the scariest sight of my life. Shirtless, with an angavastram covering his bent torso, was not my hero, the man who'd taught himself the alphabet or the illustrator who had produced over a hundred picture stories for children. It was instead a broken, numb and petrified man of fifty who wasn't ever going to make the transition from being his father's son to his son's father.

SPRING MOVES TO THE CEMETERY. ANDHRA'S MIRROR BREAKS. So read the front-page banner headlines of Telugu newspapers. One paper carried a series of photos of CG – as a child attired like a prince, as a young moustachioed poet, as a cigar-smoking fifty-year-old who had the world at his feet and as the toothless halo-haired imp I'd known all my life. That day, if the Telugus had had their own flag, it would have flown at half-mast.

A lot had happened in the last few years. We hadn't noticed, but age had finally caught up with CG. He had been spending more time with his crossword than with music directors. His muse had begun to play Ice Boys with him. It was only natural. He'd been bleeding her dry for sixty years. But, for some inexplicable reason, Father, who was then only in his forties, had begun to lose his dum, too. There was weariness in his strokes. The vibrant, sharp-edged drawings had got a little rounder. His cartoon characters had lost their sauciness and the captions their zing. Of late, he'd become more interested in playing the horses than drawing them. Though there was a lot less work being done by the men in the house, we continued with no visible change in lifestyle.

For some reason, a week after Grandfather died, Father thought it was appropriate to tell his children that we had no money, save a couple of meagre fixed deposits. I got the feeling that we were somehow to blame.

Grandfather's Padma Vibhushan, his honorary doctorates, the hundreds of songs, Father's awards, the picture stories, the greeting cards, the felicitations, the headlines – was that all it was worth? There *had* to be more somewhere. Where was it?

Maybe my expensive school and bell-bottoms had done us in.

While the heads of families we knew had solidified their savings into plots of land and, with clenched teeth, built homes, the Meghamala men had scrambled their nest egg on a slow fire to keep up appearances. Even the last little plot of land that we owned in Hyderabad had been sold a year ago for no particular reason. It wasn't as if there had been an unavoidable family event that needed to be funded. If they had needed advice on capital management, all they had had to do was ask me. The treasure of junk in the oven room had only grown in the last ten years, thanks to my judicious administration.

A fortnight later, a doped-out Dodo arrived with a pair of scissors and a box. He staggered into Father's studio, cut the wire off our phone, stuffed the instrument into the box, mumbled something that sounded like an apology and walked off while we stood watching. It felt like it was our family's turn to have a tracheostomy. We asked Father to stop him. But he couldn't because the phone belonged to Auntie Renu. Apparently, from the time we'd come to Madras, we'd been using someone's spare phone, never bothering to apply for our own connection. Why apply? Why save money? Why buy a house? Why get insurance? Why prepare for a rainy day when we had our very own giant multicoloured big top called Meghamala Radhakrishna. We could weather any storm. The troops of admirers would take the fall for us. The rich, the powerful and the connected would change the weather if they had to, and make it sunny.

I realized this was the other film in my head, the 'Coming Attraction' I hadn't been able to see.

EPILOGUE

The last time I saw our house it looked like it was lying down. But this time it wasn't an optical illusion.

We'd moved out after twenty-two years to yet another rented house in another locality. It might as well have been another planet. That January day, on my way to work, I asked the auto man to turn into Ramalingam Street on impulse. I'd sold the Amby. I needed the money to pay the advance to our new landlord and, moreover, there was no place to park the car in the new house. I'd got thirty thousand rupees for it, roughly a thousand for each year of its existence. A classic, the buyer had called it. The car may have gone but I managed to retain the upper berth. It sat packed in cellophane, hopefully dust-free, in a corner of my head.

As the auto puttered into my old street, everything looked different. I couldn't figure out what I was comparing it with, the street we'd left or the street we'd come to in '73?

I asked the auto driver to stop near what had been the Maharani's house. Instaglued matchbox flats had swallowed the once spacious compound. Marutis stood where the horses ought to have been. I looked in the direction of our place. A gaping hole stared at me from where our house used to be. I looked up roughly at the area from where Pandu had given me his one-handed greeting and made our house the Ice Boys Capital of the World. There was no coconut tree. (Try swinging now – show-off.) In fact, there was no frangipani, no garage and no hairy neighbour, he'd died years ago.

I wondered what Grandfather would have done if he had had a song to write from one of the flats that was coming up. No foliage to study, searching for his tricky muse. Then again, the old guy could have always reverted to the evergreen forest in his head.

I walked closer. Workers were trying to organize the doors, windows and girders into neat little piles on one side, wood and metal separated for easy weighing. The waste merchants didn't have time to waste. I recognized the gate. The metal was still bent where I'd reversed the Amby into it in my maiden driving effort. Broken bricks lay in mounds, a few pieces mutinously holding on to the paint and concrete. A lone corner of what used to be the Raghavans' living room still stood with its jagged edges, like the survivor of an air raid.

I felt foolish. This wasn't my house. It had never been. It was just the family home of a retired railway employee. Poets and artists don't build family homes, their domain is castles in the air. What right did I have to feel anything for this place? Sekhar himself had tied up the ten grounds, the trees, his childhood and his dad's efforts, both honest and otherwise, into a neat little bundle, exchanged it for one transaction on the computer and left for San Jose, California. And here I was, hanging around feeling all profound.

'Hey, Gopi – what are you doing here?'

I turned around and saw Mahesh, the fifty-year-old Yuvaraja of Devagiri. The Man Who Wouldn't Be King, still dressed like a commoner. He gave me a pat that had the makings of a hug.

'What happened to your place?' I said. When you don't have an answer, question.

'Poof!' he said, slapping his hands together like someone who'd eaten mixture and was trying to get rid of the crumbs. 'Co-developed with SRS Builders. Good deal. Managed to retain four flats. We stay in one. Rented out the others.'

'Great.'

'What about you people? What did you get from Sekhar?'

'What do you mean?'

'You know – as tenants for...what was it, twenty, twenty-five years, you could have asked for two, three flats – at least.'

'Didn't ask.'

Mahesh shook his head.

'Silly fellows, man.'

'You don't know the half of it.'

'Why don't you come in...have a cup of coffee?'

I looked at the auto man. He was looking at his watch.

'Thanks. Some other time perhaps.'

ACKNOWLEDGEMENTS

My thanks first to Keshav Desiraju, for bringing south Delhi closer to south Madras for my sake;

To V.K. Karthika, for fighting not one but two severe throat infections while making sure my voice remained intact;

To Shantanu Ray Chaudhuri, fellow film buff, and angry young man, for helping me with the final cut;

To Kuri Abraham, secret agent among literary agents, for holding my hand with one hand (even though I'm not his client) while holding a Scotch in the other;

To S. Sreeram, martial fine artist (also fine martial artist), for his invaluable suggestions for the cover design; and

To Chitra, the reason I write.